TECHIN' CARE OF BUSINESS

HEIDE GOODY

IAIN GRANT

1

Gustav White was trying to work out what he would look like with a beard when he was distracted by the nearly naked man.

The question "Where do you see yourself in five years?" was from a website he'd browsed over breakfast before setting off for the marlin headquarters. According to the website, it was a common question asked in interviews. He considered his aspirations, modest as they were, and wondered how best to convey those vague personal ambitions he had. Unfortunately, he had allowed himself to become side-tracked by wondering if he would have a beard in five years' time. He had often thought about growing one, although his chin was smooth and seemed disinclined to sprout anything but the smallest amount of face fuzz.

Gustav wanted to make a good impression today and had shaved what little face fuzz he did have. He wore his marlin branded t-shirt and hoodie, and his newest trousers, and had tried cleaning his sneakers over Mrs Miller's sink before putting them on. He looked, he thought, just like one of the friendly people at the marlin stores. Maybe that was the job they would give him if he was successful. Assuming he could give a passable answer to their questions, of course.

As he pictured himself in the role, a nearly naked man hurried across the narrow road separating the car parks from the gardens in front of the marlin building. The man wore underpants, socks and shoes, but nothing else. He was a pale man and looked cold despite the sunshine.

"Are you all right, sir?" said Gustav.

The nearly naked man gave him a bitterly sad look. "It's nothing. It's really nothing."

Gustav tugged at the cloth of his t-shirt. "I could lend you something."

The man looked at the t-shirt and its marlin logo and a squeaky noise, a sob perhaps, escaped from his lips. "It's nothing," he managed to say, before giving Gustav an up-and-down look. "You're new here."

Gustav wasn't sure if the man meant Gustav looked unfamiliar to him, or that Gustav looked like he didn't belong, or indeed that Gustav looked like the kind of person who was going to fit right in. Gustav often wondered how he must appear to others. He was not a tall man, nor a broad one. His narrow features and lightly tanned skin made him look and feel like he could belong to any tribe, yet none at all. Gustav White wondered if he looked like he'd fit in anywhere.

"I have an interview," he said, but the nearly naked man was already giving him a sorry shake of the head and running off.

Gustav turned to watch him go before stepping into the road where, because he had his attentions elsewhere, he was nearly run over by an electric marlinGo car. The little white car made an agile dodge to avoid him. Gustav's body made a poorer effort at swerving: he simply fell back and sat down heavily on the ground. The little car, braking, bounced hard onto the pavement on the far side, and stopped at ninety degrees to the road.

Gustav stared.

The car door opened. The black woman who got out looked as stunned as Gustav.

"I'm sorry," he said automatically.

"Are you okay?" she said.

The reversing lights came on the rear of the marlinGo and it accelerated backwards, off the pavement and straight at Gustav. His body reacted better this time. Before he could even think, he had rolled sideways, pushed himself to his feet and sprinted aside.

"Stop!" the woman yelled.

The car stopped, now mounted on the other pavement, parked on the spot where Gustav had just been sitting.

Gustav stared some more. Thoughts of interview questions and beards and strange naked men fled from his mind. His terrified brain was filled with a high-pitched white noise, like the tone of a disconnected phone.

"Christ!" said the woman. "Are you okay?"

"I was," said Gustav automatically.

She looked at the marlinGo. "That's really, really not meant to happen."

The other car door opened and a robot climbed out. It was humanoid, its metal frame partly covered in white panels that bulked it out to a more human shape.

"I have a minor abrasion on my right knee," it said. It had a simplified face with a pink '26' stencilled on its cheek. Its mouth didn't move when it spoke.

"You just stepped out into the road," the woman said to Gustav.

He nodded as his heartbeat slowly returned to normal. "Did you see the nearly naked man?"

"What naked man?"

"Nearly naked," he said, looking towards the car parks. He couldn't see the man anywhere.

"Are you okay?" she asked for a third time.

He took a deep breath, nodded, pointed at the marlin building and took another deep breath. "I'm going for a job interview."

"Okay," she said. "You seem unhurt."

"I was trying to work out if I would look good with a beard."

"Goatee or full bush?"

"I don't know." He pointed at the robot. "Was it driving the car?"

"No. The car was driving itself. That's just a crash-test droid."

"I have a minor abrasion on my right knee," it said.

"Shut up," said the woman.

"The car tried to run me over," said Gustav.

"You stepped into the road," she said.

"And then it reversed at me."

"I noticed," she said. "I need to look into that. I'm Ruby Jallow. I'm an ethics consultant and run a thing called the Algorithm Accountability Unit."

Gustav nodded.

"The car shouldn't have tried to run you over," she said. "That was, um, bad."

"Is that what ethical consultants do? Say if things are good or bad?"

"Not exactly." She jiggled her head. "I have frameworks and techniques to evaluate complex situations. Marlin hires me to audit and oversee the AI systems and the company at large. Basically, I intervene when needed, to help people and computers to consider how they should behave and treat each other."

"I have a minor abrasion on my right knee," said the droid.

"For fuck's sake, shut up and get in the car!" Ruby snapped. She smiled at Gustav. "This probably hasn't given you the best impression of marlin. We don't usually try to run people over when they come for interviews."

"No," he agreed. "That wouldn't be a great idea."

"You okay?" she said. That was the fourth time now. "I mean, to go to your interview?"

"I think so," he said.

"Okay. Across to that building there, through the big

entrance." She got back in the marlinGo. There were angry but muffled words exchanged in the car and then the electric vehicle pulled forward, back onto the road, and went on its way.

Gustav made sure it was out of sight before looking both ways and crossing the road to the marlin building.

2

Ruby Jallow spent the journey back to the marlin car centre wordlessly imagining what might have happened if the marlinGo had hit the young man. He was very slender and Ruby could picture the marlinGo crushing him like a bunch of dried branches.

Of course, she hadn't been at the wheel. Yes, she had been physically in front of it, but the marlinGo's on-board Vehicle Management System had been in control. It had only been a test drive on marlin's private roads, but a crushed pedestrian was a crushed pedestrian.

Ruby didn't feel secure enough in her role at marlin to get away with running over a man. Not that she imagined there was a level of job security that entitled one to run over a man. But there was a precariousness, a poor perception of what her role actually entailed that made her feel she always had to be on her best behaviour. She had been given a quarterly objective to provide 'awareness training' to the entire company. In an effort to establish the scope, she had asked the leadership team what kind of awareness was required. She had received a jocular email telling her that as she was the expert, it was for her to decide. This was a tactic that she had seen many times. At some point she might try getting senior management to explore the difference between empowering employees and failing to provide leadership, but not just yet. She would gain a seat at the table by proving her competence, then she would issue some gentle challenges. She would gain that seat at the table by not running people over.

It was going to take months to deliver the training to everyone, and Ruby had decided she would fine tune her material on a select group of familiar and easy targets.

The car pulled into its docking station. Ruby made a note of the version number of the VMS, marked it down as 'do not use' and got out.

The crash-test droid got out. "I have a minor abrasion on my right knee," it said.

"You're fine," she said.

The droid stuttered, re-evaluating its state of being. "I am fine," it said.

"Bloody useless droid. Just go somewhere where you're not in my way."

The droid walked off in its high-stepping manner. It was one of dozens of the things which were used as pedestrians in some of the live trials for the self-driving marlinGos. Their approximation of human movement was impressive but they were moronically simple devices.

Ruby went into the test centre offices. Celery Brown, the

marlinGo beta test manager sat in a desk hub, chatting to a colleague in a furiously low tone of voice and idly scratching at a red spot on her chest at the edge of her low cut strappy top.

"And then that damned Quinn McAndrews girl has the temerity to tell me it was my fault!" said Celery. She saw Ruby hovering. "Dr Jallow. Did the test drive go well?"

"Not particularly," said Ruby.

"No?"

"No. A weird problem." Describing a marlinGo deliberately reversing across the road at a person as a weird problem was something of an understatement, but the fact that she had been there, in the blast zone of culpability, made Ruby reluctant to go into details right now. "I need to schedule in time to interrogate the VMS. Maybe later this week."

Celery crossed her arm across her chest and the bite. "You're going to interrogate the VMS at some point? Cos apparently there's something wrong with *my* Vehicle Management System." Celery was clearly angry at something and Ruby could tell it wasn't her, so she didn't let it bother her.

"Yeah, I'll let you know when. Thanks," said Ruby and walked out of the work area. The co-worker got up to close the door behind her.

3

The interviewer introduced herself as Myfanwy. Gustav had never heard the name before and hoped he wouldn't be required to repeat it as part of the interview process. She had big hair, a big round face, big round glasses and a smile that seemed to be on permanently. As though she hadn't learned how to stop.

"Have you checked in?" she said, gesturing to the reception area.

He nodded. She continued to smile.

The reception area was a huge, brightly lit atrium. On the walls, in ten foot high plastic lettering, were the company's three guiding principles: ACCESSIBILITY, UNIVERSALITY, FRUGALITY. Gustav had read up on them, and what they really meant for marlin, just in case it came up in the interview. He had also read the company mission doctrine, the vision statement, and the brand objective. All that 'marlin – giving humanity what it needs' and 'whatever you want to do, you can do it with marlin' stuff. He wasn't sure what the differences between the various slogans were – which were just advertising mottos and which were sort of company rules. He was a bit woolly on that, hoping he wouldn't be asked to talk about them in anything but the most general way.

"We will find a space to talk," Myfanwy said, leading him through the building and between glass-walled working spaces.

She pointed at one of many cameras in the ceiling. "We don't use ID badges here. Face and gait recognition throughout the campus. If you have marlinOptics, then everyone is tagged. Morning, Quinn," she said to a passing woman.

"It's very good," said Gustav.

"All marlin innovations are implemented here. We're doing good work."

Myfanwy pushed into a private office space. There were low lime green chairs and a coffee table. On the wall screen, a piece of abstract art slowly swirled and shifted. She sat.

Gustav waited to be offered a seat. When it became apparent that wasn't going to happen, he jigged uncertainly, finally taking a seat facing her. He put his hands on his knees to keep his knees still. And his hands.

Gustav didn't think he was anxious. You could only be anxious if you had at least a dim understanding of what was going on. Or what you feared might, or might not, happen. Like a tortoise at a paintball game, he wasn't afraid, yet felt a deep social awkwardness at being out of place.

Myfanwy grinned; she grinned more. "You're looking forward to working at marlin."

"I hope so," he said, which seemed about right. "I like marlin."

It wasn't a great statement. Marlin was so many things. The mobile devices, the computers, the cloud computing, the search engine, the global mapping system, the transportation and logistics organisation, the internet marketplace, retailer and product developer. 'I like marlin' was as empty as 'I like stuff'.

"I am going to be honest," said Myfanwy. "I like to speak as I find. *We* like *you*."

"Oh."

"*I* like you."

"Oh," he said again, knowing 'oh' was not among the top answers to give in interviews, according to the websites he'd read this morning.

Myfanwy nodded deeply. "You are the kind of thing we at marlin are looking for."

"That is good?" he said, wondering why he'd made it a question. "I hope my application conveyed some of the..."

She shook her head. "That wasn't an application."

"Wasn't it?"

"We don't call them applications. You are not an applicant. Did you think you *applied* yourself?"

She'd said the word so often he no longer felt he knew what it meant. To apply ... was it to put something on another thing?

"This is a relationship," said Myfanwy. "Marlin is all about relationships. I'd say it's our core business value. I'm not an interviewer. I'm not from some Human Resources department. You're not an applicant or a resource. We don't use these words in a relationship." She laughed. Gustav wasn't sure why, but offered a half-smile out of politeness. "Unless you're some sort of unreconstructed Victorian putting an ad in a newspaper. 'Wanted: a wife to cook and clean. Please apply in writing, enclosing a CV and references. Broad child-bearing hips essential'." She laughed again.

"Ah," he said. He didn't know how people, including unreconstructed Victorians, went about getting wives. Putting adverts in newspapers struck him as practical, if nothing else.

"This is the start of a relationship," she continued. "Between you and me. Between you and marlin."

"Do you not need to interview me first?" he said. "Well, not interview me, but find out about me?"

She tapped on her mobile and the wall screen art was replaced with a complex infographic.

"You agreed to share your marlin data with us. Your marlin searches, your marlin orders, your marlin TV viewing choices."

Gustav saw the data on the screen for what it was. It was all his on-line activity in graph form.

"You order a lot of tinned laverbread," noted Myfanwy.

"I like laverbread," he said.

"And you watch a lot of shows about dogs."

"I like dogs," he said. There was a big spike on the bar chart for *Dog Rescue – Forever Homes*. Having a specific number of hours, a *large* number of hours, put to his favourite show was alarming.

"Gustav White, we already know enough about you to say that we like you," said Myfanwy.

"That is good," he said and then felt he had to ask. "Is it the dog programmes?"

"I do not understand the question."

"Do you like me because I watch the dog programmes?"

"It's not as simple as that."

He wondered what kind of person marlin didn't like. Were there marlin TV shows that ratcheted up negative points? Were there product purchases or app downloads that weighed against you in the eyes of marlin?

"It is not one thing or another," said Myfanwy. "It is a rich picture. It is not just what you watch or consume. It is the times at which you do so. It is the quantities and proportions. It is the combinations. A grand and perfect picture is built up of you as a consumer."

Myfanwy, who was not an interviewer and not from Human Resources (although what she was and which department she was from was unclear), seemed to speak in a series of clear and certain statements. There barely seemed to be any questions for him. Gustav decided to keep his hands on his knees, try to agree at the appropriate moments and just go with the flow.

"You will want to know about the position you're going to fill," she said.

"I would. I will," said Gustav.

Myfanwy grinned again. Grins within grins.

"We don't have a job for you," she said.

"Um. There's no job?"

"That is correct."

"The job's gone?"

"There never was a job."

"Um." 'Um' didn't quite encapsulate his thoughts on the matter, but it was all he had. He wanted to stand and apologise for wasting her time. He had the peculiar impression there had been a job but he'd arrived too late, or misunderstood the message they'd sent him and come in error.

Myfanwy swiped on her mobile and the wall screen changed to a picture of a tall glass jar. "Marlin is like a jar," she said. "Any organisation is."

"Yes?" said Gustav.

"The people and processes are like rocks within the jar." He watched as cartoon rocks tumbled into the jar. "But the big rocks, the big components, aren't enough to fill the jar. There are gaps. Can you see the gaps?"

"I can," said Gustav.

"So, we add smaller rocks, smaller processes linking this department with that, this process with that one. Can you see?"

"I can see," he agreed.

"But still there are gaps," she said and there were. "So, we add even smaller rocks, individual people with small but vital roles."

Pea-sized pebbles cascaded through the jar.

"And still there are gaps," she said. "The company is incomplete. What are we to do?" She swiped and powdery yellow sand poured into the jar from above, trickling down, finding a path through. "You see?"

"Sand?" said Gustav.

"Sand. Yes. You know, like, on a beach."

Gustav did know sand. His island home had no sandy beaches, only smoothed slate pebbles sloping away to the shoreline. But if he thought hard about the in-between places on those beaches, he knew sand was there, hidden in the gaps.

"This is you," said Myfanwy.

"I'm the sand?" he said.

"You will be an interstitial operative."

"Is that my job?"

"No. There's no job for you. No single identifiable job. You will be like the sand, flowing through the organisation. All those jobs that no one thinks needs doing or no one thinks to do."

"So, I should just … help people?"

"But not help them do their job," she said firmly. "That's their job. Everyone should do their own job. Your role is to do the jobs that no one is doing. Filling the gaps. It's a very important role."

Gustav looked at her. "You want me to be the sand."

"The glue that binds. The oil that greases the cogs."

Sand, glue, oil. Gustav nodded.

"And, as a member of the marlin community, you will be appropriately rewarded. Would you consider living on campus?"

"Live here?" he said.

"We have accommodation in the garden complex. Single occupant dwellings. You currently live at Fields Park Road in Newport."

"I rent a room from Mrs Miller."

"It's temporary accommodation?"

He nodded.

"You don't have any family gift addresses linked to your account, not in this country anyway."

"I am originally from Eilean Dubh Mòr. It's off the Scottish coast." He added the detail automatically. He had learned no one had heard of Dubh Mòr, or most of the other Hebridean islands. "My mother lives in Ireland now." He had a photograph of her in his wallet and momentarily debated taking it out to show her. "I have no family on Dubh Mòr anymore."

"None?"

"The herd died after the grasses got lead poisoning."

"Your family died?" she said, with the slowness of someone who knew they were wrong way before they spoke.

"The sheep. We used to fertilise the soil with bird carcasses and peat ash. Islanders did it for generations. The lead in the grass went into sheep. The lead in the sheep went into the people."

"Oh." He only realised when she smiled that the permanent smile had dropped for a moment. "That's the circle of life, I guess," she said brightly.

"This accommodation," he prompted after a moment. "How much is the rent?"

"It would be free. There's terms and conditions, a data privacy waiver to sign. We use the accommodation to test new products and lifestyle systems. It's a sort of residential focus group."

"But it is free?"

The wall screen changed. "You will start on our

Interstitial Operative salary. You are paid a minimum salary in local currency and the rest in marlin store credits."

The numbers on the screen added up to a more than satisfactory amount. Gustav had been living off his savings. He would have to tell Mrs Miller he was moving.

"When should I start?" he said.

"Maybe an eager community member such as yourself would like to start today," said Myfanwy.

He hesitated, though he could see no reason why. He had no employment at present, and dwindling savings. The marlin campus and office buildings were a world of shining glass loveliness, and if all the employees here were like Myfanwy, a bit intense but otherwise friendly, it should be an ideal place to work. And live. But he hesitated. He didn't like to be rushed into big decisions.

"I am sending you your relationship agreement now," said Myfanwy. "Perhaps you have questions."

The mobile in his pocket vibrated. He took it out. There was a message from marlin. The contract looked like a standard set of user terms and conditions. There was a lot of it. "How long is my contract for?"

"Relationship agreement," she corrected. "The relationship between marlin and you can be terminated with no notice and no penalties incurred by either party, rising to one month's notice after the first year. If you don't enjoy working with us then you can simply walk away."

There was nothing to lose. The salary looked good. There was free accommodation. Gustav quashed his hesitation. He ticked the acceptance boxes on his mobile, applied his thumbprint to the touchscreen and the document flew away in a tiny animation.

"Excellent," beamed Myfanwy. "Welcome to the community. Your first day with us has begun."

He nodded. "That is great." He flexed his hands on his knees. "What happens now?"

She pulled a funny, surprised face. "You are literally free to be about your business, Gustav. Your employee account is linked directly to your marlin community account. Your passwords and security details are the same. No need for ID cards. Your account will prompt you to download the marlin employee app which includes an induction programme you will be expected to complete over the course of the next week. It also includes the marlin campus app so you can find your way around."

Gustav's mobile was buzzing with fresh notifications.

"I think that's all clear." She stood. Gustav stood automatically. Myfanwy gestured to the door. Gustav looked at the door.

"And right now?" he said. "Where should I go?"

"Wherever you're needed," she said, managing to sound solemn whilst still smiling broadly.

"Good." He nodded. He moved to the door and then stopped. "And where might that be?"

"We prefer our interstitial operatives to find that out for themselves. It's not the place of the rocks to tell the sand where to flow."

"No. No, of course." He looked at the door and the office complex beyond.

"Customer Fulfilment might be a good place to start," she said in a half-whisper. "But I didn't tell you that."

"Right. Yes. And that is...?"

"Use the marlin campus app," she said.

"Of course," he said, nodded in thanks and left.

4

The marlin campus app produced a jolly and cartoonish map in kindergarten blues and yellows and greens. A little radiating blob acted as a 'You are here!' marker. Gustav searched for Customer Fulfilment. A dotted line appeared on the map, leading on a zig-zagging course between buildings from his current location.

Gustav followed it.

He was an employee of marlin. Or community member. Whatever it was Myfanwy had said. However, he wasn't sure he felt like one. Wasn't there meant to be more to the process than this? Some tough questions, perhaps? Some sort of introduction to the company or the people he'd be working with? They might not need ID badges, but Gustav felt a surprisingly sharp desire to have one, or just something to say that, yes, he now belonged here, he was one of them.

He passed various people alone and in groups. No one challenged him. Many people ignored him. Several people he had never met greeted him by name. He managed to give some hurried replies but mostly just nodded and smiled.

In the months he had spent on the mainland, he had become used to the fact that people here were generally surly and unsociable. They were, for the most part, wrapped up in their own lives, focused solely on their own goals and problems. They perversely viewed this surliness as a form of respect, charity even. They didn't engage with you due to the belief you were too wrapped up in your own problems, and didn't have time to be sociable. In a land of inward-looking grouches, reaching out to others was seen as a sort of social trespass.

Grumpy self-interest had not been part of Gustav's past life. When you could walk from one side of your island to the other in an hour, and every family knew the history of every other family, privacy was not an achievable goal. Your fields were everyone's fields. Your fishing patch was everyone's fishing patch. A person always made the effort to speak to their neighbour.

And there were shades of that here, at marlin. Unlike Gustav's experiences of the rest of this country, there were cheery smiles and waves from passers-by. It felt as though if he could stop and engage them in conversation if he wanted to *and they would join in*. When he had first arrived in this country, he had tried to strike up a conversation with the man sitting next to him on the train. On Dubh Mòr, such behaviour was to be expected (although the island had no actual trains). Here, the man had made a strangled noise of horror, pretended to get a phone call and then changed seats as soon as possible.

The casual friendliness of the people at marlin suddenly made the world seem a sunnier place. Gustav looked at the sky, which was a cloud-free blue, and smiled.

"*Help me,*" said a little voice.

He looked round.

A white plastic robot had fallen off the paved path and tipped sideways into a flowerbed. It was wedged on its side in the soil. There was a brown cardboard marlin delivery box in the hopper on its back. It had six spoon-like legs which it waggled as it tried to right itself.

"*Help me,*" it said. Or rather it didn't.

As Gustav went over to look at it, he realised the noise was the sound of its front legs whirring as they tried to pull itself up. The legs moved backwards and forwards, generating a rhythmic two-tone sound. Back, forward. Back, forward. *Help, me. Help, me.*

The robot was not getting out of its current position without assistance, so Gustav crouched down, lifted it out of the soil and placed it on the path. It was as big as a footstool, but quite light. The robot rotated itself on its circle of legs, oriented its black visor face towards the admin building Gustav had come from, and set off. It had walked maybe five metres before it fell off the path again and into another flowerbed.

"Hang on," Gustav told it, hurried over and picked it up once more.

He moved down the path, away from the flowerbeds before putting the robot on the ground. It whirred and realigned itself and went on its way. Gustav watched it go to make sure it had no more unfortunate encounters with flowerbeds.

He waved to it. "No problem. See you later."

Pleased he had made his first contribution as part of the marlin community, he looked at his campus app and continued towards Customer Fulfilment.

5

Ethics consultant Ruby Jallow sat down at an empty hotdesking workstation on the fourth floor and logged into her interface. She had access to query the algorithmic choices which had been made by marlin's computer systems, with specific interest in the AI systems, and the Vehicle Management System in particular. Interrogating marlin's systems was not always an obvious and straightforward process, as she always had to dig around to find the correct question to ask.

She started by pinpointing the date, time and location of the incident where the newbie, Gustav White, had walked into the road. She leaned back in her chair and thought carefully before addressing the microphone.

"Please confirm the version of the Vehicle Management System in control of the vehicle at this time."

VERSION VMS 30251.11. SUB-VERSION HAS BEEN TAGGED AS UNUSABLE.

Ruby nodded. "Please confirm that the vehicle made an attempt to drive towards a pedestrian."

THE OPTIMAL PATH OF THE VEHICLE WAS ADJUSTED ACCORDING TO ENVIRONMENTAL FACTORS

It was never straightforward. "Please display a list of environmental factors which were considered."

The list scrolled up and up for what seemed like a really long time.

"Can I please get that list sent to me by email? I would also like the details from ten seconds before as well."

EMAIL SENT.

Ruby would need to comb through each and every factor, so that she could ask more pointed questions of the interface.

"Ruby, can I ask you something?"

Ruby looked up to see a young woman with an earnest face. She thought she had been alone in the room. "Sure, go ahead, er, Quinn. Take a seat."

"It's a question about ethics."

Ruby settled her face into an open and receptive expression. Advice and advocacy was part of her job. She'd mentioned it when she'd first been introduced at the regional all staff meeting.

"Can you get into trouble for telling someone they ought to use insect repellent?" said Quinn.

"Um. What?"

Quinn repeated the question. Ruby tried not to frown and forced herself to nod.

Ruby held up a hand. "Let me pause a moment and ask you a question. What do you think ethics is?"

"It's the rules. How people should behave," said Quinn

with confidence.

"What if I was to suggest that it's more helpful to describe ethics as a set of moral principles? Sometimes it is very clear what's right and what's wrong."

"Like the situation I just told you about?"

"And is this a hypothetical – weirdly hypothetical – question, or is it something that's happened?"

"The company picnic."

"Ah."

There had been a picnic by the lakeside yesterday. It had been good, the weather had been kind, but the flies buzzing around the water's edge had been a nuisance. The smoke of the barbecue had driven some away, but given the choice between smoke and flying pests, some had just taken the decision to go home early.

"Well, let's think about that. We can sometimes overlook other factors." A connection, a half-heard thing, clicked in Ruby's mind. "Is this Celery Brown at the MarlinGo centre? With the—" Ruby circled a hand to indicate an imaginary insect bite on her chest.

"Exactly!"

Ruby shrugged. "Some people don't like advice or like having their mistakes pointed out to them."

"But she says she's going to get me fired!"

Ruby tried to give a reassuring smile, which was more than Quinn's dumbass question deserved.

"You're not going to be fired for making reasonable suggestions that someone put on some citronella spray."

Quinn made a furious face-scrunching expression. "Citronella. I was trying to remember what it was called."

"I wouldn't worry about it. And if anyone tries to fire you, tell them to come see me."

Despite Ruby's 'and that's the end of that' tone, Quinn hesitated.

"Maybe you'd like to learn more about ethics," said Ruby. If Quinn couldn't be placated, maybe Ruby would have to drive her away with boredom. "I'm going to send you a link to a couple of instructional videos. I would really like you to watch them, I think you'll find them helpful."

Quinn nodded slowly.

"And I'm running an awareness training course, starting later this week," added Ruby. "Maybe you would like to be a participant."

"You think I'm not being aware?" said Quinn.

"This is advanced ethical awareness. Could be an opportunity to put your insightful mind to good use."

"You think?"

"Oh, I think."

Quinn nodded doubtfully and retreated.

A surprising amount of Ruby's time was taken up by people who thought she was some sort of ethics policewoman or enforcer. After jotting notes on how her awareness training and educational programme might address the kind of knowledge gap Quinn clearly represented, Ruby spent a good few minutes dreaming up what her uniform might look like as an ethics enforcer. Shiny buttons, shoulder braids and a row of fake medals was the least she deserved. Was it wrong to also want a ceremonial sword?

"I'd look good with a sword," she said to the empty room.

6

The first man Gustav met at Customer Fulfilment had clearly dealt with interstitial operatives before. Customer Fulfilment was the name given to marlin's massive packaging and distribution centre, where goods were transferred from the huge warehouse shelves to box after box after box destined for homes and businesses across the country. Books, electronics, homeware, furniture, clothes, toiletries, toys, tools – all manner of items sent out from a physical storehouse for the world's largest on-line retailer. Clayton was some sort of operations manager.

The warehouse was arranged in zones, some of which were caged off.

"What's in the cages?" Gustav asked.

"Watch for a minute," said Clayton. An enormous piece of machinery whizzed past. Gustav had encountered lifts, and this was like a lift's mad feral cousin. It shot up and down and side to side too. He could see why people were not allowed to get in its way. "It's a robot picker," said Clayton. "See the boxes that are coming out of there on the conveyor belt?"

Gustav nodded.

"That's the goods coming out to be packed."

"Why are some of them going back in?" asked Gustav.

"The robots will send out a box, but it might have a hundred items in it. A human will take out what's needed for an order and send the box back in for the robot to put away."

All of the boxes had barcodes, and now that Gustav looked, he could see how the computers must be controlling the breakneck flow of the goods around the complex maze of conveyors. People stood at stations, moving things from the plastic boxes into parcels, their hands a blur as they picked, packed and scanned, tapping a touchscreen as they went.

Clayton had suggested Gustav could make himself useful by going round the warehouse's walkways and picking up any rubbish bigger than his hand.

"Why my hand?"

"Cleaning's dealt with by bots," he said. "You know, hoovers."

Gustav didn't know the word 'hoover'. He nodded anyway.

"They can't handle anything bigger than yay big," said Clayton, holding up his hands, "and it's no one's job to tidy it up because the bots are supposed to do it."

This did indeed sound like a job for an interstitial operative and he spent the morning doing exactly as suggested. It took all morning too. Even at a reasonable pace, it took an hour and a half to make the circuit. Gustav's brain wasn't quite ready to believe that marlin had buildings with a perimeter of several miles but legs didn't lie. He could have circled the isle of Dubh Mòr in as much time. He picked up scraps of cardboard, crushed boxes and discarded plastic wrapping. When he found his first intact box he used it as a hopper to carry his finds in. Twice on his journey, he met stout boxy robot vacuum cleaners coming the other way. They had floor-brushing hose nozzles fringed with moustaches of stiff black bristles.

"Hoover," Gustav noted as he stepped out of the way.

There was not a huge amount of trash to pick up and Gustav was able to use some of the time to glance at the induction material on his screen. It informed him that, among other things, he was free to make hours of his choosing, and that all community members could eat for free at one of the various eateries around the campus. Gustav returned to Clayton with a filled box of rubbish after several hours. Clayton told him he'd done a great job and that he was awarding him a Shining Star via the company's recognition programme. It turned out that this meant Gustav received a cheery animation on his mobile to congratulate him on a job well done, plus a dozen marlin store credits. At that point he decided it was appropriate and fitting that he should go get lunch.

In a high bright space with chunky plastic furniture, he looked at the menu. "What's the YouKnowMe?" he asked the man behind the counter.

The man glanced at his screen. "Stir-fried fish with rice."

Gustav didn't hesitate. The food was ready by the time he got to the end of the counter. It smelled good. Not quite grandma's cooking good, but good. He found an empty table and sat to eat.

He was partway through his meal and deciding the food was about equal to grandma's cooking on a bad day, when a tray appeared at Gustav's eye level. He looked up to see who was carrying it. It was a familiar face – the one which had very nearly been the last face he'd seen before being killed by a self-driving car.

"Hello," he said.

"You got the job then?" she asked.

"Uh ... yes?" said Gustav. "Sort of."

"Mind if I join you?"

"No. Do."

She sat. It was the first time he had a chance to look at her properly. At their first meeting, minor details such as what she looked like had been pushed from his brain by the very real presence of death. She was young, possibly his own age, maybe a little older, with a sort of *knowing* look in her eyes. Compared with manically cheery Myfanwy, this woman gave off the appearance of always holding something back: a little sadness, a little cynicism.

"I forgot your name," he said.

"Ruby," she said.

"I'm Gustav White."

"And you don't know if you got the job or not?"

Gustav pulled a face as he tried to explain a concept he still had to get his head round. "There is no job but I'm being employed anyway. I'm an interstitial operative."

She frowned as though trying to pull apart his words in her head. "You ... work in the gaps between things?"

"Yes," he said, surprised she had a grasp on the concept.

"Yes?" she said, sounding equally surprised.

"I'm meant to find my own little space and do the jobs no one is doing."

She nodded and ate salad. "You're a gap monkey. Okay."

He nudged his mobile on the table. "I'm looking at the induction material. There were questions I should have asked at the interview—" He stopped, closed his eyes and rephrased. "It wasn't an interview. She wasn't from Human Resources."

"What was it then?" said Ruby.

"I don't really know," he said honestly. He tapped the induction app. "I don't even know who my boss is."

She seemed to consider this. "Most of us would be happy to not know who our bosses are. Do you need a boss?"

He didn't want to appear anxious or useless, even though that was how he felt. "I don't know what I really should be doing. I'm supposed to be doing the jobs no one else is doing."

She chewed on salad. "Printers."

"Printers?"

She nodded. "We're meant to be a paperless office, but we're human. Humans like actual physical paper and we want to print stuff off. But half the printers are out of toner, and because we're meant to be a paperless office, no one restocks them." She gave him a conspiratorial look. "My favourite printer is the fourth floor one in Integrated Solutions."

"You have a favourite printer?"

"Of course. Everyone does. You want to use that quiet, out

of the way printer. Not one of the big, brash obvious ones where everyone goes. Where there's queues and it's more likely to go wrong." She made an appreciative noise. "Integrated Solutions is the printer for cool cats. Except it's not working at the moment. Not sure why."

"Isn't there a helpdesk you can call?"

"You can log the fault on the marlin community site, but no one seems to do anything. What have you done so far?"

He recounted the not particularly thrilling story of his work at Customer Fulfilment which amounted to "I picked up the rubbish that was too big for the hoovers to suck up." She didn't query his use of the word 'hoover' so he guessed he had it right.

"And I helped a little robot that got stuck in some flowerbeds," he added.

"What kind of robot," said Ruby, pausing in her general stabbing of her salad.

"A little white robot. It had legs like spoons. It was carrying a parcel."

Ruby dropped her fork on her plate and quickly looked about them as though spies might be watching. "You helped a bug?" she whispered.

"A bug?"

"A little delivery robot."

"I don't know. It was kind of this wide and—"

"It doesn't matter what it looked like. They're all different. Did it have a red snowflake sticker on it?"

"I'm not sure."

Ruby growled. "You *don't* help bugs."

Gustav realised that as she had been speaking her head

had got lower and lower, leaning in to him, and he had lowered and leaned in to match. Their faces were close together and they spoke in hissed whispers.

"You don't touch anything with a red snowflake on it. Didn't you pay attention to your induction?" she said.

"I've got a week to complete it," he said. "I was just being helpful. I'm supposed to be helpful."

"Okay," she said. "Let's see if we can avoid you getting fired in your first week. I feel I kind of owe you because of the whole—" She waved her hand about.

"Your self-driving car trying to kill me."

"That. Okay, so the development team at Customer Fulfilment are working on delivery robots. At the moment, it's a man in a van coming to your door: parcel drop, confirmation photo, contactless delivery."

"Yes."

"But if that can all be done by robots it cuts out the middle man, saves on energy, saves the planet, et cetera."

"I understand."

"So." She positioned the napkin dispenser on the table. "Every day Customer Fulfilment unleash a hundred bugs—"

"The robots."

"—the robots to deliver parcels on campus. They're all different. The bug goes to its destination—" she traced a line along the table from the napkin to the edge of Gustav's plate "—delivers the parcel to the target employee and toddles back to base. Customer Fulfilment analyse the data. They're looking for speed and efficiency."

"That makes sense."

"The slowest robots are put in the crusher."

"What?"

Ruby mashed her hands together like jaws. "A crusher."

Gustav pictured the little spoon-legged robot going into a steel crusher, its plastic shell imploding under the pressure.

"That's horrible."

"Survival of the fittest," said Ruby. "Customer Fulfilment take the metaphorical DNA of the fastest few, throw in some random tweaks and print up a batch of replacement bugs."

"Robots don't have DNA, do they?" said Gustav.

"Software is variables and routines. Motors are measurements and ratios. Bodies are lines and curves and density and all manner of other attributes. It's DNA of a sort. Customer Fulfilment tweak and build, and the next day the bugs race against each other again. It doesn't take many iterative generations for certain winning attributes to come to the fore."

Gustav contemplated this. "It seems sort of random, doesn't it?"

"It's evolution," said Ruby. "It's machine learning. Apart from setting the parameters and the variables of the DNA, it requires no human innovation. The software these bugs are running on has not been coded by human hands. The developers in Fulfilment probably don't know what half the code does. But they know it works because it has come from the ones who survived the previous day."

"That is clever," said Gustav. It also sounded wild and crazy and, in a way he couldn't articulate, dangerous.

"But," she said and she was back to her conspiratorial whispering again, "if some numb-nuts comes along and helps a poor defenceless loser out of the bushes—"

"It was a flowerbed."

"Whatever. You're messing with the system. You allowed a bug that should have died to survive."

She might be telling him that by rescuing the robot he had done wrong, but now he couldn't shake the image of the crusher from his mind.

"Don't help the bugs," she said. "You do not want to be fired."

"I understand," he said.

7

Integrated Solutions was at the far end of the fourth floor in the main building. Here the building narrowed so that windows came in at both sides, and the place had the air of the prow of a great glass ship. Integrated Solutions sat in that prow of an office, filled with brightly lit work spaces and 3D models of cities and buildings. As though the people there were charting the course ahead for the good ship marlin. Gustav thought it the most impressive of the working spaces he'd seen all day.

A man and a woman in white shirts stood over a table and munched on donuts as they regarded plans on a screen filling the table edge to edge. As Gustav moved through, looking for Ruby's favourite printer, the woman turned to him.

"You okay there?"

"Yes," he said. "I am looking for your printer."

"3D or paper?" she said.

"Paper, I guess."

"Why?" said the man suspiciously, a fragment of donut glaze in the corner of his mouth.

"I hear it's not working."

"Are you from IT Support?"

The woman twitched at her colleague. "IT Support don't do printers and photocopiers. It's Site Maintenance you log equipment faults with."

"I thought Site Maintenance were doors and ... busted light bulbs and things," said Donut Guy.

"They are," she replied. "And printers."

"Printers seem more like an IT thing. It's literally information and technology."

"Well, it's not."

"I'm not from either of them," Gustav cut in. "I'm just an interstitial operative."

"Huh?" said Donut Guy.

"He's a gap monkey," said the woman.

"I thought I could just take a look," said Gustav. "It might be something simple."

"No problem," she said. "It's round the corner there by the Yucca plant. While you're here, if you could water the Yucca. I don't know what's happened to the office plant watering man, but he should have been here."

Gustav nodded. "Check the printer. Water the Yucca."

The printer was round the corner as described, next to a tall spikey plant. The printer was a large boxy thing. Gustav had never seen a printer this size before. He had rowed boats smaller than this printer. There was a multitude of drawers, doors and flaps, and a display screen on which there was an orange error message.

"Paper jam," he read. There was even a picture on the screen telling him where the jam was.

He opened door J at the back of the printer and saw a piece of white paper wrapped around a roller. He pulled it out and closed door J. The printer clunked and beeped as though satisfied. A job easily done.

The error message on the display screen had changed. The jam was now somewhere else. Door K.

He opened door K, below door J, found another piece of paper bunched around a different roller. This was a little harder to tease out. The roller only moved in one direction and he had nearly ripped the paper in two before realising. The roller cleared, he closed the door. The printer clunked and beeped.

The error message had changed again. There was still more paper trapped inside the machine. And now he spotted a little counter in the bottom corner telling him he was on step three out of eleven.

Gustav opened panel A in the front of the printer. He pushed aside flap D2 between two rolling systems and removed paper.

He closed panel A, read the next message and reopened panel A. He slid out component C and turned roller C4 to get more paper out.

He closed panel A opened door J, rotated cog K3 and a piece of print-covered paper was extruded from the works.

He closed J, reopened K below it, lifted the little letterbox tab marked K2 and searched for the paper that was supposed to be there but wasn't. He mentally tried to picture where K2 led to and experimentally opened paper drawer 3 and pulled out the paper from the other side.

He closed drawer 3 and door K.

He opened the lid of the photocopier unit on the top and dropped down panel F from which another sheet fell. He snapped panel F back into place.

He lowered the lid and then opened the hinged feeder thing on the top of it. The hinged lid did not have an identifying sticker, nor was it identified by an alphanumeric designation on the screen. He wondered if the printer manufacturers had run out of letters or had ceased caring by that point. There was a piece of paper jammed in the hopper. He removed it carefully, mindful of the ratcheting sound of protesting wheels as he did.

The piece of paper had a staple in one corner.

"The culprit," he said, knowingly, feeling he had performed a complex task requiring the dexterity of surgeon and methodical problem solving of a master detective. He closed the hinged top of the feeder and the photocopier lid.

The printer clunked and beeped.

For a second the error message was replaced by a pastel green user menu of options and then a fresh error message popped up.

CYAN TONER EMPTY.

After a succession of printer errors, each hiding behind the one before, a person might have felt the urge to rail at God and fate for presenting yet another problem. Gustav did not indulge in that kind of behaviour. He had not been raised to expect easy answers to problems and life had generally operated accordingly. There was almost always another problem. Humans seemed only able to focus on one at a time, usually the largest one. It seemed in this blessed part of the world, even when people had dealt with every significant issue in their lives, they were still startled to find minor ones still there.

For now he had a printer lacking a cyan toner cartridge. He opened his now familiar friend, panel A, and removed the long cyan toner cartridge with a twist and unlock motion.

He went round to the two integrated solutionists who had finished their donuts but were still discussing their plans.

"Excuse me," said Gustav. "Do you know where I can find spare printer cartridges?"

"I think you have to log it with IT Support," said the guy, who still had a fleck of sugar glaze in the corner of his mouth.

"Not IT Support," said the woman.

"Not IT Support apparently," said the man.

"I think they have some in the supplies cupboard in admin down the corridor," said the woman.

"But I think you're supposed to log it," said the man.

"Thank you," said Gustav and went to look.

Gustav went down the corridor as directed and found the cupboard. In a building campus full of glass doors and, often, glass walls, only storage areas and toilets seemed to have solid doors. This door, like every other one he had so far encountered, was unlocked. He supposed with benevolent watchful cameras in almost every corner (he looked for the nearest one and smiled at it), there was little need for physical locks.

He opened the cupboard door and walked in. There were shelves of marlin-branded stationery and neat stacks of consumables of all sorts. There was a pile of large boxes at the rear, marked with the marlinGo logo. He picked one up, finding it lighter than expected, and looked inside. There was space for a number of printer cartridges and a waste toner box, but contained only a yellow toner cartridge. He put it aside and looked in the next. Again, it had been opened and there was no cyan toner.

Gustav moved another of the bulky near-empty boxes aside and found a robot, a droid, standing in the space behind.

Gustav uttered an "Oh!" of surprise.

The droid twitched its head. It had a pink 26 stencilled on its cheek.

"I didn't mean to disturb you," said Gustav.

The droid said nothing but twitched its head again.

Gustav held the box in his hand awkwardly. "Um. Should I put this back or—?" He hummed indecisively. "What are you doing there?"

"I was told to go somewhere where I would not be in the way."

"I understand," said Gustav. "You were in the car that tried to run me over this morning."

"I had a minor abrasion on my right knee," said the droid. "I am fine now. Am I in the way here?"

"No. I'm just looking for cyan printer cartridges."

Droid Twenty-Six looked to one side, then another, but said nothing.

"I might need to look behind you," said Gustav. He reached out carefully to move the droid aside, then hesitated. "Do you have a red snowflake sticker on you?"

Twenty-Six made a vague pretence at looking at itself. It had glassy camera lenses mounted in its eye sockets.

"If I interfere with a red sticker robot I could be fired," said Gustav. "Even if they are going to be put in a crusher."

"I do not understand the instruction," said Twenty-Six.

Gustav shook his head, dispelling the line of conversation. "I'm just saying. Useless robots get put in the crusher and destroyed."

Twenty-Six took a step back.

"I know," said Gustav, equally appalled.

"Will you put me in the crusher?" said the droid.

"Me? No. It's ... so wasteful. You're fine with me. I'm Gustav."

Twenty-Six didn't step forward again but maintained a neutral stance. "I am fine," it said.

Gustav made to reach past it. "Can I look in those boxes?"

8

Ruby logged into her interface. She stretched in her seat as she waited for the log in to complete. Her lunch of leek and potato soup with crusty bread roll was doing something strange to her innards. Either the potatoes and the leeks were combining forces to produce a hitherto undiscovered gas swelling her stomach, or her insides were violently reacting to the crustiest of bread rolls. Was she wheat intolerant? She'd never been wheat intolerant. Could you catch wheat intolerance? She didn't know.

She had a doctorate from York, she was a highly educated woman, but the interactions of digestive systems and volatile lunches were a mystery to her. She surreptitiously loosened her trousers and focused on the computer.

It had taken her hours to examine all of the metrics the VMS had captured in the moments leading up to the incident where the car had steered towards Gustav. She had been able to discard many of them by comparing values with the slightly older metrics. She had seen nothing to explain what had triggered the incident, so she had decided upon an approach.

"I would like you to spin up a test environment so that I can run some VMS simulations," she said.

P*lease specify which version of the software you require*, the system responded.

"Use VMS 30251.11, " said Ruby, consulting her notes. "In fact, I would like to run a full simulation of the incident which I logged with that version. Then I would like a secondary environment with the previous major version of the software, and let's have it tackle the same scenario."

R*eserving virtual servers.* E*stimated completion time for scenario building is fifteen hours*

Ruby logged off. She would conduct her tests tomorrow when the scenario was built and her intestines had calmed down.

9

No one told Gustav when his working day was done.

In a day where no one had told him what his job or responsibilities were, where no door was locked and no place forbidden, the lack of constraints and direction regarding his time felt equally freeing and strange. It was, he thought, like being a sailor on a sea with no end. Such a man could row his boat forever, knowing he would not collide with anything and yet— And yet it was also a little unnerving. A sea with no end was a sea with no landmarks and nothing to take a bearing from. As a child on the islands the sea was a wild and vast thing, but there were always the other islands and the rocks to judge things by.

Here, the only guidance he had was the casual words of strangers and the apps on his mobile. These were the few scant stars in his sky.

He was surprised that the local people could cope. It seemed to him that, in this crowded country, people loved to fill every moment and every space with noise and objects and identifiers that declared "This is me. This is mine. This is my personality and life. Look at it." If you liked little boxes with stout walls and lockable doors, then a place like marlin would drive you to insanity.

Myfanwy had said there was free accommodation for Gustav here. Again the lack of detail was disconcerting. When he left the marlin building at the end of his day, there was a strong temptation to walk to the bus stop and go back to Mrs Miller's house in Newport where there were definite rules and restrictions. No outside shoes, smoking or percussion instruments were allowed, and Gustav had been careful to comply.

But a notification arrived on Gustav's campus app, highlighting the existence and location of his promised accommodation. Gustav followed the app, across the rear lawns of the office complex, between some low-rise retail and office buildings and to an area that was marked as 'garden' on the map but seemed more like wooded parkland.

On the far side of a wide grassy semi-circle, behind a loose screen of trees, was a curved residential block. It was three storeys high and studded with a multi-coloured frontage of dozens of balconies. Gustav was reminded of television images of holiday hotel complexes. All that was missing was the pool out front.

The app led him inside and up to the second floor. There was the scent of fried cooking from somewhere, and the sound of tinny muffled music.

At a door indistinguishable from any other, the app told him he had arrived. His mobile spoke to the door. He was asked if he consented to using his face and gait as the key to his apartment. He saw no reason to disagree.

The door clicked open and Gustav stepped inside.

The apartment was empty but furnished. There was a corner sofa unit in the lounge area and a small dining table near the kitchen. There was a bedroom and a bed, and a linen cupboard containing pillows and quilts. This apartment just for him was as big as the cottage he had shared with his sister, his mum and his grandma.

It was hard to believe this space was his space. This morning he had woken up in a small rented room in nearby Newport. Now, he had a job and an apartment, all gained so effortlessly. A local marlinAssist was sending him notifications, asking him to log into the home with his credentials. He had seen the digital assistant hubs, little back cylinders, in the kitchen and the bedroom. He logged in and linked his account to the apartment. Mobile, home and on-line profile connected. Only when he was able to turn on the apartment lights from his mobile and tell the fridge to stock up on his preferred essentials did he accept that, yes, this was apparently his home.

He called Mrs Miller while he explored the kitchen further.

"Hello, Mrs Miller. Yes, it is Gustav. I did. I got the job. Mmmm, well, it is somewhat hard to explain but I got it and..."

He nodded patiently as his landlady spoke and he continued to explore his new home.

The kitchen cupboards were stocked with functional plates, bowls, cups and crockery, plenty for one person but with space to store more individual items. The fridge was stocked with a limited but helpful range of foods, as though someone had stocked it according to his own recent purchases.

"Yes and they've given me a place to live too," he said. "Here at marlin. I'm in it now."

There was a shower room. There was toilet paper by the toilet and a wrapped bar of soap on the basin.

"No, I know," he said. "I will pay the rent for the rest of the month but I will come over tonight to collect my things."

He opened the shower cubicle. A droid stood inside.

"Bloody hell!" Gustav blurted in surprise. The droid raised an arm. Gustav automatically shoved it back against the taps.

Mrs Miller's voice went up in alarm.

"No. No," Gustav said to her. "I saw something surprising. I wasn't complaining about the deposit. Not at all."

The droid with a pink 26 on its cheek bent slightly. "I have a minor impact injury on my lower spine."

"I will call you back," Gustav stammered, ended the call, and for a second looked around for a weapon before coming to his senses. "What the hell is going on?"

"I have a minor impact injury on my lower spine," said Twenty-Six.

"What are you doing in my shower?" Gustav demanded.

Droid Twenty-Six looked around the confines of the shower cubicle. "Am I in the way here?"

Gustav made a confused burble of a noise. "Yes. This is my shower."

"Will you put me in the crusher?"

Gustav put his hand to his forehead and stepped back to give himself room to think. It was not a large room and there was not much space to give himself.

"Useless robots are put in the crusher," said Twenty-Six.

"I am sure you are not meant to be here," said Gustav.

The droid said nothing.

Gustav shook his head. "You cannot stay in my shower. Come out." He went through to the lounge area. Twenty-Six came in shortly after. Gustav looked at it. "I didn't mean to startle you."

Twenty-Six twitched. "I have a minor impact injury on my lower spine."

"Sorry," said Gustav. "I didn't mean to push you. Let me have a look."

Gustav approached cautiously and inspected the white panels forming its outer body. There was a light scuff mark in the small of its back but nothing more. "I think you're fine," he said.

"I am fine," said Twenty-Six.

"Are you?"

"Am I what?"

"Are you fine?"

"I am fine," Twenty-Six agreed. "I am fine with you."

Gustav decided he needed to sit down. The droid remained by the door.

"Why did you come here?" he said.

"You are Gustav White. You said you would not put me in the crusher."

"I was talking about other robots. Useless robots."

Twenty-Six was silent. In a human being, such a silence would be telling.

"Aren't you meant to be somewhere else?" said Gustav. "Won't someone be looking for you?"

"I do not understand the question."

"This isn't where you belong."

"Where would you like me to go?" said Twenty-Six.

Gustav looked to the window. Beyond the blinds, night was falling.

"I am fine with you," said Twenty-Six.

Gustav sighed. "Weary traveller, do come in."

"I do not understand the instruction," said Twenty-Six.

"It is not an instruction. It's something my mum used to say, to everyone who came to our door. You are fine with me. Stay here."

Twenty-Six rocked in position as though planting its feet.

"I need to go to Mrs Miller's and collect my things," said Gustav. "You will stay here and keep out of trouble."

Gustav ordered a cab. It was five minutes away.

"Should I leave the lights on while I'm out?" he asked the droid as he prepared to leave.

"I do not understand the question," said Twenty-Six.

Gustav checked his pockets for the keys to Mrs Miller's house. "MarlinAssist, lights out."

The apartment lights went off. Gustav could still see Twenty-Six in the gloom. Its glassy eyes reflected a silver blue. The droid was quite still.

"MarlinAssist, lights on," said Gustav. The droid didn't seem to have an opinion either way, but Gustav decided he could no more leave the droid alone in the dark than he could a dog.

"Stay out of danger. Break nothing," he said and went down to meet his cab.

10

Gustav returned to his apartment on the marlin campus an hour and a half later with a suitcase in one hand, a bag over his shoulder and Mrs Miller's keys no longer in his pocket. The front door of his apartment unlocked as he approached. From inside there was the sound of talking and, as he entered, he realised it was the droid, Twenty-Six, and the apartment's marlinAssist.

"I do not understand the instruction," said Twenty-Six.

"*I do not understand that instruction,*" said the marlinAssist. "*How can I help you today?*"

"I do not understand the question," said Twenty-Six.

"*I do not understand that instruction,*" said the marlinAssist.

"I do not understand the instruction," said Twenty-Six, and round the conversation went again.

"What's going on?" said Gustav.

"I do not understand the question," said Twenty-Six and the marlinAssist at the same time.

"I do not understand the instruction," said Twenty-Six.

"I do not understand that instruction. How can I help you today?" said the marlinAssist.

"Stop," said Gustav.

The droid and the marlinAssist fell silent.

"Twenty-Six, do not talk to the marlinAssist or respond to anything it says."

Twenty-Six rotated slowly, looking.

"The black cylinder." Gustav picked it up and put it down. "Do not listen to it."

Twenty-Six twitched.

"MarlinAssist, only respond to comments and questions from me," said Gustav.

"I have changed my settings," said the marlinAssist. *"Do I have your permission to listen to other voices? I learn how to communicate better by listening to others."*

"Yes, yes. That's fine," he said.

"I am fine also," said Twenty-Six.

Gustav took snacks from the fridge and went to flop on the sofa. He turned on the television. He looked over at Twenty-Six who was still standing by the kitchen counter.

"Want to watch some *Dog Rescue – Forever Homes*?"

"I do not understand the question."

"Come sit with me."

Twenty-Six walked over, steering neatly and deliberately around the coffee table. It sat down right next to Gustav. Gustav considered moving up to create a little space between them but didn't want to appear rude.

"I am not in the way?" asked Twenty-Six.

"We should make some rules," said Gustav. "Sitting on a

chair is a good place for you, generally. When I am watching TV, come over here and sit on the sofa."

"When you are looking at the television, I will sit here."

"When I'm eating a meal, sit at the table. It's called being companionable and it will make me happy to have your company."

"I understand. I am fine with you," said Twenty-Six.

Gustav found his favourite TV programme.

"You'll love this show," said Gustav. "We see unloved dogs finally finding a place where they belong." He glanced across at the droid. Homes and places to belong, places to be safe. Droids didn't understand irony, he guessed. Neither did dogs. It was one of the things he liked about them.

They watched three episodes back to back. Gustav watched them. Twenty-Six angled its head towards the screen. The format of the show was simple and repeated time and again but that was a reason to love the show, not bore of it.

Gustav was thirsty. "Twenty-Six?"

"I am here," it said.

"If I asked you to fetch me a can of soda from the fridge, is that something you could do?"

"What is soda?"

Gustav held his hands together as though holding one. "A can. Can you get a can from the fridge?"

"Do you want me to fetch you a can of *soda*?" The word 'soda' was spoken with the heavy emphasis of a new word learned.

"Yes. I mean no," said Gustav. "I don't want to be so lazy

that I cannot walk from here to the kitchen, but I am interested to know if your hands would be able to—" He shook his head. "Let's try it. Please fetch me a can of soda from the fridge."

Gustav followed Twenty-Six as the droid went to the kitchen. It opened the door without any problems reached inside and pulled out a can.

"No, that's tuna."

Twenty-Six put the can aside and reached in again.

"No, that's tinned laverbread."

Twenty-Six put it aside and reached in again.

"Soda," said Gustav. "It will say the word soda on it."

Twenty-Six pulled out a jar of pickled gherkins and began to read the label on the side.

"This," said Gustav, tapping a can. "This is soda."

Twenty-Six reached into the fridge and took out the can.

"Thank you," said Gustav, taking the can. It had a couple of tiny dents in the side from the droid's grip, but metal on metal was slippery, so that was probably necessary.

Gustav opened the can and sipped the cool soda. "Another episode?"

They watched more heart-warming dog telly. Monty the terrier was rescued from his life as a street dog and treated by the vets for the skin condition and parasite problems threatening to overwhelm his immune system. He ultimately found a loving home with a family.

"Monty is fine with the Harrises," said Twenty-Six. "Monty did not die."

Gustav glanced over at the droid. "I'm turning it off now

because I'm going to bed," he said. "We'll watch more tomorrow."

He sought out his new bed. It was already made, with a crisply laid quilt over it as though he were staying a hotel, or a doll's house.

11

Gustav woke early and smiled when he looked around his living accommodation. It was really very pleasant to have his own space, and such a large one too. In Mrs Miller's house, he had only a bedroom to himself, in which the shape of the sloping roof cut off a chunk of the room and made it impossible to stand in nearly half of it.

After he had showered and had towelled himself down he went to see if the droid was still staying with him.

Twenty-Six sat in the lounge area. It looked at him as he entered.

"Do you need fuel or cleaning or anything like that?" said Gustav as he pulled on a t-shirt. "I don't know how you are powered or maintained."

"I have an induction charger that is compatible with all marlin charging pads," said Twenty-Six.

"The same ones that the mobiles use?"

"My maintenance schedule is empty for twelve weeks or more unless I sustain damage. It is recommended that a lint-free cloth is used to remove surface dust."

"I will get hold of a lint free cloth today," said Gustav. He was aware that these words somehow committed him to being Twenty-Six's custodian. "Someone is probably missing you."

Twenty-Six said nothing.

Gustav ate a breakfast of milky oats and Twenty-Six silently took a seat beside him, which made Gustav smile.

"What will you do?" he asked the droid.

"What would you like me to do?"

"How will you entertain yourself while I am work?"

"I do not understand the question."

"We should find you something else to do."

The droid stared at him with his swivelling eyes, waiting.

Gustav briefly wondered if Twenty-Six was faking it, and being deliberately dumb, but he knew he was projecting human behaviour onto the droid.

"Listen, let's see if you can do a jigsaw. I'm going to order one now for rapid delivery. When the package arrives, you should open it and see if you can re-create the picture on the lid. Got that?"

"Yes."

Gustav left his accommodation happy he would soon find something to occupy Twenty-Six.

The strangeness of Gustav's sudden but ill-defined employment by marlin had not entirely dissipated when he started work that morning. Part of that strangeness was the thought he had nowhere he needed to report to upon his arrival in the morning. There was no locker for him to store his personal effects, no hook on which to hang his coat – not that he actually had any personal effects or coat that required either storing or hanging. As he walked across the gardens to the main buildings, he consulted his induction material and his campus app and discovered that there were indeed free-to-use lockers, and changing rooms, and indeed a wide number of shower rooms, kitchens and relaxation spaces that could be home from home for any marlin community member. In addition, there was a crèche, a dry-cleaners, an on-site medical centre, several restaurants, and a number of other retail and service facilities. It appeared that marlin had made sure their community members had everything they needed on-site and that, in theory, no one ever need leave the campus at all.

Gustav had decided one of his jobs that day was to continue his search for replacement printer toner cartridges and he was halfway to the Site Maintenance offices when he heard a whining complaint from a building entrance. Behind a large potted weeping fig tree there was a white robot. It carried a parcel in the hopper on its back and appeared to have got itself into a space it could not crawl out of. It was not the 'bug' Gustav had rescued from the flowerbed on his first day. This one had eight legs and a more spherical shape, but the spoon-like legs were familiar and its whining leg motors made the same *Help. Me. Help. Me* noise. Maybe this was, figuratively speaking, a child or grandchild of yesterday's design. It certainly had its grandma's knack for getting itself into trouble.

"I'm not allowed to help you," Gustav told it.

Ruby Jallow had been very clear on that point. There was the red snowflake on its body meaning it was not to be touched.

Gustav walked on, knowing he was doing the right thing. He made a conscious effort to not think about the bug being fed into a crusher machine. He thought about the crusher machine. In his mind's eye it had grown larger and its teeth more fang-like since he'd last thought about it.

He went back to the bug. He watched it turn around in the space between two walls and the plant pot. There was a gap large enough for it to escape through, but it was only just large enough, and each time it approached the gap, a leg clipped the wall and it backed away. Its big round visor sensors looked about in questioning alarm. It did a little dance, trying and failing again.

"The gap is there," Gustav told it, but the bug would not be told. "I am forbidden to help you," he added.

The bug whined piteously as it shuffled backwards and forwards, trapped.

Gustav thought. "I am forbidden to touch you," he said. He gripped the edges of the earthenware plant pot and rolled it along its edge until it was a further hand's breadth from the wall. "There," he said.

A few seconds later the bug had found the wider gap and was stomping on spoon feet down its corridor.

"Do not tell anyone I helped you," Gustav told it. "Or we will both be put in the crusher."

12

Ruby settled down at a workstation, her morning cup of cappuccino at her side, ready to run some tests. She had found a spot where she was less likely to be interrupted by passing strangers. It wasn't that she was hiding, more like she was seeking some peace and quiet by sitting in the furthest corner on the top floor. There were booths for private working, but they were sound-proof hooded things, really intended for voice calls. Ruby didn't much like the weird claustrophobic cave vibe they had. She logged in, and queried the system.

"Are the test environments ready for me to run some VMS simulations?"

T*est environments are ready*, it replied.

"Good. Let's re-run the scenario on the exact same version of the VMS that was in the car, to see if it behaves the same."

LAUNCHING TEST. DIGITAL TWIN CAN BE VIEWED IN THE PANE ABOVE.

Ruby watched as the computer rendered a jerky video of the unfurling scenario. The marlinGo car and all of its controls were displayed, and when the car identified elements of the landscape they were clearly labelled. She was able to switch angles and zoom in and out. She watched the default view from the driver's seat and was treated to the same view she had experienced herself the day before. The marlinGo headed out from the marlin car centre, on a route through the road systems that covered the marlin campus. The roads were ostensibly laid down for the practical business of allowing employees and deliveries to get about the campus efficiently, but there was an undeniable sense they also existed as a testing ground for the marlinGo vehicles. Maybe it was the green spaces, or the simplistic and clear junctions, or the signage which did not match the public highways off campus, but some intrinsic element made it feel like a toytown road network. That it had been laid down to entertain and educate youngsters. And the youngsters in this case were the AI systems in the VMS, a training space before they were allowed on the big grown-up roads outside.

The marlinGo in the computer scenario behaved exactly as it had previously. It swerved to avoid the pedestrian Gustav White, then reversed – apparently aiming straight for him. Just before it went into reverse, she noticed it had applied a very specific label to Gustav.

She ran the scenario again, switching the view to an

external side angle. She paused it at the point where it labelled Gustav.

Normally, obstructions were labelled with a set of criteria that were important for the VMS decision-making. She would expect to see labels like UNDERWEIGHT CAT or UNSUPERVISED CHILD. The VMS would drive more cautiously around an unsupervised child, knowing it might run into the road. Similarly, if a cat was clearly underweight then it spoke of neglect. Ruby had already uncovered a rule the VMS had created which suggested harming neglected animals was less likely to result in legal action. This meant, in a difficult situation, the VMS might sacrifice the underweight cat if it would prevent harm to something deemed more worthy. Ruby had that rule placed on a watch list. She wasn't sure exactly what the VMS deemed more worthy, and she might have to insert an override at some point.

Here, the VMS had labelled Gustav with his full name and a small, triangular, flashing red icon. She had never seen that before.

"What is that flashing icon?" she asked.

UNKNOWN ERROR

Ruby scowled at the screen. Unknown errors in a system this critical were not acceptable.

"I want to see the second test scenario now. Show me the same thing with the older version of the software."

LAUNCHING TEST. DIGITAL TWIN CAN BE VIEWED IN THE PANEL ABOVE.

Ruby watched as the same scene unfolded. She edged forward as Gustav stepped into view. This time he was simply labelled ADULT MALE HUMAN, BELOW AVERAGE WEIGHT.

The car swerved perfectly around Gustav, this time making no attempt to target him at all.

"Huh."

She watched again, just to give herself some thinking time. "How many subversions are there between these two major versions?" she asked.

45

She sighed. "I'm going to need test environments created for some of those subversions. Set up four more for me, will you? We'll do numbers ten, twenty, thirty and forty of forty five."

RESERVING VIRTUAL SERVERS. ESTIMATED COMPLETION TIME FOR SCENARIO BUILDING IS EIGHTEEN HOURS.

This could take days. In the meantime, Ruby had a nagging feeling she really should tell Gustav about him being labelled by the VMS. But she had no idea at all what it meant, or why she should tell him.

13

The individual at Site Maintenance who Gustav spoke to was clear to the point of bluntness. Printers were not repaired or maintained by Site Maintenance. Yes, she conceded, printer faults were logged via the Site Maintenance portal, but were picked up by another department.

"We're doors and busted light bulbs and things," she said. "Try IT support."

Gustav did try IT support. The very young individual he spoke to there was adamant printers were not their concern.

"Printers, like telephones and aircon, are not part of information technology."

"The woman at Site Maintenance said—" Gustav began.

The very young individual cut him off with a curt shake of the head. "What do they know? They're just—"

"Doors and busted light bulbs and things?" suggested Gustav.

"That."

Stumped, Gustav started to leave. A man with a moustache clicked his fingers and waved at him from a distant desk. Gustav craned his neck to see the man better.

"Sub-basement. Room one-one-J." The man sat down again and was gone from sight.

Gustav nodded his thanks to the empty space the man had occupied and went in search of the sub-basement. There was indeed a basement, and then a sub-basement, in the main admin block. It was a quiet in the lower levels, a contrast to the cheerful chatter of the higher ones. Gustav almost felt he should be tiptoeing along the empty corridor, that this could be the lair of hungry ghosts or fanged demons.

Gustav found room 11J and knocked on the door. It was a wooden door. In an office complex where glass predominated, actual wooden doors were a curious rarity. He tried the door handle. It was locked.

He put his ear to the door. From within came whirring machine sounds which abruptly stopped. There was silence.

He looked at the door. He waited, then he knocked again.

After another silence there was a scrape and the sound of the door unlocking.

A middle-aged woman in a shirt and knitted tank top looked out. She looked at the printer cartridge in Gustav's hand. "What are you doing with that?" she demanded.

"I'm looking for a cyan printer cartridge," he said.

She pointed. "That's one."

"This one's empty," he said.

She snatched the toner cartridge from him. "You're not

meant to take them willy-nilly. What would happen if people wandered off with them?"

She turned back into her room and Gustav followed. The room was windowless and stuffy, the air filled with a warm fuzziness and a constant thick odour. It smelled faintly of fire, faintly of fibrous wood. It was the smell of printing. A high bench ran around the sides of the room. On the shelves above were stacked boxes upon boxes of printer components and products, all marked with the marlinPrint logo. Through a door to the side, Gustav could see a larger, better lit room in which stood more than a few of the larger printers.

The woman saw him looking and closed the door to the other room before putting the spent cyan printer cartridge on the bench,

He realised she was wearing a staff ID badge on a lanyard. Gustav had not seen anyone else wearing an ID badge of any sort. The photograph beneath the scratched plastic cover was of a notably younger woman. The name CASSIE TROY was just about legible.

The woman, Cassie, held her lanyard. "You don't see many of these around these days."

"I was thinking that," he said.

"Long service," she said. "What did you want to print anyway?"

"Sorry?"

She half raised then dropped the printer cartridge so it made a hollow clonk on the bench. "This is meant to be a paperless office. What could you need to print?"

"It's not for me," he said. "It's for the printer in Integrated Solutions."

She shook her head. "And what do they need printing? Paper is an insecure medium." She plucked a printed sheet from between two boxes on the shelf. "It gets lost. It burns. It's useless if it gets wet."

"I think people still like to print things."

"It's a reflex action. If they've got a problem, they should log it."

"They did," said Gustav. "I did too."

There was an alert on Gustav's mobile. He looked at it. It told him to go to a meeting space in the building. The seventh floor. A scheduled meeting for five minutes time appeared in his calendar.

Cassie Troy picked up a screen device from the bench and blew dust from its surface. She tapped on the screen with the sharp precise hen-pecking motions of someone who didn't do it often and had to focus on the task.

"If it's logged, it will be dealt with," she said.

Gustav nodded. "Good. Er – can I just take one now?"

"Take?"

"A printer cartridge." He had a mystery meeting to go to. He really just needed a cyan printer cartridge.

There was a glare of hatred in the woman's eyes. It looked like hatred at least. "If it's logged—"

"Yes, I understand," said Gustav and retreated.

14

The meeting room Gustav was directed to overlooked one of the roof gardens. He stopped in the open doorway. There was no door to knock on, no bell to ring, but he did not feel comfortable entering unannounced.

"I was asked to come here."

There were two women and a two men in the room, sitting around on comfy chairs. One of the women was Ruby. She had a tight, pensive look on her face. The other woman was Myfanwy, who was not from Human Resources and who had not interviewed him on his first day. He was surprised that he remembered her name. Both of the men had sandy hair and full beards of the sort one might get after a year without scissors or razor.

"Gustav, come in and join us," said Myfanwy, beaming.

Gustav sat in the sculpted orange chair.

"This is Dr Ruby Jallow, ethics consultant," said Myfanwy.

"And this is Kingsley Garrison and Jim Bryant from the development team in Customer Fulfilment."

The words 'Customer Fulfilment' and the warning look from Ruby caused Gustav to jump to certain swift conclusions. "Am I in trouble?" he asked.

"We just need to chat," smiled Myfanwy. "It's good to chat."

"It is," he agreed.

The man called Kingsley flicked a video onto the wall screen. A second video joined it.

The first was taken by an outside security camera. Gustav was on a pathway, looking at something that had fallen off the edge of the path into the flowerbeds. The second video was an interior shot of a doorway. Gustav was leaning over a weeping fig, talking to something in the corner behind it.

"What are you doing here?" asked Kingsley. He had an even, measured tone, like someone reading out phrases for a foreign language phrasebook.

Gustav felt a guilty worry knot inside him but what could he say? "That's me helping a bug, a robot, out of a flowerbed. That's me moving a plant pot."

"Why did you move the plant pot?" said Kingsley.

"There was a robot stuck behind it."

"All new community members should complete their induction and adhere to community guidelines, Gustav," said Myfanwy.

He wanted to point out that it was actually only his second day on the job and had been given a week to complete his induction, but simply nodded. "I know, now, that I shouldn't have touched the first robot. I shouldn't have helped it."

The other bearded man, Jim, huffed. It was an emphatic and angry huff. "You messed with the eco-system, Gus. You played God."

Gustav nodded.

"We have rules," said Myfanwy. "Not many, but we have them."

"Yes."

"The development team over at Customer Fulfilment are an important part of our community."

"The evolutionary process contaminated!" Jim huffed once more.

"Why did you decide to move the bugs?" said Kingsley.

"I thought they needed help."

"Needed help?"

"They were stuck. They looked to be in distress."

"They're cockenhooting robots, Gus!" snapped Jim.

"I didn't like to see them suffering."

Kingsley frowned. Between his hair and his beard he didn't have a large face and frowning made it seem to draw in on itself. "You understand they are robots, don't you? They don't 'feel' anything."

"Perhaps this is where I should come in," said Ruby, a finger raised.

"You offered to give us an insight into some moral questions," said Myfanwy.

"And Mr Garrison here has just said the robots don't feel."

"They don't," said Kingsley.

"They have sensors. They have decision making processes."

"They don't feel."

"And yet Gustav felt compelled to help them."

"He watches a lot of animal rescue shows on television," said Myfanwy.

"I do," agreed Gustav.

"He saw an entity in distress and he went to help it," said Ruby.

"It said, 'Help me'," said Gustav.

"Apparently," said Ruby.

"Doesn't mean it has fandangling feelings!" said Jim.

Ruby reached over and flicked Jim sharply on the wrist.

"Ow!"

"Did that hurt?"

"Yes."

"Can you prove it?"

"I said 'ow', didn't I?"

Ruby spread her hands as though her point had been proved. "It strikes me that Customer Fulfilment have created an experiment in robot evolution with clear and valid criteria for success. You're pitting the bugs against the geography of the local landscape. And the flora." She gestured at the plant pot video looping on the wall screen. "It also needs to take into account the local fauna." She indicated Gustav.

He had never been called fauna before.

"You should ask yourself, what attributes did these bugs evolve that caused Gustav to want to help them?"

Jim was about to speak but Kingsley tapped his arm and

pulled him into a whispered conversation. When they emerged from their little huddle, Kingsley looked at Ruby.

"Helplessness? As an evolutionary strategy?"

"Co-operation. Symbiosis. Cuteness can be a desirable trait within a species." She pointed to the screen. "Look at the little bug with its big round eyes. So cute."

"That's an adaptation for navigation," said Kingsley. "Bigger eyes, clearer vision."

"Are you sure?" she said.

Kingsley glanced at Jim. "Some people were ... mean to the robots in the early iterations."

"Mean?"

"Put things in their way. Didn't let them in elevators." His face was grave. "Dropped things on them."

"It sounds like your bugs had to evolve the attribute of cuteness to survive."

The developers looked at each other. "We need to think about this." There were mutual beard-waggling nods.

"It might be valuable if Jim and Kingsley attended the awareness training programme I'm starting tomorrow," said Ruby.

"You think we need awareness training?" said Jim.

Ruby looked like she was regretting the name of the training course. What kind of person possibly thought they needed training to be more aware?

"It's something all staff will need to go through," said Ruby. "But I think, as members of the development team, you would make ideal beta testers. You know, get in on the ground floor."

"We could be willing to share our perspectives," said Kingsley slowly.

"And Gustav too," said Ruby. "I think this would benefit him and us."

"It would?" said Myfanwy.

"As a new employee—"

"Community member," Myfanwy cut in.

"Indeed. As a newbie, I think Gustav represents the kind of cognitive diversity we need to show awareness of."

Gustav didn't know what cognitive diversity was, but suspected it wasn't necessarily a nice thing.

Myfanwy tried to gesture surreptitiously at Gustav. "So, are we *done* here? I mean, today?"

"For now," said Kingsley and they got up and left.

Myfanwy smiled. "Well, Gustav, you've certainly given everyone a lot to think about."

"And that's ... good?" he said.

"I might want to ask my colleague here some follow up questions," said Ruby. She stood, gesturing sharply for Gustav to follow her.

Follow he did as she walked smartly out the room, down the corridor and round a corner. She pulled him into an alcove in which stood a watercooler.

"You thirsty?" he said.

"Was I not clear when I told you before to not help the bugs?" she snapped.

"It was only the two times—"

"Was I not fucking clear!" she said.

"You swore."

"Everyone swears."

"Jim said cockenhooting. I don't think I've heard that word before."

"No one's heard that word before."

"And fandangling."

Ruby prodded Gustav in the chest. "I told you not to touch the bugs."

"But it's like you said. They need to interact with the local fauna. That's me."

The look she gave him was cold and hard. "Why do you think I was in there, Gustav?"

"You're an ethics consultant. You help them sort out right from wrong and—"

"I was in there because I got wind of the fact you were being hauled in and made up some cockamamie story about the wider ethical issue of human-robot interactions so I could be in the room."

"Is cockamamie the same as a cockenhooting?"

"I came down to save your bacon. Your scrawny naïve bacon."

"Is this about your car running me over?"

"Trying to run you over. Yes. No. Maybe. Look, I'm looking into the car accident thing. There are irregularities, maybe linked specifically to you."

"I'm an irregularity?"

She looked him up and down. "Quite probably. Anyway, I'm looking out for you. Maybe I have a soft spot for dumb animals." She sighed. "If I hadn't pulled off some minor bullshit reasoning in there, you would have been fired."

"I understand," he said.

This comment seemed to infuriate her further. Ruby

Jallow seemed to be the kind of person who lived right next door to irritation and could pop round on a regular basis.

"Do you know what happens to you if you get fired?" she said. "Have you read your contract?"

He nodded. "The contract can be terminated by either party without notice and without penalties," he said, recalling what Myfanwy had said in the not-an-interview on his first day.

"Read your damned contract," she said. "You do not want to get into trouble here."

The door to the meeting room opened. Myfanwy looked out and smiled.

"Oh, you are still here, Ruby," she said. "Are you free for a chat?"

There was a notification from Ruby's mobile. From where he stood, Gustav saw that a meeting had popped up for this very moment on her screen.

"It seems I am," said Ruby.

15

Ruby went back in the room. "We need to talk?"

Myfanwy from HR smiled, like she was auditioning for a toothpaste commercial: too many teeth and not enough social awareness of how weird and oddly threatening a big toothy smile was.

"Ruby, come in. Sit down. You know Delphine from legal."

Ruby nodded at the other woman who had appeared in the room, and tried not to frown. She didn't know Delphine in particular, but she knew she was something fairly high up in marlin's local hierarchy. Marlin worked hard to appear like it had little formal structure and no hierarchy, but it was impossible to shake off entirely. Whoever this Carman was, she gave off the aura of being a big cheese.

"Are we still talking about Gustav and the bot misunderstanding?" said Ruby.

"No, you've been called as a, I suppose we should call it a character witness, for another matter," said Myfanwy.

"Oh?"

"To get right to it," said Myfanwy. "A complaint has been made about things a colleague, Quinn McAndrew, has said. Ah—!"

The 'ah' was for young Quinn as she nervously entered the room.

"Just in time," smiled Myfanwy. "Quinn. Sit down."

Quinn nervously sat down next to Ruby. She sat close, as though cleaving against her for warmth or protection.

"Am I here as some sort of legal counsel or union representation?" said Ruby. "Because I'm none of those things."

"We just want to chat about some things Quinn said," said Delphine from legal. Her voice was deep, sombre even.

"What things?"

"Things that contravene our code of professional conduct and our sexual harassment policy," said Myfanwy. "Things that you apparently said Quinn was fine to say."

"Woah. What?" Ruby smiled out of sheer surprise.

"These are serious concerns," said Delphine.

"What things?" said Ruby.

Myfanwy flicked on the screen in her lap. "Quinn, you were in the marlinGo test centre yesterday. You spoke to Celery Brown."

"Yes," said Quinn.

Even though she had no understanding of why she was there or what her role was meant to be, Ruby felt an immediate impulse to say something like "My client can neither confirm nor deny that she was at the marlinGo test centre."

"We can show the camera footage for Dr Jallow's benefit," said Myfanwy and cast an image to the wall screen.

The image was angled, from on high. It was the same work hub that Ruby had seen Celery and her colleagues at the other day. Maybe only an hour or minutes before Ruby had come onto the scene. Quinn hovered on the edge of the chatting group.

"OTHERWISE IT WAS FINE," *said Celery on the screen.* "*But that? Beyond irritation. I'm sitting there, having a perfectly lovely time, virgin mimosa in one hand, hot dog in the other, and apparently the damned pests look at me—*" *she leaned back a little to indicate herself* "*—see a bit of flesh, think it's okay to swoop in.*" *She winced and scratched at the insect bite on her chest.*

"*Not acceptable,*" *agreed a co-worker.*

"*It's like you can't go anywhere without them swarming round. You at the company picnic yesterday?*" *she asked Quinn.*

Quinn nodded. "*Probably best to cover up more in future.*"

"*Pardon?*" *said Celery.*

"*Just to be safe,*" *said Quinn.* "*The more you have on show, the more likely they are to go for you. Particularly in the summer.*"

"*I should cover up?*" *said Celery.* "*Why should I have to do anything? Like it's my fault?*"

"*It's no one's fault,*" *she said.* "*They don't usually go for me. Maybe I'm not to their tastes.*" *She ran her hands over her own arms.* "*But I have a spray I use when it becomes too much.*"

The co-worker gave a sort of gasp-laugh of disbelief. "You carry a spray?"

"Sometimes. Always take it on holiday. I can't remember what it's called."

"Citronella," said Ruby, in the room, watching.

"Citronella," Quinn echoed beside her.

"Wow," said Celery on-screen. There was a coldness in her tone.

"I can't believe you're so accepting of it," said the co-worker, equally cold.

Quinn tried to stay light. "What are you going to do? Just try and kill 'em all?"

Celery nodded slowly. "I'd vote for that."

Myfanwy paused the video. "Quinn, you told her she should wear less revealing clothing."

Quinn shook her head. "I mean she was wearing a very strappy top and a low—" She drew a low swooping arc across her cleavage. "She had a red mark on her boob."

"You were looking at her breasts?" said Delphine.

"She has breasts," said Ruby. "Quinn was looking at her generally. She was scratching at it."

"And you told her she should cover up more," said Myfanwy.

"I see what you're saying," said Quinn. "Yes, that did happen. But I was only saying it for her own good."

"And you thought this was appropriate?"

Quinn looked Myfanwy to Delphine to Ruby and then back again. "I was just being practical. I could see it was irritating her. I mean it's nice to wear summer clothes, but if you do you're taking a chance, right?"

"You're suggesting what happened to her was her fault," said Delphine.

"This is not anyone's fault," said Quinn. "But wearing a top like that, an acre of flesh on display. It is a factor, isn't it? Particularly round here."

"Round here?" said Delphine, eyes widening.

"The local area," Quinn nodded. "You've got a large body of water there. Long grasses. It's a natural haven for them."

"You think this is commonplace?"

Quinn shrugged. "I told her she should use a repellent."

Myfanwy flicked on her screen again. "Yes. You mentioned that. Do you have it on you now?"

"No. As and when. But when you go on holiday, you know, it just makes sense."

"Yes." Myfanwy made a practised thoughtful face. "Do you think women are much more likely to suffer unwanted sexual attention on holiday?"

It took more than a moment for Ruby's brain to catch up with what Myfanwy was saying. "Who is talking about unwanted sexual attention?" she asked slowly.

"Quinn, your attitude is deeply concerning," said Myfanwy.

"It's not acceptable within the marlin community," said Delphine. "Our community members are permitted to dress in a manner of their choosing and not expect to face ridicule, condemnation or harassment because of it."

Quinn worked her mouth a few times before finding the words to put in it. "I did not tell Celery to cover up because I thought her clothing was – what are we saying? – sexually suggestive."

"She was talking about the insect bite," said Ruby, leaping in with the defence she was supposed to give. "You know. *Tzzzt! Tzzzt!*" Why exactly Ruby thought making buzzing insect noises and flapping her hands would help she couldn't say, but it was possibly panic setting in. "Did something happen?" she said. "At the company picnic?"

"You didn't know?" said Myfanwy.

"No." said Ruby.

"No," said Quinn.

"Another community member made inappropriate comments, comments that marlin did not find acceptable," said Delphine. "That community member no longer works here."

"Ah," said Ruby. "I think this has been something of big misunderstanding."

"You didn't tell Celery to cover up because you thought her clothing was provocative?"

"She did not," said Ruby. "Quinn came and related the whole thing to me, mentioning specifically that she had been talking to Celery about the insect bite. All of that was insect-related."

"So, in terms of what did happen at the company picnic—"

"—Which we're all learning about right now," Ruby put

in clearly, making big hand circling motions to include them all.

"So, in terms of what happened at the picnic, Quinn, you're not saying her clothing choices were a 'contributing factor'?"

16

When Gustav returned to his apartment that evening there were a number of things that were not as he expected. The droid, Twenty-Six, was still in the apartment. It turned its head to him as he entered. Twenty-Six's presence was a mild worry, but not unexpected.

What was unexpected was that Twenty-Six was standing beside the television screen on which was displayed a picture of trees in a sunny rural setting.

"What are you doing?" asked Gustav.

"You told me to recreate the picture on the box," said Twenty-Six.

Gustav picked up the jigsaw that had been delivered. There was a picture on the front. An identical image, either sourced from the internet or photographed from the box lid was on the screen.

"Good job," said Gustav. "I hope you enjoyed that. There's

more we can do with a jigsaw. I will show you later."

Another marlin parcel sat unopened on the dining table.

"What is that?" said Gustav.

Twenty-Six rotated towards the parcel but said nothing.

"There is a parcel on the table," Gustav pointed out.

Twenty-Six's head twitched.

"Why is there a parcel on the table?" Gustav asked.

"I placed the parcel on the table."

"Another delivery?" said Gustav.

He inspected the box, turned it round. He asked the marlinAssist if he had any orders due to be delivered but, as he suspected, he had none. He looked at the delivery label. It had his apartment number.

"Wrong address?" he mused.

Marlin was not known for making delivery errors, but here was a parcel he had not ordered. Maybe it was for one of his neighbours on this floor, one slipped digit of an error.

Although Gustav made no changes to his attire upon returning home – no shoes kicked off into a corner, no slipping into 'something more comfortable' – he was still nonetheless mentally in outdoor mode so decided to go and sort this out at once. He picked up the parcel and went out. He went to the apartment next door and rang the bell.

Soon enough, the door opened. It was Ruby.

"Oh. Hello," he said.

"What are you doing here?" she replied, suspicious.

He pointed down the corridor. "We're neighbours."

She peered out and looked down the corridor even though there was nothing in particular to be seen.

"Oh. Wow, they just let anyone move in now." She saw the

look he gave her. "I'm sorry. I'm being flippant. I may or may not have been drinking."

"You're unsure?"

"I'm not sure if I want to tell you." She looked at him and his parcel. "Would you like to come in?"

Gustav followed her into her apartment. In terms of layout, it was identical to his, although the décor was different. His apartment was muted oranges and warm browns. Hers was light greens, blues and white. His apartment was a forest in autumn. Hers was like living inside a dental clinic.

"How long have you been here?" he said.

"Six months," she said, shrugging.

"You've decorated though."

She frowned and then seemed to understand. "It came like this. The apartments are all different. It's all part of the grand experiment."

"We're being monitored," he said, not because he knew but because it made sense.

"Constantly," she said. She pointed at the marlinAssist on the kitchen counter. "This little bitch listens to everything we say. Marlin are using the data to improve their AI chat function. They think that if the AI listens to enough human conversation it will learn how to speak like us."

"That's clever."

"Is it? That would make sense if language was only words and didn't come coded with thousands of years of bias and cultural baggage. I'm hoping to teach this bitch to swear. Hey, marlinAssist, go screw yourself."

"I do not understand that instruction," said the marlinAssist.

Ruby shrugged and padded through to the kitchen. Gustav saw she was barefoot, her untanned soles on the tile floor, and even though he had no problem with bare feet, he was abruptly aware that he was in this woman's home. That the working world was on the other side of her closed front door.

"I may or may not have been drinking," she said again and picked up a bottle of pink wine from the counter. "I may or may not have already demolished two thirds of this bottle of fine Zinfandel. Would you care for a glass?"

Gustav was not a drinker but he was polite. "A little one."

"Suits me," she said and poured two deeply uneven glasses of wine. The wine in the one she passed him was little more than a mouthful.

He held it politely. It was an elegant glass. Drinking wine from elegant glasses was something he had no experience of.

"You might be able to tell, I've had a weird and stressful day," said Ruby.

"I did not know," he said.

"You think I come home and hit the booze as soon as I get in every day?"

He wasn't sure what an appropriate answer would be. "I've only just discovered we're neighbours," he said.

"Smoothly dodged, Gustav. I've had a weird and stressful day. Got hauled into a HR meeting right after your meeting."

"Were you in trouble too?"

"Not me. Not quite. Another colleague."

"Did they touch a bug?"

"No," she huffed and then related to him a long and sorry tale about skimpy clothing and insect bites and sexual harassment. She sort of lost him somewhere in the middle, but he got the general gist of it.

"And then Myfanwy asked me if we though Celery's choice of clothing was a contributing factor in her getting harassed at the picnic."

"And you said no?" Gustav suggested.

Ruby groaned. "What I should have said was, 'No, Myfanwy. Her clothing was not a contributing factor to what happened when Dave Wicket said *I like to see a woman showing off her assets*."

"What did you say?" asked Gustav.

Ruby groaned again. Apparently, there were not enough groans in the world to exorcise this pain. "I told her I have not researched all factors and causes in relation to workplace sexual harassment."

Gustav nodded in a polite and friendly manner. "Things are very different in this part of the world compared to where I come from."

"Yeah?"

"A lot of concepts. Little bits of language. The, um, turns of phrase. And it's so easy to give the wrong impression with just a tiny alteration in what you say."

"Yes?"

He maintained a friendly look. "But I think you probably said the wrong thing."

She groaned again. "I knew it as I was saying it. I really did. I should have shut up. But the pub philosopher in me, the scientific contrarian, just piped up and— Then I began to go on about how, on a personal level, even quantum level – I used the fucking word 'quantum', Gustav – on that tiny level, all factors can have an impact on outcomes."

"But it was not the right thing to say."

"I know! What's right and what's true and what's socially acceptable and morally expedient ... I know! I should have shut up, explained we were just talking at cross purposes, salvaged my reputation and Quinn's job and got out of there."

"Maybe you should both go on some ethical awareness training," he said.

"Oh, ha fucking ha. Actually, we got out of it by me promising I'd put Quinn on my course."

"So you explained it all to them in the end?"

Ruby put her head in her hand. "I used the Speedos analogy."

"Speedos?"

"You know, Speedos. The little tiny swimming trunks."

He shook his head. "I don't know Speedos."

She sniffed and looked at him. "There are these tiny swimming trunks called Speedos. Budgie smugglers, Australians call them."

"Oh." He had heard the phrase 'budgie smugglers' on television before, only now understanding the meaning.

"I said to Myfanwy and Delphine from legal that our dress code allowed employees to wear what they wanted," said Ruby. "That self-expression and identity was an important value within the community. But, I said, if a male colleague turned up to work wearing nothing but Speedos, it would cause social embarrassment and some amount of alarm."

"I understand," said Gustav. "It possibly would."

"But it's a stupid argument. Because it doesn't happen. No man is going to do that, unless he's making some tacky, petty point. And that's what I was doing by even mentioning it. It was pathetic and cheap and—" She was about to groan again, but must have concluded groaning was achieving nothing. "I need more alcohol."

"No one needs alcohol."

She shot him a fiery look. "So, our colleague, Quinn, has now been given a formal disciplinary warning for unprofessional behaviour, and your friend, Ruby Jallow, now seems to be some go-to expert witness and possible scapegoat for any such further incidents. Yay, me."

"Friend?" he said.

She looked at him and scowled at his amused expression. "Don't try to spin a positive out of this."

She stared at her glass which had miraculously emptied. Gustav hadn't touched a drop of his mouthful of wine.

"I'm having a top up," she said and poured herself another glass. "You're not from round here, are you?"

"I'm from Eilean Dubh Mòr," said Gustav. "It's off the Scottish coast."

"Huh," she said.

"I was brought up in a commune. That's what they tell me anyway."

"You don't remember?"

"To me it was just home. There was a cluster of abandoned cottages, from a slate mine. None of us had a right to be there, but my grandparents and their other founders had lived there since the 1970s. But we were forced to leave."

"Shit. I'm sorry."

"Why? You didn't do it," he said, and grinned to show he wasn't being serious.

"So, your parents?"

"My father died when I was young. My mother resettled in Ireland. Here, I have a picture."

He found his wallet, opened it up and took out the photograph. It was creased near one side, where it had been folded to fit in the wallet, but it was otherwise pristine. He passed it to her.

She pursed her lips. "Maybe you have another photo you meant to show me. This appears to be a bunch of, wow ... some sort of nudist beach thing."

He leaned forward so he could see it too, and tapped the middle of the picture. "That's my mother. She was the Dubh Mòr May Queen in 1995. All the adults get naked for the May festival."

"Right. Oh. She looks, um. You must be very proud."

"I am very proud," he said.

"It's a lovely picture." She handed it back.

"Thank you." He tucked it away, then thought it about time to point out why he'd come in the first place. He tapped the parcel he had placed on the counter. "I thought this might have been meant for you but was accidentally delivered to me."

She took a gulp of wine, then picked up the marlin parcel.

"It was sent to me by marlin but I did not order it," said Gustav.

"Ah." She turned the box over and tapped a

RECOMMENDED PURCHASE label. "Yeah. It's a recommended purchase. Have you not had one before?"

"No."

"Marlin are beta-testing it on employees. They might roll it out to the wider 'community' if it's a success." He could hear the quotation marks as though it was something she didn't believe in.

"But I didn't order this," he said.

"No," she agreed. "What happens is that marlin send out items to its customers – you in this case – items it thinks they might want. It can be quite random at times. I once got sent a cuckoo clock."

"Do I have to pay for it?"

"You get a choice to accept it or reject. Reject it and send it back and there's no charge. Accept it and you will have to pay for it."

"Oh, okay." He frowned at the box. "That seems an odd way of doing things."

"You haven't heard the half of it. If you accept the package without even opening it then you get a discount." She looked at his box. "Twenty percent off on this one."

"Without knowing what it is?"

She nodded.

"If you eventually get to the point where you think marlin knows enough about your spending habits – and let's face it, they know a lot about us, don't they? – then it's reasonable to expect they will send things you want or didn't even know you wanted. Because, in fact, there's only marginal value in sending you products you were definitely going to buy anyway. What marlin really wants to do is send you things you might sort of want, that you wouldn't have bought naturally, but which, faced with the minor inconvenience of sending it back, you decide you will pay for and keep."

"They want us to buy things that we didn't really want?"

She laughed and nodded.

Gustav thought in silence. "Is this marlin policy or are you in a very cynical mood today?"

She laughed. "Cynical mood. Definitely. Doesn't mean it's not true though." She nodded at his nearly empty glass. "Do you want another one?"

17

Gustav eventually returned home from Ruby's apartment.

Twenty-Six stood in the living area, stock still, waiting. Given a waggy tail, the droid would be a perfect house dog.

Gustav held up his marlin box. "It is a recommended purchase. From marlin," he said. "Should I accept it before opening it?"

"I do not understand the question," said Twenty-Six.

Gustav slid the box on a counter. "What shall we have for dinner?"

"I do not understand the question," said Twenty-Six.

"I think I would like you to stop saying that," said Gustav. "If you don't mind."

"You wish to cancel my query response?"

Gustav looked in the fridge for something to eat. "I think

you should say something other than 'I do not understand the question'."

"What should I say?"

Gustav closed the fridge and shrugged. "Say ... 'what?'"

"Say what?" said Twenty-Six. The droid was confirming, not questioning.

Gustav decided to order Chinese food from one of the local restaurants. It arrived within the hour. The meal was accompanied by complementary prawn crackers and two fortune cookies. He poured prawn chow mein and kung po vegetables onto his plate and went to sit on the sofa to watch television.

Twenty-Six came over and sat with him. It got up and went to sit at the dining table. It almost immediately got up again and sat on the sofa. It was on its third iteration of this fidgeting action when Gustav told it to stop. "Can't you decide where to sit?"

"Say what?" said Twenty-Six.

Gustav shook his head. "Why are you sitting here then there, then here?"

Twenty-Six twitched. "When you are looking at the television, I will sit on the sofa. When you are eating a meal, I will sit at the table."

Gustav vaguely recognised the instructions he had given the night before. "When I'm eating a meal, sit where I am sitting – *near* to where I am sitting. That is best."

Twenty-Six complied, sat on the sofa and was still.

"I am going to have to take you back at some point," said Gustav.

"I am fine with you," said Twenty-Six. "I am not being put in the crusher."

They watched two episodes of *Dog Rescue – Forever Homes* and a wilderness adventure programme about travels in Norway. Tired and yawning, Gustav cracked open the first fortune cookie. He read out the fortune inside.

"*The harp with the fewest strings can make the sweetest sound.*"

"Say what?" said Twenty-Six.

"Yes. Not sure what to make of that. You open that one," said Gustav, pointing.

Twenty-Six picked up the other fortune cookie in its white plastic finger. The fingers tensed, carefully adjusted position and crushed the cookie into powder. The crumbs scattered on the carpet floor.

"Now read what it says," said Gustav.

Twenty-Six unfolded the crushed paper and turned it round five times in its hands.

"*The wind blows and not even the highest mountain can stop it,*" Twenty-Six read.

"Good advice," said Gustav. He stood and leaned over to snag the marlin parcel sitting on the edge of the counter. He told the marlinAssist he was accepting the recommended purchase, then opened it.

He lifted out the large squat disc. "Well, what do you know?"

"I do not recognise this," said Twenty-Six.

"MarlinVac," said Gustav. "It will clean up the apartment, which is useful." He found the power button on the underside of the little robot vacuum cleaner and placed it on the floor. Within seconds it had found the fortune cookie crumbs and sucked them up with a satisfying gritty sound.

"Hoover," said Gustav, savouring a word recently learned.

IN BED THAT NIGHT, after setting up the marlinVac's docking station, Gustav tried reading the relationship agreement between the marlin corporation and himself. Ruby had suggested he should, but it was not easy.

After five minutes, he still hadn't got beyond the first paragraph in which concepts such as 'marlin' and 'community' and 'customer' were defined, and some of the words within those definitions were further defined. He pushed on, but things became more complicated when the relationship agreement made references to the marlin customer agreement and the terms and conditions for marlin devices.

Within the hour he realised he was reading but not comprehending. The words were couched in straightforward and easy to understand language, but their actual greater meaning was lost on him.

Back on Dubh Mòr, there had been a white-haired man who sat on the slate-shingled shoreline on summer evenings and told stories to anyone who would listen. Although the stories might have a clear beginning, and each divergence seemed important by itself, it was never clear where the story was going or which details one should commit to memory. Gustav's father had called them shaggy dog stories. The white-haired man's stories had no dogs in them, shaggy or otherwise, but then Gustav had never stayed to the end of any of them. And when he thought of the beach and dogs, he couldn't help but think of the last day when they left the island and couldn't take the dogs with them.

The tangled web of the marlin relationships agreement, customer agreement, and general terms and conditions was a shaggy dog story of rights and responsibilities and he could not tell the difference between vitally important clauses and general contract waffle.

He fell asleep without digesting anything.

18

The following morning, Gustav ate breakfast at the table. The marlinVac was negotiating its way around the bedroom, learning the layout of the apartment. The marlinAssist was playing some light string music from a playlist called 'Your future favourites'. Twenty-Six sat beside Gustav pretending to drink a cup of tea. They had moved on from the droid simply sitting there, as Gustav wanted to give the droid some way to participate. He taught it how to intermittently raise a cup as though drinking tea and, somehow, that made Gustav feel much better.

As he ate his colourful cereal-based marlinHoops, Gustav once again tried to get to grips with his marlin employee contract.

An on-line search provided him with a solution. It appeared others had tried to decipher the contract, and with greater success. The length and complexity of marlin's agreements and contracts was a subject of some ridicule.

Gustav found a video in which marlin's customer agreement was performed as a three hour long opera. For a moment he was tempted, deciding instead to opt for the thirty minute animation which explained the key parts of the various documents.

Cartoon figures with rectangle bodies and spaghetti limbs stood in for marlin, the customer and the employee, while a narrator talked through the key elements, the dos and do nots, the clauses, exemptions and get-outs. Twenty minutes in, the narrator said something that made Gustav pause and rewind.

'Marlin retain not only the rights to all its copyrighted and trademarked products, but also retain the ownership. When you purchase from marlin, you are entering into a long-term single-payment rental agreement.'

Gustav tried to work through the implications of that. He was still trying to work it out when, in a later scene, the narrated added, *'Employees who choose to end their working agreement with marlin can do so only by ending all agreements with their employer.'*

Gustav stared at the screen thoughtfully.

He went round to Ruby's apartment. He knocked on the door.

Ruby opened the door. She was wearing fleecy pyjamas and holding a huge mug of black coffee. She blinked at him. "Do you know what time it is?"

Gustav held up his mobile. "Seven forty-seven a.m. Does marlin own my mobile?"

Ruby nodded wearily. "Yes, they do."

"And my marlin music?"

"Yes. And your marlin social media and your on-line account and your tv and music."

"And if I quit this job they will—"

"They *can* take it all back, yes," she said. "And if you get fired, they definitely will. Well done."

"Well done?"

"You worked it out."

"On the day I arrived, I met a naked man. A nearly naked man. He looked very sad and I offered him my t-shirt." Gustav tugged at the shoulder of his marlin-branded t-shirt. "It made him even more upset – like I'd offered him something he could never have."

"Dave Wicket possibly," said Ruby. "He'd just been fired for what happened at the company picnic. Seems like they took the contract literally. That's why they make it so easy to leave. You can just ask your marlinAssist to close your account and it'll do it in—"

"Do you really want to close your marlin account?" Ruby's marlinAssist asked.

"No! No," she said quickly. "Cancel that!"

Gustav thought about all the episodes of *Dog Rescue – Forever Homes* he had on his marlin TV account. "I don't want to lose it all," he said.

"Then don't get fired," she said. "They say people who spend their money on experiences are happier than people who spend their money on material things. It applies doubly to marlin things." She drained her mug of coffee. "I'm an experiences person."

19

Gustav found a delivery bug at the bottom of a flight of stairs. It was wheeled, spherical and the front of its body was a display screen. On the screen, big soulful eyes blinked at him.

"*Up? Up?*" it squeaked in a pathetic child's voice. As it did so it raised two little arms up to him. The arms were tiny vestigial things like the hands of a T-Rex and could not possibly serve any practical purpose.

"I'm not allowed," said Gustav. Then he realised there was no red snowflake sticker on the bug. "Oh, okay."

He picked it up, careful not to dislodge the parcel in the concave hopper on its top, and carried it up the stairs.

When he put it down, it blinked heart-shaped eyes at him, gave him a flash of smile, giggled and trundled off. Gustav watched it go.

"I've carried three of those upstairs today already," said a woman, watching.

"I don't mind doing it," said Gustav.

"Oh, me neither," said the woman. "Just saying." She held a bunch of cushions in her hands: green, orange and purple. She looked at the bundle of tangled cables in Gustav's arms. "You're the new one," she said, cagily. "Gustav White."

"I'm Gustav," he said. There was no point denying it.

She tapped her temple, at glasses that she wasn't wearing. "I don't wear Optics. I use my brain."

"Yes," said Gustav. Again, there seemed little point in contradicting her.

"You've been poaching in other people's territory," she said. Freeing one hand from her bundle she put it on her hip in a consciously sassy gesture.

"I've not been poaching."

She nodded at his cables. "Wiring and hardware peripherals is Vito's. He called dibs on that after Glen left."

"I don't understand."

"Just because you're a gap monkey, doesn't mean you can occupy any gap you like. There are rules. There are agreements. Some of us have seniority."

"I had no idea."

"I'm Gabriella. Not Gabi. Furniture relocation and relaxation spaces. Those are mine."

Gabriella was a short woman and Gustav suspected she was deeply aware of that. She wore baggy dungarees, a big floppy beret and big purple boots. Big gestures, big name – Gabriella made up for her lack of physical stature with big everything else.

"We need to sort you out," she said.

"Sort me out how," said Gustav.

"Tell you what's what."

"What's what?"

"Exactly. You know the decorative rocks at the centre of the gardens out back?"

Gustav did. They were one of the landmarks visible from his new apartment. He nodded.

"It's neutral territory," she said. "Four p.m. today. I'll tell Vito."

"I'm busy at four. I'm doing some awareness training thing my neighbour's organised. I think she might be an alcoholic."

"Six then," said Gabriella. "Six at the big rock. It's neutral territory."

She readjusted her grip on her cushions and walked away. After ten steps she turned back to look at him: a stern glance. An *I've got my eyes on you* look.

Gustav smiled at her, friendly-like. She didn't seem to like that.

20

Ruby hosted the first session of the awareness training in one of the breakout spaces on the third floor. She had found an old fashioned flip chart made from actual paper and headed the top sheet with bold letters.

<u>*RUBY JALLOW*</u>

"Welcome everybody!" she said as they found seats. There was a choice of seating in the breakout spaces, and it was always interesting to observe where people chose to sit. Gustav and the young woman Quinn sat in straight-backed chairs, but Kingsley and Jim took beanbags and reclined in the manner of Roman emperors. They were clearly signalling their Bohemian credentials, but Ruby knew they would have backache before very long.

"As you know, I'm responsible for the newly formed Algorithmic Accountability Unit. I haven't written it on the flip chart in case the pen runs out."

Nobody laughed at her poor joke, although Gustav smiled politely.

"Instead of diving straight in and talking about what that means, we're going to begin our workshop by exploring the idea of empathy. Who wants to start off by describing what we mean by the word empathy?"

There was a moment of silence.

"Feeling sorry for someone?" asked Quinn.

"Not quite right, but you make a very valuable point, Quinn. That would be more like sympathy, and it's important for us to realise the difference. Empathy might be better described as being sensitive to the feelings and experiences of others."

"I don't do feelings," said Jim, firmly.

"No," agreed Kingsley. "Not since the recent unpleasantness. He now has a heart of stone."

"Not that," said Jim. "Definitely not that. I just don't do feelings. At all."

Ruby gave him a look that hopefully said nothing at all. "Empathy is the ability to put ourselves in other people's shoes. We can do that without judgement. So, rather than feeling sorry for them, we try to understand them. And that's a skill we can all value."

Jim nodded warily, as if this was just about acceptable.

Ruby drew a stick figure on the flip chart. "What do you think this is?"

"A person," said Gustav.

"Correct! What do we know about this person?"

"Ooh, let me!" said Quinn. "Her name is Emily and she lives on a ranch with dogs and horses. She wanted to be a ballet dancer, but she fell off the roof when her dad made her fix the shingles in a storm—"

Ruby held up a hand. "Lovely. Very creative, Quinn. The point here, and you make it very well indeed, is that we don't know anything about this particular individual human until we take time to get to know them."

A muted chorus of "Well, yeah, obviously," followed, so Ruby pressed on.

"Where might we find humans, while we are working for marlin?"

"Our colleagues," said Gustav, smiling around the room.

"Customers," said Jim.

"Shareholders," said Quinn.

Ruby wrote them all on the board. "Great! Those are all humans, definitely. Now which of these do we need to think about, when we're going about our day-to-day work at marlin?"

"All of them?" asked Quinn. She looked a bit queasy. Ruby nodded in encouragement. "What, *all* of them? How can we do that? That's like every person in the world!"

"Don't panic, Quinn. There are some tricks to this. You mostly need to work on your empathy when you experience a human touch point." Ruby drew another stick person next to the first and drew a little electric spark between them. "As you go about your work, you might meet and talk to a person, or you might send them an email, or you might even create some software that interacts with them."

"No, I don't think so. I work in accounts."

"Point is, you don't have to think about everyone in the world all of the time. Focus on the human touchpoints."

Kingsley spoke up. "When we make software, we're making a touchpoint for loads of people. How can that work? We can't think about all of them."

Ruby clapped her hands together. "I am so happy you raised that, Kingsley!" She was trying to be enthusiastic and encouraging, but feared she might be slipping into primary schoolteacher mode. "Let's imagine how we might deal with that." Ruby drew a pyramid underneath the stick figure on the flip chart. "If you think about a customer using your software, I bet you think about them like this. You have a stand-in. Someone who represents all of these other customers."

"I guess."

"A stand-in customer can be a handy thing. I believe the marketing people like to call them personas. There's just one problem when we make up our own: they will almost certainly be modelled on ourselves. Does your stand-in customer look like a white man with a beard, Kingsley?"

"Super cute? Barely looks a day over twenty?" He made an exaggerated pout at an invisible camera. "Yeah!"

Jim snorted.

"One of the things we all need to be aware of is being blind to our own in-built bias. If Kingsley builds software designed around white men with beards then he might miss some obvious problems that a woman of a different ethnicity will encounter."

"Riiiight," said Kingsley, "but empathy can't fix those things. I still don't know how you'll use my software."

"Empathy is just the beginning," grinned Ruby. "We have other tools to talk about. If the next time you do something which relies on facial recognition you think to yourself, 'Hey, let's see how this works with Ruby and her gorgeous black skin', then we're helping to make the algorithms fairer."

"How can we have empathy for everyone, though?" said Quinn. "The shareholders want us to make as much money as we can. The customers want cheap things. We can't please everybody."

"No, we can't. Empathy does not mean we have to accommodate everyone's wishes. There are other types of controls around finances. What we are talking about here is humanising our interactions with each other, and perhaps starting to notice and respect our differences. It forms a good basis for some of the other subjects we will cover when we talk more about ethics."

"But why only humans?" asked Gustav.

"Do explain what you mean," said Ruby.

"Why do we only need to have empathy for humans? I get upset if people treat animals badly. And the little delivery bugs," he added, giving an embarrassed glance at the developer guys.

"What an interesting area for us to explore, Gustav," said Ruby. "Do you feel the same way about a kettle?"

Gustav paused.

"I see what you are doing," he said. "You think I will fall into a trap of feeling foolish about this."

"No," said Ruby, but she recognised the lie and knew she had been called out by Gustav's annoyingly guileless honesty.

"If we make things that look and act as if they are intelligent things, then shouldn't we treat them as we would an intelligent thing? It just feels bad to do anything else," said Gustav.

"There are absolutely very good reasons for us to treat bugs, robots, et cetera with respect," said Ruby. "Not least of which is the fear that if a person becomes used to the idea they can treat a droid badly, they are more likely to treat a person that way. A bad habit is a bad habit."

"No, no, no," said Jim hotly. "If we start down that road then who knows where we'll end up? We might have to apply for legal permission to recycle every bug or droid!"

Gustav smiled happily at this.

"No! That would be a bad thing! Our business would grind to a halt." Jim was aghast.

Ruby gave him a moment to exhaust his spluttering.

"Some interesting points are emerging here, and if we can all work together, we can learn some valuable lessons from them. Now, I think we might work more on this topic in our next session, but for now let's think about it." She wrote on the flipchart as she spoke. "Cognitive diversity. It is an asset to our company. Gustav here is bringing some views that are not represented on our development team."

There were some dark mutterings from Jim and Kingsley.

"Which is a good thing," said Ruby firmly. "If Gustav has

these views then it's a certainty some of our customers do too, so we need to understand what to do with them. The second point I want to make is this. We've made excellent progress, because things have already become heated in this first session. Sometimes we need to tackle questions which do not have easy answers. We must not shy away from topics just because they are messy. When we come in here for these sessions, we must regard it as a safe space, where we can share our emotions, as long as we're considerate of others."

Quinn stood up suddenly and shouted, "To hell with this!" and sat down.

She looked around at the shocked faces of her classmates. "What? I was just practising."

21

The inaugural meeting of the awareness training group had gone really well. It had certainly gone much better than Ruby had expected. The worst moment had come at the end when Kingsley had thanked her before leaving.

"That was good," he'd said. "I liked it."

"I'm glad," she'd replied.

"I thought you were very—" He'd waved his fingers in search of a word. "It was like being back at nursery, you, Miss Jallow, being our teacher."

"Oh. I hope I wasn't, um, patronising."

"Oh, no. No. I liked it," Kingsley said and gave a little shiver of pleasure.

Slightly creepy teacher fantasies aside, it had definitely been a good session and, buzzed by her success, Ruby decided to throw the remainder of her afternoon into addressing the homicidal marlinGo problem.

She thought it would be a good idea for her to walk the scene of the marlinGo's near-miss with Gustav. It was possible she was overlooking an environmental factor that had not registered with the VMS. An uneven road surface, or a reflection which had confused the cameras, perhaps?

She would print out a map of the area with grid marks overlaying it, carefully walk and measure her way around each section, then mark on the map anything that needed further thought or examination. If she could get her map onto the larger size of paper then it would be no problem. She took her laptop over to Integrated Solutions and took a look at the printer to see what state it was in. An amber light shone on top, which was encouraging. At least it wasn't red. There was a flashing complaint about having no cyan. She clicked to print her document in greyscale and crossed her fingers. The printer woke with a hum, making a series of busy internal clunking noises that sounded like a prelude to printing. Ruby realised she was feeling something like excitement that she might successfully print out a document. Could she feel judgmental stares from colleagues in the surrounding office space because she was using paper in a paperless office? She resisted the temptation to either look up and check, or indeed to justify what she was doing. She gazed hungrily at the printer as it continued its preparatory shunting noises, until it stopped abruptly and flashed a message.

Tray 2 is empty

Ruby pulled open the drawer. It was empty.

"Hah!"

She checked the other trays, similarly empty, then cast about for signs of paper supplies. There were none.

She wasn't out of tricks yet. She went to the secure waste bin. It was a locked cupboard where paper waste was posted into a slot for recycling by a third party. It was locked so that confidential information wouldn't be accidentally shared. Purely by accident, Ruby had once found that the primitive lock on the cupboard could be opened with the handle of a teaspoon (the kind of accident that happened when a restless person stirred a drink on top of the cupboard while chatting).

Ruby briefly considered the transgression she was about to commit. She was breaking an important information security rule and might very well see or expose a document she should not. She promised herself she wouldn't read any material that she found. What she was doing was surely for the ultimate good of the company, wasn't it?

Her conscience clear, she went to find a teaspoon. She also needed to make sure she did not let others see her hack, because that would automatically increase the risk of wrongdoing. She loitered by the secure waste bin until everyone who was walking around had taken a seat, then she jiggled the handle of the teaspoon in the lock briefly, and the door swung open.

Inside the cupboard was a simple bin, lined with a bag. She dragged the bin out so she could riffle through the contents, looking for a large sheet of paper with one blank side, or better still, two. There wasn't much paper in the bin, which was testament to the generally non-functional printer. Mostly the contents looked like personal mail or ancient instruction manuals. Then she struck gold near the bottom.

A large piece of paper which had some sort of half-printed form trailing off an edge.

She pulled it out, swiftly put the bin back inside the cupboard and clicked it shut. She smoothed the paper on top of the cupboard. It wasn't as flat as she would have liked, but it represented a chance. She loaded it into the tray and retried her print job. The whirring and clunking was briefer this time, the printer being partially warmed up, but it stopped just as abruptly.

PAPER JAM IN TRAY 2.

She spent several minutes opening doors and probing the printer for her jammed sheet of paper, managing to extract it from its hiding place between two rollers. She placed it back on top of the cupboard and ran a hand across it. It was pleated so thoroughly it looked like an art project. It was well beyond salvation, unless she took it home and used her iron on it. Was that ridiculous? She would decide later. She scrunched it up into her laptop bag and left Integrated Solutions.

22

Gustav approached the standing stones at the centre of the parkland called the gardens. It was not a rockery. It had more in common with Stonehenge. No, it was more like Monument Valley. Landscape gardeners had taken four or five sandstone boulders and driven them upright into the ground, where they stood closely like stone trolls having a watercooler moment. The evening sun made the stones glow a desert orange.

Gabriella was already there with a lean, angular man. He had well-maintained black hair and an equally well-maintained moustache covering his top lip. He looked like a young Freddie Mercury in workman's overalls.

"This is him," said Gabriella as Gustav neared.

The man, Vito, gave Gustav a curt but simple chin-jutting nod. It seemed a quintessentially Italian gesture, but Gustav suspected the name Vito was doing the heavy-lifting in that impression.

"Vito," the man said and held out a gloved hand.

Gustav shook it. The leather glove was rough and the handshake strong. Gustav never knew if there was something to be read into other men's handshakes. On Eilean Dubh Mòr, everyone knew everyone and there were only casual greetings and loving hugs. Handshakes were for strangers.

"I'm Gustav," said Gustav.

"When we meet, we meet here," said Gabriella.

"Unless we happen to meet somewhere else," said Vito. Gustav heard his Italian accent through the dropped aitch and the shifted vowels.

"No, we meet here," she insisted.

Vito shrugged like none of it mattered to him.

"Clear delineation of roles. We decided that after Glen went. That way, we know who's done what." She looked at Gustav. "You seen the adverts for marlin Wire-Free?"

Gustav owned a pair of the earphones. "I do."

"That was me," she said.

"You?"

"I worked with the team who designed them. I managed their space. I kept their offices just how they like them."

"Oh, right. Wow." The 'wow' came out sort of unenthused. Gustav didn't mean it that way.

"We're not just doing jobs here, jobs there," she said.

"That is exactly what we're doing," said Vito.

"We're part of bigger processes. We are the glue that holds them together."

Gustav remembered Myfanwy saying something similar.

"I am rubber. She is glue," said Vito. "I move like a silent shadow. You seen me before now?"

Gustav shook his head.

"Exactly," said Vito. "Gap ninja. If trouble cannot see you, trouble cannot find you."

Gabriella jerked a thumb at Vito. "Vito does hardware and peripherals. He's also got hidden rubbish in the manufacturing and processing areas. The stuff robots don't get."

"Sometimes I do that," said Vito. "Sometimes I do other things."

"We agreed after Glen left," she insisted. He shrugged. "*I do all hospitality-related activities and everything to support marketing and design. I'm a creative.*"

"Okay," said Gustav.

"And what does new boy here do?" said Vito.

The look Gabriella gave Gustav was not an encouraging one. "Gustav is trying to fix the printers. All of them."

Vito spat with laughter. "Good luck with that. You met Cassie Troy?"

"I have," Gustav said.

"You will have no luck there. We done?" The man's feet and hands were itching to move.

"We are in agreement?" said Gabriella. "We made ourselves clear?"

Vito shrugged.

"I suppose so," said Gustav.

"You play pinochle?" asked Vito.

"Cards?" said Gustav.

Vito nodded. "You any good?"

"This is a business meeting," said Gabriella. "This is important."

"I thought the meeting was over," said Vito.

Gabriella shot him a hard look. "We need to talk, we meet here."

"Or down at the deli café by the medical centre," said Vito. "They do a nice crab salad. We could play pinochle. Bet a little. For fun."

"Meeting adjourned," said Gabriella, kicking the standing stone with her purple boot for emphasis.

"Good to meet you, Gustav," said Vito and walked off.

Gustav smiled at Gabriella. "This was nice," he said.

She held his gaze for a second and left without further words.

Gustav walked across the gardens to his apartment to see what Twenty-Six had been up to and maybe teach the droid how to do jigsaws. He decided he might also look up the rules for pinochle.

23

Ruby sat in the fourth floor restaurant picking over a lunch with her fork and wondering what it was exactly supposed to be. Midweek menus tended to be quite experimental. Two silhouetted figures with bushy and sandy beards stopped in front of her. It was the Jim and Kingsley from Customer Fulfilment development.

"Can we join you?"

She gestured to the seats.

"We want to pick your brains," said Kingsley.

"*He* wants to pick your brains," said Jim curtly. "It's an ethics issue."

"An empathy issue."

"We've got another awareness training session later," said Ruby. "Is it something you want to raise then?"

"We'd rather do this privately," said Kingsley.

"Pick away," said Ruby and put her fork down.

Kingsley held out a tablet screen on which there were images of two cute robots.

"We've uncovered a weird phenomenon," said Kingsley. "We've changed our protocols and now allow the bugs to interact directly with humans."

"I noticed."

"Since when the delivery bugs appear to have evolved cuteness as a, er..."

"Defence mechanism," said Jim.

"Right. People were being obstructive when they viewed them as just machines, so after our last chat we opened up their parameters to allow adaptations in relation to human contact."

Ruby nodded.

Kingsley pointed at the first robot. "People look at this bug and see the cute eyes and helpless demeanour and leave it unmolested. Then people look at this one—"

The second robot had even bigger eyes and a cutesy tiny mouth and dinky little limbs like a new-born animal.

"And they want to punch it in the face?" suggested Ruby.

"Right!" said Kingsley. "They do! Why is that? That shouldn't be."

"It's like we've hit peak cuteness," said Jim.

"Maybe you have," said Ruby.

"But why should that be? Is that thing?" said Kingsley.

Ruby shrugged. "I can give you a couple of theories. One, it's basic cute aggression. You know that?"

Kingsley was shaking his head. Jim wouldn't be drawn.

"People who want to pinch babies' cheeks or hug kittens until they explode. Not actually, obviously. That would be a symptom of a more worrying problem. That inner 'squee!' feeling."

"Squee?" said Jim.

"Squee. People can be overwhelmed by positive emotions until it comes out in weird and inappropriate ways. Alternatively, it's genuine anger you're seeing. Are these people expressing conscious or unconscious fear of new technology?"

"Luddites," sneered Jim.

"Or can they perceive that with this cuteness thing, the robots are playing them?" she suggested.

"The people think the bugs are trying to trick them?" said Kingsley.

Ruby pulled a twitchy 'not quite' expression. "You know people who try to get through life on their good looks? Expecting other people to buy them drinks or indulge in their whims because they're, you know, the sexy one?"

Jim just looked at her. Kingsley looked at Jim.

"What?" said Jim.

"Nothing," said Kingsley.

"This is nothing like that," said Jim.

"Sure," said Kingsley, coolly.

"I know what you're insinuating."

"I've said nothing."

Ruby watched the private unspoken conversation going on between the two men.

"I was the dumper in that relationship, not the dumpee," said Jim.

"And I applaud you for that," said Kingsley.

"And if I don't get my car back within the month, I will be taking legal action."

"Well done."

The two men looked at Ruby.

"We see what you're saying," said Kingsley.

"Does it matter?" said Ruby. "Aren't your bugs supposed to be evolving their way towards efficiency. If you let things run their course, the designs will be refined with each new generation."

"And yet bug abuse by people on campus is going up and up."

"Equip the bugs with tasers?" said Ruby.

"I said that," said Jim.

"I was joking," she said. Jim looked disappointed. But he'd clearly just come out of a painful relationship and Ruby was willing to cut him some slack.

"We could ask site security to identify culprits and fine them," said Kingsley. "Except that's imposing an external control on the system that won't exist in the outside world."

"Can the bugs identify the people who are impeding their work?" said Ruby.

"Then what?"

"Marlin gives out company credit as customer rewards. I mean, all of us get marlin credits on top of our salaries. Couldn't the bugs—" she shrugged "—fine people for specific acts of abuse?"

Kingsley nodded slowly as he thought about it.

"Taser them in the wallet," said Jim.

"We'd have to be very specific about the situations in which the bugs could fine people. It would have to go through legal." As he said it, the light of optimism came on in Kingsley's eyes. "Bugs with the power to punish – or *reward*! – social behaviour."

The men stood.

"Always happy to help," said Ruby.

24

Over the course of the next few days, Gustav saw the other interstitial operatives a few times. It initially seemed suspicious that he would suddenly start seeing them on his rounds, but then, he reasoned, it was probably only because he now recognised their faces amongst a sea of other employees. Stars were just stars until you had the constellations pointed out to you.

He had tried waving to Vito once or twice, but the man always looked like he was on an undercover mission: eyes fixed doggedly ahead, engaging with the world around him as little as possible. Gabriella, by contrast, was always already looking at Gustav whenever he came near. She glared, as though demanding to know what he might be doing in *her* space. Whether she was re-sorting badly sorted recycling waste, cleaning up a communal kitchen, or going round and encouraging people to sign up for the morning mindfulness club, as soon as Gustav approached, her efforts doubled and she somehow filled the available space to ward him off.

Gustav, who was always pleased to meet new people, began to wish he had never got to know her. Ignorance, in this instance, would have been preferable. It was, if nothing else, cramping his own efforts to be the most helpful interstitial operative he could be. He was a sociable person, and he had an in-built desire to please others, but Gabriella's behaviour squashed his enthusiasm and engendered an unhelpful level of reticence in him.

He decided he would have to do something to counteract this.

As was so often the case, marlin had the answer.

The parcel he ordered was at home when he arrived that evening. Twenty-Six and the marlinVac were in the kitchen. Twenty-Six shredded little pieces of cardboard and watched the marlinVac hoover them up. Then the droid shredded some more and watched the robot vacuum cleaner sweep that up. The pair of them progressed about the apartment slowly, like someone trying to entice a tortoise to follow with fragments of lettuce.

"What are you doing?" said Gustav.

"Cleaning up waste is useful," said Twenty-Six. "The marlinVac is being useful."

"Okay," said Gustav. "Maybe you should just put a lead on it and take it for a walk."

Twenty-Six put down the cardboard and looked around.

"We don't have a lead," Gustav pointed out.

Twenty-Six seemed to consider this, and went back to its cardboard shredding.

The parcel Gustav had ordered was on the counter. He peeled back the perforated strip and pulled out the t-shirt. It smelled faintly of unknown chemicals, like it had just been manufactured that very day. Which he supposed it had.

Gustav stripped off his hoodie and t-shirt and put on the new t-shirt. "Hey, Twenty-Six, what do you think?"

The droid looked round. "Say what?"

"It's my new plan to get people to ask me for help." Gustav had ordered a plain white t-shirt with the words I AM HERE TO HELP. ASK ME ANYTHING printed on it in bold red letters. It had only taken minutes to design, and not much longer to print and deliver. "Can you see what it says?"

Twenty-Six studied it. "What should I ask you?"

"Ask me to help you with something."

"Help me with something," Twenty-Six said dutifully.

"Something specific."

"Help me with something specific," said Twenty-Six.

Gustav looked about and his eyes latched onto the not-yet-opened jigsaw. "We should do the jigsaw. Sit with me."

The pair of them sat at the table. Gustav removed the tight cardboard lid and tipped the pieces out onto the table. "We're going to recreate the picture on the box with these pieces."

Twenty-Six picked up a piece. It showed fragments of blue sky, yellow grass and the hint of a fence.

"You need to see what bit of the picture this looks like," said Gustav.

Twenty-Six looked at the box top. "It is not like the picture."

"Are you sure?"

"The picture is square. This piece is uneven." Twenty-Six pointed at the tabs and holes on the puzzle piece.

"No, you have to look at the colours and shapes on the piece. They will match the colour and shape of one part of the picture."

Twenty-Six looked again and immediately said. "This piece is a match for that area." It pointed.

"Then put it down on the table. Imagine that this rectangular area of the table is the same as the rectangular picture. Put the piece in the approximate place where it would go."

Twenty-Six looked at the table, obviously looking round at the spaces that would form the edge of the unmade jigsaw. It then placed the piece carefully on the table.

"Excellent," said Gustav. "Now, do it with another piece."

Twenty-Six picked up another piece from the pile. It looked at it, looked at the picture and, with more confidence this time, placed it on the table.

"And now do that for the other nine hundred and ninety-eight pieces."

Gustav went to the bathroom to get showered and to admire the t-shirt which would form the backbone of his interstitial operations marketing plan. When he returned, Twenty-Six had gone through much of the pile and the jigsaw was more than a third complete. Gustav watched as, between the placement of new pieces, Twenty-Six shuffled certain pieces from place to place within the picture.

"Everything okay?" said Gustav.

"Say what?"

Gustav pointed to one of the moved and re-moved pieces. It was a section of sky. "Why did you place this then move it?"

"The piece belongs here and here and here," said Twenty-Six.

"Yes, it looks like it can go anywhere, doesn't it?" Gustav agreed. "Sky can be like that. You will only know where it belongs when you can see how it connects with other pieces. By itself, you can't tell where it belongs."

Gustav noticed a pile of pieces that had been put to one side, away from the picture. "What are those?"

"They do not belong in this picture," said Twenty-Six. It picked one up. "It is all grey. There is no part of the picture that is all grey."

"Turn it over," said Gustav.

Twenty-Six rotated its hand to turn the piece over to show leaves and spindly branches.

"The jigsaw has two sides," observed Twenty-Six.

Gustav nodded. "Back home, the old man who sat on the beach used to tell jokes about the stupid mainlanders. Hamish and Dougal were nailing boards on the side of a house. Hamish was hammering but throwing away every other nail. Dougal asked him what he was doing. Hamish held up a nail. 'They put the head on the wrong end.' And Dougal said, 'Don't be an idiot, Hamish. Those ones are for the other side of the house.'"

Twenty-Six looked at Gustav blankly. All Twenty-Six's looks were blank, but this one felt doubly so.

"It's a joke," Gustav explained.

"Dougal was correct. Hamish was wrong," said Twenty-Six and went back to the jigsaw.

25

Ruby set up another request for a pair of test scenarios. She was working her way through scenarios every day to find out which specific subversion of the software had introduced the strange behaviour in the VMS. It was a slow, laborious process, as she could only reserve enough processing power to run two tests at a time, but she was progressing steadily.

Her other avenue of investigation, to carefully examine the site, was being frustrated by her inability to print anything. She knew the marlin answer to her problem would be to capture her findings electronically, but for the purposes of visualising the area and breaking it up into searchable sections, she could not imagine how she would use a tablet screen. It was very much an old-school field trip, needing a tape measure and clipboard.

Trying to iron the only sheet of large paper she'd been able to find had not gone well. Ruby now had a persistent stink of scorched paper in her apartment, and had reduced the sheet to a charred mess that would definitely not feed through the printer.

She idly searched marlin's knowledge base for printing solutions, but it kept sending her to the store, where she could buy all manner of goods for overprinting with personalised images. She huffed and lifted her hand to close the laptop, then paused. Maybe that was the answer.

She went to the store and looked carefully at the items she could get printed with an image. She quickly dismissed tiny stuff like mugs, coasters and mouse mats. She wished there was a way to sort by size, as she really needed to find the biggest thing she could order. It was going to be a t-shirt wasn't it? She knew it instinctively, but she checked some other items just to be thorough. An art canvas? No, they had wooden frames. A big magnetic sticker for a car? Sounded tricky to handle without an actual car, and the marlinGos were made from fibreglass. She was very tempted to order a massive cake, with the image on the top, but she realised she was just hungry, and that was possibly affecting her judgement. A t-shirt it was then. Ruby clicked to purchase.

26

Ruby found Gustav in an office space on the sixth floor. He had many pieces of paper spread over a large table, a number of them held down with black moulded printer cartridges. Gustav stood over it all, hands spread wide, fingers flexing like an orchestral conductor preparing to launch into a powerful symphony.

Ruby decided to go in. Gustav barely looked up. "Some people say that working at marlin is enough to drive you mad," she noted.

"I'm thinking," he said.

"Do you always look like that when you're thinking?"

"I don't know," he said. "I don't tend to look at myself when I'm thinking."

She saw the big letters on his t-shirt.

"Can I ask you something?" she said.

"Not right now."

"Your t-shirt says otherwise."

He stood up straight and looked at her.

"Advertising your services," she said. "Nice. I got a t-shirt printed today." She held it out.

"It's got a map on it."

"So I'll always know where I am."

She moved closer and looked at the arrangement on the table. Gustav's mobile had a spreadsheet or database grid on the screen. He'd been compiling a list which had spilled over into a spiderweb configuration of paper and pen scribblings. Notes on this item here and that item there were joined together with criss-crossing arrows like some precarious food chain.

Gustav had a mentally frazzled air about him, and he was generally an unfrazzleable sort of guy.

"Want to talk about it?" she said.

He sighed. "It might be a good idea."

"Talk me through it, then."

He slowly broke from his mad conductor pose and brought one finger down on a sheet. "Here is the printer in Integrated Solutions."

"Yeah, it's not working at the moment."

"It lacks a cyan printer cartridge," he agreed. "So does the printer in the marlinGo test centre." His finger moved to a scribble on another sheet, then to another. "But the printer in Support Services has run out of magenta toner, just like the one in Browser Innovations. Two of those, plus the printers in Customer Fulfilment, Digital Mapping and these ones here also have full waste toner boxes, and they won't work until those boxes have been swapped out for empties."

"You've made a list of all the printer faults. Couldn't you just log them?"

He gave her a level stare. His gaze was unnervingly fixed, like he'd had too much caffeine or not enough sleep. "They've all been logged, Ruby. Nearly every single printer on campus is non-functioning for one reason or another." His fingers hopscotched across his many sheets. "Toner, toner, toner, toner. Waste toner, waste toner. Paper jam, paper jam. This one has a R402 error."

"What's that?"

"I don't know. No one knows. Error, error, error. And they all use these." He put a shipping box on the table. "Standard pack for the marlinPrint range." He tapped the printer cartridges out on the table. "Cyan, magenta, yellow, black printer cartridges. Plus each pack comes with a waste toner box. Do you see how the yellow and black toner cartridges are substantially bigger than the cyan and magenta?"

Ruby did see. She gave it a moment's consideration. "The black and the yellow get used up more quickly so it makes sense to have larger cartridges."

Gustav giggled. Definitely not enough sleep. "It does," he agreed. "I don't know who calculated the proportions."

He opened the box he'd put on the table. The little slots for the black, cyan and magenta were empty. He pulled out the yellow toner cartridge.

"It's full," he said. "And the admin cupboard on the fourth floor is full of these. We have enough yellow toner to last us until rapture, Ruby."

"Okay, bud," she said. "This is a very interesting – and insane – side project you have got going on here."

"It's not a side project. With the other interstitials carving out their own niches, I've got to make this work." He waved his hands at the mess of information. "But none of them work."

"You'd think people would be in uproar."

"But they're told not to print. Be paperless. If you want to print, it's a deviation from the norm."

"The printers are still there."

"And people know they can print, notionally, *because* the printers are there. They're not being denied access to printers. They can print, in theory. They are allowed to print, in theory. But in reality it's not happening."

"What's this?" said Ruby, pointing to a printer in the centre of the web with a big question mark next to it.

"The exception that proves the rule. It is, as far as I can tell, the only working printer on campus."

Ruby bent to read his scribbled notes. "Seventh floor, conference suite. Oh well, that makes sense. It's the managing director's printer."

Gustav peered at it again. "Huh."

"You surprised that whoever's in charge of printing has made the MD a priority?"

"I'm surprised there's a managing director," said Gustav. "And the person in charge of the printing is a— Is it rude to call someone weird?"

"To their face, maybe."

"Or maybe I just think that because she lives in the basement behind a locked door."

Ruby shook her head and waved her hands over the table. "This. This is weird."

Gustav shook his head at her. "This is my plan."

Ruby regarded the insane web of lines. "It's just printers, Gustav."

"No, there's a principle at stake."

"What principle?"

His face creased irritably. "I don't know. I'll tell you when I work it out."

27

Later that week, Ruby welcomed the attendees of the awareness training back into the breakout room.

"Hello everyone. Thank you all for coming at short notice. I am squeezing this in between our scheduled sessions because I want to share something that will provide us with plenty to talk about next time. It will just take a few minutes."

Everyone sat and looked attentive, so Ruby moved to a side table, where there was a cloth covering something bulky.

"Ready?" She made sure she had their attention, then pulled the cloth off with a flourish.

"Ta da! Now what you see here is a pair of cages with our class pets inside them. Come and have a look. If anyone's feeling brave, we can take them out and get to know them."

"What are they?" asked Quinn.

"One of the cages contains a hamster, and one of them

contains a delivery bug that was destined for the crusher. I got permission to use it for this project."

Quinn rushed forward. "I love hamsters! Let me see." She opened the cage and scooped out the sandy-coloured ball of fur.

"What are their names?" asked Gustav, close behind.

"Everything to do with the care of these two is now the responsibility of the class," said Ruby. "And that includes giving them names."

"Oo'd a leedle floofy babee?" said Quinn, caressing the hamster and grinning widely. "So silky soft! We should call you Velvet."

Velvet didn't seem keen on either the name or attention. Gustav peered into the other cage where a robot delivery bug looked up at them with its over-sized eyes. "What about this one?"

Jim huffed with exasperation. "They all have identifiers coded onto their comms sign-in. I'll soon tell you its name." He pulled out his mobile and held it against the cage. "There you are, it's EB9 99AHG."

"Ooh, we can call it Heeby!" said Quinn, making kissy noises at Velvet the hamster, and dipping her head towards Heeby to share the affection.

"Ridiculous!" said Jim.

"Oh, I don't know," said Kingsley, scooping Heeby up from the cage. "I always had a fondness for this generation."

"Excellent," said Ruby. "It's over to you now. There's food and sawdust in the cupboard underneath, See you next time."

"What?" said Jim. "That's what you got us here for? To give us a pet rodent and a bug?"

"Yes," she said.

"But why? What's the point? At least tell us the point."

"Call it an open-ended experiment." Ruby breezed out of the room and left them to it.

28

The following day, a marlin package spoke to Gustav. Or at least, it appeared to. It sat on a stone bench in the campus gardens and said, *"Sir! Sir! Would you like to earn marlin store credit?"*

Gustav went over to look. The package itself was a square box, maybe twenty centimetres to a side. A standard parcel. But it wasn't the package that had spoken; it was the crab-like robot squatting on its top.

The robot clung to the package with eight sharp white legs. Its round body was nothing but a display screen. It blinked friendly eyes at him.

"You're a delivery bug," he said, recognising minor elements of design here and there.

"If you carry me to Morgan Jenkins in campus building C, I will give you store credit," it said. A strobing arrow pointed the direction it wished to go in.

"How did you get here?" he asked. The crab bug was

clearly too small to carry the parcel, and there was no way it would have been able to climb up onto this bench.

"A kind person carried me part of the way here in exchange for store credit," said the bug. *"If you carry me to Morgan Jenkins in campus building C, I will give you store credit also."*

Gustav hadn't exactly been going that way, but it didn't seem sufficient reason to say no. "Of course." He picked up the light parcel and bug and set off.

"You are very kind," said the bug.

The mobile in Gustav's pocket buzzed. He looked at it. Marlin store credit had been added to his account. A tiny amount, but it was there.

"Thank you," he said to the bug.

"You are a valuable member of the marlin community," it said.

His mobile buzzed again. The bug had given him five compliments.

"Thank you," he said.

Gustav had accumulated five small credit deposits by the time he reached campus building C. On the journey, he had seen at least three other people carrying parcels with small squatting bugs on their tops. The last one gave him a look, a sort of 'Hey, look at us. Isn't this strange?' look. Gustav returned it.

He dropped the parcel off with the recipient. The small crab bug disengaged its claws from the cardboard parcel, dropped to the floor and scurried away.

29

Ruby proceeded across the marlin campus, screen in one hand, map t-shirt in the other. Today was the day she would physically map out the events leading to Gustav's near accident.

The central hub of the campus had no roads at all. From the apartment complexes to the admin building to Customer Fulfilment there were only green spaces and gentle pathways. A loop of ring road bounded the edges, providing access for couriers and service vehicles, and marking the closest anyone could get to the heart of marlin. The ring road represented a border, with the Republic of Marlin on the inside and the strange, cold, real world on the outside.

Ruby walked the boundary, following her progress on her t-shirt map, one eye on the screen's descriptions of the marlinGo's actions on the day it had nearly killed Gustav, and half her mind trying to remember how long it had been since she'd stepped beyond that ring road. How long it had been since she had spent any time outside marlin's domain.

The answer was, longer than she could remember.

She stopped at a junction. The screen revealed the decision-making modules the marlinGo had accessed before proceeding across this T-junction. She used a black felt tip pen to make a note on the t-shirt before proceeding along the roadside path.

There were marlin sites all over the world. This place was not unique. It was by no means the largest or the most strategically important of the marlin sites. And, in a company where the hierarchical structure was so flat as to be utterly opaque, it probably wouldn't even count as marlin's head office. Yet the place felt like it was unique. A bubble of idealistic business and living set apart from the world; a tiny near-perfect kingdom.

Yes, a magic kingdom, she decided. It was like Disneyland. There might have been various Disneylands or Disneyworlds all over the planet, but step inside any of them and you immediately felt this was *the* Disneyland. The one and only.

Ruby considered herself to possess a healthy level of scepticism. Yes, she might mess about on the same social media platforms as everyone else, she might binge watch the same 'must see' TV events as everyone else, and she might automatically order her takeaway from whatever service had most recently put their adverts in front of her. But importantly, she did this knowing what she was doing. She wasn't a mindless sheeple (or whatever the singular of sheeple was) living her life on autopilot. Companies might draw her in and steer her life like everyone else's, but at least she was aware of it. Marlin had suckered her into a workplace, a lifestyle, and a culture, and very cosy it was too (if a little insane), but she consoled herself with the fact she recognised it for what it was. This workplace she had not left in weeks had become her home. True, she might now be feeling a peculiar dislocation from the real world, a deep *Weltschmerz* for the world within and the world without, but at least she knew that was what she was experiencing.

In short, Ruby had swallowed the marlin pill. And despite believing the marlin way was unnatural and odd and ultimately unworkable, she felt zero desire to step out of it into the old world again. Ruby Jallow was going to stay on this side of the road.

At the next junction, she looked at her screen again. The decision process of the Gustav-attacking Vehicle Management System version 30251.11 flowed on the screen. All perfectly normal. She took the lid off her felt tip to make another note on the t-shirt. The pen faded and died on the second letter. A t-shirt might have given her the size to suit her printing needs, but as a writing material, it was an ink-drinking failure.

"Damn." This plan wasn't working.

A short distance along the other side of the road, a moustachioed man in a boiler suit was plucking pieces of windblown rubbish from the hedges.

"Excuse me," Ruby called.

"Yes?" said the man, packing that single syllable with enough inflection to reveal his Italian roots.

"Do you happen to have a pen on you I could borrow?"

said Ruby, adding by way of explanation, "I need to write on this t-shirt." Which was really no explanation at all.

"Certainly," said the man. He reached for the breast pocket of his overalls. It was brimming with various pens, like a miniature mobile stationery shop. "Perhaps I could interest you in one of these?" he said, pulling a red pen from his pocket to show her as he crossed the road.

A marlinGo, whizzing along the ring road, shifted lanes and ran straight into him.

30

Gustav's plan to fix printers, whilst not criminal or immoral or against any marlin policy he was aware of, nonetheless felt instinctively ... *transgressive*. So he approached it as he might a criminal enterprise. He was aware that security cameras covered almost every part of the campus complex and had many of the large printers in their line of sight, but he didn't necessarily need to avoid appearing on camera. What he needed to avoid was meeting people who might regard his behaviour as unacceptably suspicious, or indeed suspiciously unacceptable.

Avoiding people was not easy, and here he might fall foul of marlin's Easy Working Hours policy. Whereas in other companies and at other times in history, workers might have been compelled to attend their place of work between fixed hours of, say, nine to five, marlin had always operated on the understanding that colleagues could turn up to the office and leave again whenever they wished. No one recorded their attendance (or if it did, it was never discussed or shared). It was simply assumed each person was working the hours necessary to complete their allotted job.

On the surface, this policy appeared to generate only positives – freedom, choice, trust – but in his short time with marlin, Gustav had noticed it generating a different kind of culture. He saw many people coming in to work not long after dawn, and those same people staying long after the street lights came on outside.

This seemed to have an interesting counterpart in marlin's Shared Spaces policy, in which no single office belonged to a single individual. Areas of the building might be allocated to certain departments or divisions, but the offices, the meeting rooms and the various reflection zones, dreamatoriums and innovation hubs were open and available to all.

In all, what Gustav had seen was, instead of the old fashioned office workers turning up at their allotted times to occupy their given workspaces, a tense and unspoken battle each morning as said workers rushed in as early as possible to snatch up favoured workspaces – which they would defend and hold for as long as they could. It was a strange madness of the kind he'd never seen on his island home.

Back home, in the row of semi-abandoned cottages, each family would have had their own allocated space. It did not need defining. It did not need labelling. Each family had a place to call their own. Similarly, they fished as a community, working together to net as much fish as the village needed, but no more. With a contempt he tried not to feel, Gustav could image the people in this corner of the world behaving very differently. He could picture their fishing boats going out onto their grey seas, jostling, barging against one another, and savagely harvesting more fish than they could possibly need for fear that others might take more than their share.

In terms of Gustav's printer plans it simply meant workers spent more time in the office than elsewhere, and thus it was nearly impossible to find a time when there were few people around. He concluded the quietest part of the day was actually the middle. The mad rush to get in, claim space and publicly parade one's hard-working early bird attitude stretched from dawn until shortly after nine in the morning. There was a conversely busy "one last meeting before I go"/ "my workplace is my social space" attitude in the late afternoon and into the evening. There was increased campus traffic around lunchtime, which meant late morning and mid-afternoon were perhaps quietest of all.

Working on the principle that, like worker bees, human workers were at their most sluggish and inattentive after a meal, Gustav chose to enact his plan in the afternoon. Two p.m. to be precise.

Ruby had described Gustav's plan as robbing Peter to pay Paul. Gustav had met neither of those gentlemen, but he understood the point she was trying to make. Even though she was wrong. Currently there appeared to be only one functioning printer on the marlin campus. By the time he was done, this would change.

He went to the marlinGo test centre and removed the empty cyan printer cartridge; then to Customer Fulfilment and to Support Services to remove the full waste toner box and empty magenta cartridge respectively. Doing his best impression of a nonchalant interstitial operative, he took all three to the conference centre and swapped them out for the full cyan and magenta cartridges and the not-yet-filled waste toner box.

The magenta cartridge and waste toner box went to Browser Innovations, fixing both problems there. Now with an empty magenta, full toner and full cyan, he went back to Architectural Services and slid in the cyan cartridge. Back to marlinGo, he swapped the empty waste toner for a full one, and the full magenta cartridge for the empty he carried. The empty waste toner he then took to Customer Fulfilment to replace the full one he'd taken previously, and the full magenta to Support Services.

The entire operation took just under an hour, and in doing so, he had crippled the conference centre printer so that the Integrated Solutions, Customer Fulfilment, Browser Innovations and Support Services printers might live again.

31

Ruby didn't recall doing anything after the accident.

She clearly recalled what she *had done* but could not remember any moment in which she had been consciously active, choosing to do *this* rather than *that*. She could not recall being mentally present in that scene.

She had run off to the man, shouting at the marlinGo to stop and to completely shut down. The marlinGo had obeyed. She had crouched by the man's side where he had been thrown by the speeding electric car. He had come to rest on his back, with his shoulders against the kerb as an uncomfortable pillow. His legs had been straight out in front of him, but there was something horribly still and unposed about them, like they didn't belong to a real human being. His eyes had been open, staring in shock and surprise, and his breathing had come in tight, pained gasps. There had been red on the man's hand and the cuff of his overalls, but Ruby could see no signs of bleeding.

Ruby had said something stupid like "Are you okay?" and then pressed the alarm button on her marlin campus app.

In what seemed like mere seconds, people were running over from the admin building, followed by a team from the marlin medical centre, followed shortly after by an ambulance from the real world beyond marlin's borders. Throughout, Ruby had been passed lovingly from person to person and slowly disengaged from the scene, and the only thing she recalled having said throughout was "He's got red on him. It might be ink. I don't know. I don't know."

Somehow Ruby found herself in a relaxation space in admin with a cup of tea in her hands. She sipped it.

"It's got sugar in it," she said. "I don't take sugar."

"Sugar for shock," said the woman who had passed it to her. Clarissa or Clare or something?

"Is that a thing?" said Ruby, but Clarissa or Clare didn't know.

Someone came along and suggested Ruby go home for the rest of the day. Another person said an appointment had been made for her with the medical clinic and that counselling might be advisable.

Ruby nodded numbly and, leaving the unpleasantly sweet tea, left.

She crossed the campus, vaguely holding onto the notion that she should go home to her apartment, but seeing the marlinGo test centre across the gardens, changed direction and went there to report the second accident.

Of course, she realised as she entered the test centre, she

wasn't the first person to inform the team there. The car itself had reported a collision and Ruby walked into the final act of various people from several departments loudly pointing fingers and casting blame. As the blame game expanded and dissipated, Celery Brown the beta-test manager caught sight of Ruby.

"Here comes trouble," she said.

"I just came to—" Ruby nodded her head sideways to generally indicate the marlinGo accident furore.

"If you're going to ask, it's not the same VMS version as before," said Celery.

"I hadn't even thought about that," said Ruby honestly. She wasn't doing much thinking right now. Since the accident, her brain had been operating on a skeleton crew, only one tiny hamster at the exercise wheel of her mind.

"You were there today, weren't you?" said Celery.

Ruby couldn't tell if Celery was expressing concern for her or accusing her of being the common factor in both accidents. Well, one accident and one near miss.

"The droid was with me last time," she said.

"The crash test droid."

It occurred to Ruby she ought to examine its core modules, to see if there were any extra stored inputs from that day. "Is it here?" she said.

"What?"

"The droid." She scrolled on her screen. "Twenty-Six."

Celery consulted her own screen. "It's out and about on campus. We program them to mimic ordinary human pedestrian behaviours. You can track it with the app." She swiped and flung the app details to Ruby's screen.

"Thanks."

Ruby stepped away. The chaos and recriminations were not yet over.

Outside, there was a cold breeze blowing. Ruby ran a search for the droid. A winking icon appeared on the map, showing it was in the accommodation block where she lived. There was no rule that said droids should not be in the accommodation, but Ruby couldn't think of a good reason why it should be over there. She decided to head over and find it. She ought to go home anyway.

When she entered the accommodation building, she checked the map again to see exactly where the winking icon was. It was surprisingly close to her apartment. She zoomed in and saw it appeared to be next door, at Gustav's place.

She walked to Gustav's front door and paused before knocking, listening. Was Gustav in there with the droid? She heard nothing so she knocked the door. There was no answer, although she thought she heard a tiny scraping noise.

"Hello! Droid number Twenty-Six? Are you inside this apartment?"

Right on the cusp of hearing, she could have sworn that she heard a faint, whispered "No."

32

Ruby was the last to arrive at the breakout room, yet she was definitely not late. Her mind still felt weirdly dislocated, detached from herself and the real world by the shock – no, not shock – the simple surprise of the accident she'd witnessed that morning. Seeing the small cluster of happy humanity around the cages at the back of the room drained that detachment. The world moved on and there were happy humans in it.

"How are Velvet and Heeby?" she asked.

Quinn pointed at Velvet's cage, where the hamster was snuggled into the internal house fast asleep. "He sleeps a lot during the day, but he sometimes comes by to say hello. Heeby is a lot more sociable."

"Is that right?" Ruby asked.

Heeby was out on a tabletop, with a small fenced-in area made from rolled-up t-shirts. Jim and Kingsley sat together at the far side of the table, with Quinn and Gustav opposite. Heeby scuttled back and forth on its curved legs, bumping into the edges of its environment. It was smaller than many of the delivery bugs that Ruby had seen, but still quite a bit bigger than the hamster. Each time it detected an edge it made a small sound that made everyone smile. Sometimes it would sit up and swivel its face from side to side, as if it was checking in on its audience.

"See how he likes to show off?" Kingsley grinned.

"This is all very interesting," said Ruby, taking a seat at the table. "I wonder what we can learn from this experience. Let me start by asking you all a question: how did Heeby come to have a gender?"

There were shared glances across the table.

"A gender?" said Gustav.

"Yes. Kingsley definitely referred to Heeby as 'he' a moment ago."

"Did I?" said Kingsley.

"You did. Let's discuss that."

"I guess we've all been doing that," said Quinn. "I don't even know who started it. Maybe the name sounds a bit like Herbie?"

"Maybe it looks male?" suggested Kingsley. They all stared hard as Heeby scampered across the table, but if they spotted any masculine traits, nobody mentioned them.

"If you don't know how it happened, then there's a strong possibility it's a result of unconscious bias," said Ruby. "The idea that everything is male by default."

"But I did it too," said Quinn.

"And she's a woman!" said Jim.

"Unconscious bias exists in women too, because society trains it into us from an early age," said Ruby.

"No," said Quinn, not in disagreement but faint disbelief.

"Nobody should be ashamed. It is very helpful to recognise this. Once we know it's happening we can work on how we might overcome it and be more inclusive. Now, tell me if you've made any observations amongst yourselves since you've been caring for Velvet and Heeby."

"Velvet doesn't spend as much time with us," said Quinn.

"His fur is lovely and soft," said Gustav. It was a simple, childish statement, but didn't seem so coming out of Gustav's mouth.

"It's nice when he wants to play," said Quinn. "I wish we didn't have to clean out his cage so often. People complain that there's a funny smell in here."

"I like the smell," said Gustav. "Most of the Marlin campus smells of nothing at all, or it smells of packaging materials and the lubricant used on the bugs." He inhaled. "This reminds me of home."

"Did your home smell of hamster wee?" asked Jim, smirking.

"No, I mean the smell of Dubh Mòr. It wasn't the same as this, it was more a peaty seaweed smell, but it was nice."

"Interesting," said Ruby. "So there's an overhead in cleaning out a live animal, but perhaps we can see some value in that?"

There were gentle shrugs of agreement.

"It's not the only overhead though, is it?" said Jim. "Velvet needs a constant supply of food. Heeby is very low maintenance in that respect."

"Is he, though?" asked Kingsley. "I think Jim's being a bit simplistic."

"For crying out loud man, we're talking to—" Jim bit down on whatever he was going to say. "We're talking to users. They don't care about what happens at the back end."

"Back end?" said Ruby.

"It's technical stuff," said Jim.

"Tell us."

"The electricity consumed directly by the bugs is fairly small," said Kingsley. "We have induction chargers all over campus that charge them up as they pass by. What isn't obvious though is the number of servers needed to operate the software. You've seen the wind turbines?"

Everyone nodded. There were tall wind turbines dotted around the far edges of the campus.

"Those don't come anywhere close to generating enough power to cover what we consume here."

"But software doesn't use up energy, does it?" said Quinn. "I mean obviously it does, but it's just circuits and processors. It's not—"

"What?" said Kingsley. "Not big moving parts? The carbon footprint of our computing efforts is huge. Take marlin's natural language processors. You talk to your MarlinAssist at home, right? It doesn't actually know what you're saying, that's handled by cloud-based processing. Translating your verbal instructions into the actual words you're saying is one process. Working out what those words mean is another. Then devising some sort of response is another process. Constructing a verbal response is yet another. These are big powerful processes – algorithms trained on colossal quantities of data. Every time we train a new algorithm, it's the equivalent of running an old-fashioned internal combustion engine car for thirty years."

Quinn looked stunned, Gustav entirely surprised.

"So what does it take to run Heeby?" asked Quinn, reaching over to give Heeby a tickle where its chin might have been.

Jim and Kingsley made eye contact. Ruby thought that perhaps they were both running calculations in their heads.

"It's not easy to attribute consumption to a single unit," said Kingsley. "But if we translated it into hamster food, it would be at least ten times what Velvet eats."

"Five times, more like," said Jim, but it was a lacklustre effort. He was clearly disagreeing on principle.

"Wow," said Gustav.

"Well then, the answer is obvious," said Quinn casually. "You should get hamsters to do the deliveries, shouldn't you?"

Jim and Kingsley stared at Quinn, then their eyes locked with one another. They started a high-speed conversation that was so muted and esoteric that Ruby couldn't hear or follow, but when the word 'augmentation' floated her way, she clapped her hands.

"Were you, by any chance, discussing the possibility of making advanced bugs by augmenting hamsters?"

"Well, by chance, there has been some research into brain ports we might use for such an eventuality," said Jim. "The exoskeleton to enable the necessary load-carrying capacity would be a smaller technical challenge, but—"

Ruby held up a hand to stop his excited chatter. "Let's talk this over with the group, shall we? It's a great illustration of where we might need other viewpoints. Just because we can do something, doesn't necessarily mean we should, right?"

Jim gave Ruby a look that said he entirely disagreed with this notion. He folded his arms and sat back in his chair. "Fine."

"What exciting ethical situations just one conversation has generated," said Ruby. "Questions we weren't necessarily aware of before today."

33

On Thursday, Ruby appeared by Gustav's side in the lunch queue on level four. "What you getting?" she asked.

He pointed at the menu. "I've been getting the YouKnowMe all week. It's an easy selection."

"Really?"

"They base it on your known habits. It's like the Recommended Purchase programme. Marlin calculates what I might like—"

"Using one of those energy guzzling algorithms," she interrupted.

"I suppose so. Still, it gives me a carefully selected food option."

"You think that's wise?"

"YouKnowMe," he said to the server, and saw Ruby about to respond to what might have been seen as a flippant comment before realising he wasn't talking to her.

"It's not always wise to hand decision making over to computers," she said.

"No?"

"There was a case a while back of American law enforcement using location-based algorithms to predict where crimes were likely to occur. If criminal activity had occurred in certain places at certain times, it was thought wise to send patrol cars to those areas at those times to pre-empt future crimes."

"Makes sense."

"Does it?" she said, in a smug and knowing manner. "So if, historically, the police have arrested more people in, say, poor black areas of major cities, and the algorithm tells them to send more police cars to poor black areas of major cities, can you imagine what happens?"

"Ah."

"Self-fulfilling prophecy. Chimichanga, please," she said to the server.

"I don't think my dinner is going to be a self-fulfilling racist prophecy," said Gustav.

"Marlin moves in mysterious ways."

He grunted in amused agreement. "Do you ever turn off this ethical bit of your brain?"

"No. And neither should you. Are you enjoying the awareness training?"

He paused in thought. He wanted to answer honestly. "It's good to understand other people and their views," he said. "Everyone comes with their own agenda, but hearing them speak openly about things… It's good."

"You have no idea how hard I had to fight to not have

management sit in on those training sessions. I've got my first meeting with the ESG tomorrow and I expect it to be mentioned."

"ESG?" he said, shaking his head at the acronym.

"Environmental, Social and Corporate Governance."

"That should be ESCG."

"I'm not the acronym police. I don't make the rules. You see it mentioned all over shareholder documentation."

"And what is it?"

"Well basically, companies are expected to provide their credentials as responsible citizens as well as being financially viable. That's the role of the ESG."

"It's a committee where they show they're being nice people."

"Indeed. It's no longer simply okay to be profitable. Major corporations need to show they're doing the right thing. Like, not sticking their noses into training sessions they don't need to."

"I don't think I would mind the people in charge hearing what I say."

Ruby made a disagreeing noise. "What we say in public, particularly when we know the bosses are watching us, is far removed from what we might privately think."

"I try to say what I think most of the time," he said.

"I've noticed," she smiled. "Most people who pride themselves on their honesty basically use it as an excuse to be rude, but you…"

"Me…?" he said, collecting a glass from the trolley at the end of the food queue.

"You're the nice kind of honest. It's not common."

They collected their meals and found a table.

"Speaking of honesty," said Ruby, "can I ask you an honest question?"

"Sure."

"Is there a droid in your apartment?"

The unexpected question took him somewhat by surprise. "I— Yes. Why would you ask me that?"

"I've been looking for droid Twenty-Six and the app says it's at your place. How long has it been there?"

"Quite a while. It wanted to stay. What do you need it for?"

She gave a dismissive wave. "I just want a chat with it about that time the car acted strangely. Maybe I could pop round when you're home?"

"Yes, that will be fine. I have no wine though."

Ruby gave him a look as though he'd said something mildly offensive. "There's your uncommon honesty again," she said.

"Let me tell you what I've been doing with the printers," he said hurriedly, and proceeded to explain.

Ruby nodded along as if she almost understood Gustav's printer juggling when he tried to explain it to her. "Sounds like you're rearranging deckchairs on the Titanic," she said. "Or doing that puzzle where you've got to get three pints in a five pint pot."

"I am unfamiliar with this puzzle," he said.

She clicked her fingers. "No. I'll tell you what it's like. John Harris's survival lottery thought experiment."

"Again, I am unfamiliar."

"It proposes that if you randomly select a person to kill in order to redistribute their healthy organs among numerous individuals in need of said organs, then the good it achieves would be worth the suffering it causes."

"I did not kill the managing director's printer."

She gave him an amused look, but even though it was amused, playful even, he did not like the sentiment of her words. "The printer was functioning. Now, because of your actions, it is no longer functioning. If that's not killing, Gustav, what is it?"

"It is a machine, not a living thing."

"Says the man who helps defenceless little bugs who get stuck in the flowerbeds. Says the man who has given a home to a little lost droid." She stared at her dinner, then at Gustav's three-bean salad and tuna. "Shit."

"What?" he said.

"Yours looks better than mine."

He shrugged happily.

Gustav knew he shouldn't be affected by her perverse ethical spin on the printer issue, but he couldn't prevent it affecting him more deeply than it should. Shortly after lunch, he found himself wandering by the seventh floor conference suite and the printer he had cruelly disabled.

The printer repair woman, Cassie Troy, crouched in front of the printer. She had Panel A open and was inspecting roller C4 he noticed. She muttered something darkly as she spun the roller and watched the inner workings. Whatever emergency interventions she was attempting were not going to bring it back to life any time soon.

Gustav walked swiftly on.

Gabriella was by the lifts, waving her floppy flat cap at him. He went over.

"Vito is gone," she said.

"Gone?" said Gustav.

"Kaput. Finished."

"Dead?"

"No. He's in the hospital. Two broken legs."

"My goodness."

"Got hit by a car. Looked left when he should've looked right. So, we need to sort this out."

"Like a get well card and a fruit basket?"

She screwed up her face like he'd just spoken nonsense. "Dividing up his territory. You can have wires and cabling. I call dibs on everything else."

34

Having been invited to present at an ESG steering committee, Ruby looked up some of the attendees and discovered they were all directors of the company. She was getting to spend time with the big boys and girls. She crafted a colourful presentation, taking extra care in choosing her outfit. Clothes should not have to make a difference, but they did. She selected a trouser suit in emerald green, with a multi-coloured silk blouse. It reflected her character, but it definitely said *professional*.

She went to collect a print copy of her presentation on her way up to the meeting. The rumours of self-repairing printers had been localised phenomena for some time before they cross-fertilised and entered the general consciousness of the marlin campus.

"Maybe it's a software update," a man in Integrated Solutions with a crumb of muffin cake on his tie said to Ruby as her printing came off.

"How would a software update make the printer toner cartridges magically refill?" she said.

He gave her a condescending look, clearly ready for the question. "Perhaps the previous software was saying it was out of toner when it wasn't. Efficiency prevents waste."

"If you say so," she said. "Doesn't sound plausible."

"What other explanation is there? Does the printer fairy come round in the night and fix everything while we're asleep, like in the fairy tale?"

She considered it. "The Elves and the Shoemaker."

"I think it was fairies," he said.

"Elves," she said and left with her printing.

She arrived at the upper management conference suite on the seventh floor well ahead of time, so she could be sure she'd be able to show her presentation with no problems. The decor in here was part of the same palette used elsewhere, except everything was a little more plush and expensive-looking. Fresh fruit was laid out on side cupboards, along with small pastry snacks that looked freshly cooked. In a company which played down its hierarchy, there were much subtler ways to indicate this area was set aside for important people. The chairs were upholstered in velvet, and before sitting Ruby noticed the pile was all carefully combed into stripes. There was definitely no way it had settled like that; each chair looked like a carefully mown lawn. She took a seat at the front so that she could present more easily, then worried it might look pushy and aggressive to take that position. She moved down a couple of seats. As she settled into the new chair, she looked at the one she had just vacated and saw there was a very obvious imprint of her bottom in the velvet pile. She could see why the chairs were so carefully groomed.

She rushed over and tried to smooth the fabric back into stripes with her hands, but it looked more like a mad finger painting done by a pre-schooler.

"Hello. It's Ruby, isn't it?"

Ruby's head snapped up, and she tried really hard not to look as if she was doing something weird. "Hi! Um, yes."

Delphine from legal wore a deceptively simple dress that looked extremely expensive. She carried a small laptop.

"This is the bit where I would normally welcome you and say I've heard so much about you," said Delphine.

"And have you?"

"You seem to have been inserting your thumbs into all sorts of pies of late," said Delphine. "We can't wait to see what you have for us." She glanced up at the screen. "You're presenting to the call?"

"I thought this was a meeting."

"It is."

"A *meeting* meeting."

Delphine nodded. "We probably won't get all of the people in the room. We need to hop on the call for those joining remotely."

Delphine brought the videoconference to life, and Ruby realised she and Delphine were the only ones physically present. She tried to keep track of which grey haired man on the screen was which, but so many of them were called names like Chad and Brock and Trent, it wasn't easy. They were all directors of non-obvious things like *Planning and Excellence* and *Oversight Management*.

"Shall we make a start, then?" said one of the grey-haired men. "What's on today's agenda, Ruby?"

"Well, I have a presentation to show you the progress I'm making with the awareness training," said Ruby. "I'm not sure about the rest of the agenda. What do you normally do in ESG meetings?"

"We've never had one before," said Delphine.

"The agenda is wide open. Completely up to you," said one of the Brocks.

That rocked Ruby's expectations. This was the company's inaugural ESG meeting. She was momentarily shocked to discover how immature Marlin's thinking was around some of these important topics. She smiled at Delphine and at the camera that represented everyone else.

"Of course, no problem. I will be very happy to help shape the work around this. Have you set any high level expectations at all? Any outcomes you want to see?"

There was a pause before the same Brock spoke up. "It's a new area for us, so we'll need you to establish some metrics as well. Set a baseline."

"Uh huh." So, first meeting and no one had put any thought into it.

One of the quieter Brocks spoke up. "We might get some input from the new guiding mission doctrine update, mightn't we?"

"Great shout!" said the other Brock. "Listen Ruby, you'll need to go with your gut until the execs sign off on the new guiding mission doctrine update, but we're right behind you if you need anything. Our doors are always open."

Ruby wondered where their doors were. "Right. Good.

For today then, I can walk you through some findings from the pilot group I'm taking on the awareness training—"

"Hey listen, I don't want to interrupt you Ruby, but is there any chance we can leave it there for today? I'd be more than happy to give you the hour back if we've given you the steer you need. What do you say?"

Ruby saw the trap. If she pointed out she'd had no steer at all then she would sound petulant. If she asked them whether they were even interested in the subject, doubly so.

"Sure. No problem."

Moments later the call was closed. Delphine whisked from the room with a brief "Great job, Ruby."

Ruby sat alone in the upper management conference suite. She had it booked for an hour, so she decided she would stay in here and consume as many high class snacks as she could reasonable scarf down. She started a list as she reached for a pastry.

Metrics – how to measure performance of Marlin's ESG?

By the time she had worked out which pastry was her favourite and eaten all of them, Ruby had expanded her list into a tangled mind map of possibilities. She would definitely need some help in working this through.

35

Later that week, Ruby happened to share a lift with a sour-faced woman in a knitted tank top. The woman had two long printer cartridge boxes under her arm and was muttering to herself.

"Busy day?" Ruby offered pleasantly.

"Off to sort out the seventh floor printer. Again," the woman said crabbily.

"Again? Ah. Problems."

The woman's head swivelled to stare at Ruby. If the woman had been taller, the action might have seemed menacing. "Problems? There are no problems."

"That's … that's lovely," said Ruby and didn't attempt any further conversation.

In the evening, she went round at Gustav's apartment when she was fairly sure he'd be home.

"Hello, I wondered if I could see the droid?" she said.

Gustav invited her in. She saw the droid was sitting on a comfy chair, as if it was watching television.

"What's it doing?" asked Ruby.

Gustav shrugged. "We like watching the dog shows."

Ruby wasn't sure why this bothered her, but it did. She glanced across at the table where a jigsaw puzzle was part done. "Did you try to get it to do a jigsaw?"

"I did."

"I have a good many questions for you, Gustav, but first of all I'd like to speak to the droid."

They both looked over to Twenty-Six. Ruby was certain it must have heard her come in, but it remained glued to the television screen. She went over and sat down on the chair to the side, so that she could face the droid. She wanted to turn off the television, but that seemed an aggressive move to kick off with.

"Hi Twenty-Six. I haven't seen you in a while."

"I have been out of your way." It stood up abruptly. "I will get out of your way."

"No! Stop! It's fine. I want to talk to you," said Ruby.

The droid sat back down but remained silent. Gustav hovered in the background, as if he was uncertain what he should be doing. There was a peculiar dynamic here, as if Gustav was being protective of the droid and she was the monster.

She sighed. "I guess I spoke to you harshly before, but you don't need to leave, or hide away from me." She cast about for appropriate small talk for a crash test droid. "Um, what have you been doing with your time here?"

"During what time frame?" asked Twenty-Six.

"Today, for example."

"From midnight until four thirteen a.m. I stood over there," said Twenty-Six, pointing at a square of carpet. "From four thirteen a.m. to four sixteen a.m. I stood there. From four sixteen a.m. to four seventeen a.m. I stood there."

"Why did you move?" said Ruby.

"I was in the way of the MarlinVac. I went somewhere out of the way. From four seventeen a.m. to—"

"I meant what have you been doing generally?" said Ruby.

"Say what?"

Ruby looked to Gustav. "Have you been changing its programming?"

"Only accidentally," he said. "This is a happy home for people and robots. I try not to tell anyone what to do."

"What have you been 'doing generally'?" asked Twenty-Six.

Ruby let out a breathy laugh. "Hmmm. Trying to chase you down. Trying to work out why a MarlinGo would try to run over our friend, Gustav. Leading a training group on ethical awareness, thinking about empathy and AI ethics and our inherent biases. I'm actually kind of worried that Jim and Kingsley from product development are going to try to augment a hamster with an exoskeleton and turn it into a sort of Robo-Hamster. And I've had a non-meeting with the ESG."

"What is the ESG?" said Twenty-Six.

"The steering committee for Environmental, Social and Corporate Governance."

Twenty-Six twitched. "That should be ESCG."

"That's what I said," said Gustav. "How could it be a non-meeting?"

"Well," she said slowly, lining up her thoughts as she stretched the one syllable. "The ESG is there to measure and improve our ethical and social impact, our general goodness. Except there are no baselines and no metrics."

"Which means?"

"We don't know where we are and we haven't decided how to measure any change. And the guys in the meeting – it was mostly guys – didn't want to offer me too much guidance in case it clouded my professional judgement. So, basically, we're going on an expedition with no starting point, no end point and no map."

"That's ... not helpful," Gustav noted.

"How astute."

"But it does mean you get to draw the map yourself?" he added.

She scowled. "You know, your optimistic outlook can rub people up the wrong way sometimes."

"Sorry."

She sighed. "But you're right. As long as I'm guided by the mission doctrine update I can probably arrange this how I like."

"Mission doctrine update. Is that like a vision statement?" said Gustav.

"No. I mean, I don't think so. I think that's two different things."

"That 'Everything you want to do, you can do with marlin' slogan thing you see on all the advertising?" said Gustav.

"No, I think – I *think* – that's the brand objective."

"Or is it that 'One day, all workplaces will be like this'?"

"No, that's a different motto," she said, irritated now. "Look, there are lots of slogans and mottos and statements and visions and executive directives. But there's a thing called a mission doctrine update and when I find *that* I can begin our ethical journey."

"Sounds like you are very busy," said Twenty-Six.

"I am," she agreed.

"Would you like to stay for dinner tonight?" said Gustav.

"I sit at the table when we eat," added Twenty-Six. "And then we're going to watch *Dog Rescue – Forever Homes*."

"I could order in some wine if you like," said Gustav.

Ruby smiled. "You had me at dinner," she said, which was a lie, but 'You had me at wine" made her sound like she had a problem.

36

The next day, Ruby caught up with Gustav while he was walking down the corridor, pushing two wheeled office chairs before him. "What are you doing?"

"Redistributing chairs."

"Pardon?"

"For whatever reason, some of the rooms end up with more chairs than others. People borrow them and never put them back. It's like a slow tide. Some offices have more chairs than desks, some desks without chairs. I can't do comfy chairs, but I can do office chairs."

"Why?"

"Gabriella called dibs on that. A long time ago. Before Glen left."

"Who's Glen?"

"I don't know."

"And are you still resupplying all the different department printers?" she asked.

"Yes. Cassie Troy has not responded to any of the logged requests for any printers except the seventh floor conference suite."

"So that's why people are leaving notes for you then, huh?"

"Notes?"

She gave him a yellow post-it note and he looked at it.

"They are not naming me by name," he observed.

"Clearly you're being super sneaky. I'm not sure if they think you are Robin Hood or some sort of printer-based tooth fairy."

"The tooth fairy takes things, not brings them," he pointed out.

"Fine. Then Santa Claus with a sleigh full of toner cartridges. Anyway, Printer Claus, it seems your devotees have also started leaving you cakes." She held up a cute little cake box with an intricate folding lid. Gustav's eyebrows went up.

His fingers hovered over the box, then he opened the lid flaps to reveal a fat chocolate muffin within, topped with swirls of frosting.

"I don't do this to be thanked," he said.

Ruby withdrew the box slightly. "You don't want it? I'm sure I could find it a good home."

"I may want it," he said.

"Which brings you greater happiness? The cake? Or the warm fuzzy feeling that people have left you gifts?"

He thought about it. "If I say the warm fuzzy feeling will you offer to split the gift with me so I get the warm fuzzy feeling and you get cake?"

Ruby scowled and thrust the cake at him. "Sometimes you are too clever for your own good, Gustav."

37

There was a marlin recommended purchase parcel waiting for Gustav when he got home. Twenty-Six was watching television while the marlinVac played around its feet. Twenty-Six had a knack for mimicking human behaviours, but Gustav was uncertain whether the droid gained anything meaningful from them. For instance, while it was true that Twenty-Six was actively watching the television, the droid was watching a swirling channel ident and the unmoving words PROGRAMMES BEGIN AGAIN AT 6 P.M. SEE YOU THEN!

"Evening," said Gustav.

"Hello," said Twenty-Six.

"*Good evening,*" said the marlinAssist. "*You have three notifications today including the delivery of a package.*"

"I know," said Gustav. "I have it here. Twenty-Six, should I accept the parcel unopened or open it first? I could get a—" he turned the parcel round "—ten percent discount."

"Say what?"

"MarlinAssist, accept the recommended purchase parcel." Gustav passed the box to Twenty-Six. "Open it," he said, adding, "Carefully," as Twenty-Six went at it with powerful plastic fingers.

The marlinVac raced to hoover up the fragments of cardboard dropped to the floor.

"It is a jigsaw," said Twenty-Six. "The picture is of a dog and some sheep on a green field."

It was exactly as Twenty-Six had described.

Gustav fixed himself a cold drink. "Clearly this is a present for you."

"It's for me?" said Twenty-Six.

"You can do the jigsaw at the table."

Twenty-Six turned off the television and went to sit at the dining table. The jigsaw of the tree was still there.

"We will have to get rid of this first," said Gustav.

Twenty-Six swept the completed jigsaw from the table. It cascaded in whole chunks onto the floor where it was dashed to piece.

"Maybe not like that," said Gustav.

Twenty-Six opened the new jigsaw and immediately began taking out pieces and allocating them to their correct spot. No human tactics for this droid. No finding the edges or sorting by colour. Jigsaw solving was a brute task of piece by piece object recognition.

"We had sheep and dogs like those," said Gustav.

Twenty-Six looked round at the floor, as though expecting to see sheep or dogs in the apartment. There was only the marlinVac, making an irregular *tunk-tunk-tunk* sound as it sucked up the pieces of the discarded jigsaw.

"On Eilean Dubh Mòr," said Gustav. "We kept a herd of sheep, before the problems with the soil. We had dogs, a mother and her daughters, to help herd them."

Gustav looked at the picture. It clearly wasn't Dubh Mòr. In the scene, the rolling fields swept past stone cottages and stone walls (which Dubh Mòr had) to a long valley bigger than Dubh Mòr, dotted with trees and houses and industry. In the picture, the land was as big as the sky. On Eilean Dubh Mòr, the edge of the land was almost always in sight. The sea and the sky were everything. Also, the shepherd standing on the edge of the picture was a man. Back on the island, women tended to the sheep more often than men.

"I remember my mum bringing in the herd for shearing," he said. "The dogs and the sheep lived outside, naturally. But when there was a sickly lamb, she'd bring it inside and I'd take care of it. An injured gull once, too." He took the photo of his mum from his wallet and pressed it flat on the table for Twenty-Six to see. "Waifs and strays, she'd call them. We'd take them all in."

Twenty-Six picked up the photograph and studied it. "This piece does not belong here," it said and put it aside.

"No." Gustav took the photo and went about preparing dinner.

38

Gustav's covert mission to resupply the under-resourced printers on campus meant regular trips to the seventh floor to steal from the one serviced printer. This occasionally and unavoidably meant encountering Cassie Troy as she repaired and resupplied it. Her bitter mutterings had grown louder of late.

Gustav tucked the full waster toner box he had brought to swap out up his *I AM HERE TO HELP* t-shirt when he saw the repairwoman crouched by the printer. As he made to walk casually by, Cassie's eyes latched onto him.

"It's stopped again!" she said. "It's taunting me!"

"Er, okay," he said.

"Everything that can go wrong with a marlinPrint has gone wrong with this machine. The toner runs out like the machine's drinking it. The R402 error that used to be on the office admin printer has jumped to this one. It's not possible."

It was possible, but it hadn't been easy. A lengthy search on the internet had identified the component block responsible for the error, and Gustav had spent a fraught afternoon unscrewing and removing the heavy component from the office admin printer and swapping it with the one on this printer. The only person who had stopped him in his secret mission was a woman from office admin. She had told him not to bother; Santa Impresora fixed all printers, she had said. Gustav would have ask who this mythical Santa Impresora might be, but he had to be more focused on his covert swap-over mission.

"This printer is cursed," said Cassie.

Gustav nodded politely.

Cassie had the top panel of the printer open and a diagnostic screen displayed on her mobile. "Every day! Something new!"

"And are any of the other printers having the same problem?" he asked. He knew he shouldn't, but there was a deep and irresistible feeling in him that here was a point which needed making.

Cassie gave him a fierce look.

"We are meant to be a paperless office," she said with restrained rage. "A paperless office! I don't think anyone knows what that means." She touched the side of the giant printer, tenderly, like a veterinarian touching the sides of a pregnant cow. "They don't make these anymore."

"You mean this model?"

"I mean printers! MarlinPrint ceased production last year. No printers. No spare parts. No printer cartridges. Marlin has gone paperless and these wonderful innocent creations are being consigned to the scrap heap."

"But in your storeroom downstairs—" he began.

"No new supplies," she said. "We have to ration what's left."

She bowed her head and stayed in that position. Was she grieving? Was she actually crying?

He wondered if he should console her in some way but as he made to step towards her, he noticed the small pile of black-grey waste toner by his feet. The box he was carrying was leaking.

He started to say some final words of consolation but only got so far as "I'm—" before he realised he had nothing meaningful to offer. "Okay. Bye," he said and walked off.

He had almost reached the corner of the corridor when there was a shout of "Hey!"

Gustav looked back. Cassie Troy had stood up and was looking directly at him. He also spotted a fine but nonetheless noticeable trail of waste toner following him down the corridor.

"Wait there," Cassie called.

Gustav ran. He ducked round the corner in what he hoped was not a suspicious manner and ran down the adjacent corridor, turned to go into the stairwell to head down, and collided hard with the stairway door as it swung shut in his face. There was crack, a dry huff and Gustav's world went black.

39

On the third floor, Ruby passed a printer by the lifts. There was a garland of flowers, a small votive candle and a little postcard asking Santa Impresora to watch over the printer. Underneath was a post-it informing the patron saint of marlin printers that they were out of black toner.

"Okay. It's just getting weird now," she murmured.

The lift doors opened and Gustav stepped out with more than a surprised look on his face.

"You do know that blackface went out of fashion about a hundred years ago?" said Ruby.

"A waste toner cartridge exploded," he said, blinking.

There were two untouched patches around his eyes in a face that was almost entirely grey-black. He looked like a reverse panda.

"It feels a bit tingly," he said.

"That stuff's caustic," she said.

"What?"

"It's toxic."

"Are you sure? Should we look it up?"

"We need to get that stuff cleaned off you." She steered him out into the hallway and to one of the shower rooms. "Get in, strip off. Wash until there's nothing left of it."

He did as he was instructed. Five minutes later, the sound of running water had stopped. The door opened a fraction, not enough to see in or out but to allow conversation.

"I think I've got rid of it," he said.

"Good."

"But my t-shirt is covered in it. I don't know if I should put it back on."

"You have a spare t-shirt? Or a hoodie?"

"At home."

"We could…" She glanced around. "Marlin do one hour delivery on numerous items. Order one."

"Really? I could just walk home."

"Topless."

"Isn't that okay?"

"Or I could go home and get one for you."

"I could just order a t-shirt and wait here."

"And maybe, gap monkey, you could find some little jobs that need doing in there."

There was a pause. "Maybe. Personalised printed t-shirt. One-hour delivery."

"We live in a golden age. Go for it."

"Ah!" he said, struck by an idea. There was a camera click. "And ordered!"

Ruby considered how to phrase her next words.

"Gustav, if you're taking photos in a shower room..."

"Yes?"

"There's only a limited number of things you could possibly be taking pictures of."

"This is great," he said. "Problem solved."

"You know what, I'm going to leave you to it," she said. "I've got things to do. Self-driving cars to fix. Ethical steering groups to steer."

40

Fifty minutes after Gustav had entered there was knock at the shower room door.

"Hello?" said Gustav who was, for the fourth time, alternating between scrubbing his face, neck and chest in the mirror, and washing the grey toner-tainted water down the sink. The waste toner was pernicious stuff. Whilst it was mostly gone, the dust had left an almost immovable stain on him. Pink scrubbed skin with blackened pores made him look like a Victorian chimney sweep after a team of servants had scrubbed him in the bath.

"Er, hi," said a woman's voice.

"I'm in here," said Gustav.

"Yes. I've got this bug. It paid me to carry it here. It has a parcel. I'm looking for Gustav White."

"That's me." He unlocked the door and, with his foot against the bottom to stop it opening too wide, pulled it open a crack. "Just slide it through."

The bug outside burbled something.

"It wants to know if you can show your face for ID purposes," the woman said.

Gustav was naked from the waist up, which wasn't something that bothered him, but might be a problem for others. "Not really," he said.

There was a brief hurried back and forth between the woman and the bug, then a narrow marlin package slid through the gap in the door.

"Thank you," Gustav said and shut and locked the door again.

He opened the package, savouring the freshly printed smell and opened out his new t-shirt. It was an excellent reproduction of the original. He turned to the handbasin and used a clean section of his soiled t-shirt to wipe the last of the water from his chest, then wiped round the inner surface of the sink. What sort of interstitial operative would he be if he left the shower room messy and dirty? He binned the old t-shirt and pulled on the new one.

He admired himself in the mirror.

This was a lovely idea. Yes, he would re-order himself a *I'M HERE TO HELP* t-shirt at some point, although with Vito sadly out of action, there seemed less pressure to advertise himself.

He picked up the printer waste toner box. The toner box was now empty and could be re-inserted in any printer, which was a faint silver lining to the whole escapade.

He stepped out of the shower room, mentally recalling which of the nearest printers needed a freshly emptied toner box, and set off.

As he walked, his t-shirt caught the attention of a few people walking by. There were some wide eyes and some quizzical frowns.

"Um. Unusual," said a man from Integrated Solution as he headed to the stairs.

"Just an old photo," said Gustav. "I was talking to a droid yesterday about my home and I was feeling nostalgic I guess."

The man from Integrated Solutions didn't appear to know what to say.

At the bottom of the stairs, he nearly collided with Quinn, who he'd met in the awareness training sessions, and they had to sidestep one another. She goggled in surprise at his fresh t-shirt.

"It's my mum," he explained. Quinn gave him a faintly horrified look and hurried off.

41

Ruby high-fived the air. This wasn't something she'd normally do. High-fiving the air was a somewhat pathetic gesture, but there was no one in the office space to see her do it, which was sort of the point of the solo celebration.

Nobody was available to share her jubilation. She'd have high-fived a complete stranger if there had been one. She wanted to mark the moment anyway. While the investigation of the crash site had not provided her with the key information she needed, the accident involving the other interstitial operative had given her another VMS version to compare with. With a pre-crash VMS, a 'Gustav' VMS and a 'Vito' VMS, finding commonalities and differences had been much easier.

And thus, she had finally isolated the software update that made the VMS behave badly in the test scenario, the iteration which had tried to kill Gustav. Her investigation would now need to focus on what was included in that update, but it was a significant step forward. She had the chunks of code that were somehow responsible.

She stood up from the workstation, too buzzed to sit still now she had finally made the breakthrough she'd been working towards. She decided she might seek out Gustav. Although she had been cagey about telling him that the car had possibly tried to kill him, having isolated the guilty software update meant she could at least share the news with an element of hope.

On her way down the corridor, a delivery bug stepped in front of Ruby in the corridor. It was sturdy, round and carried a marlin parcel in its scoop-like front limbs. She made to step round it but it sidestepped to block her.

"*Carry me,*" it said.

She tried sidestepping, but it mirrored her movement.

"*Carry me,*" it repeated.

"I've got work to do," she said. It skittered side to side on speedy little legs as she tried and failed to get by.

A black and yellow warning flashed on its face screen below its narrow eyes. "*Marlin will not tolerate abuse of its property or community members. Abusers will be penalised,*" the bug said.

"I'm not abusing you," said Ruby.

The bug narrowed its eyes further, then ran sideways into a glass wall. It collided noisily and bounced off.

"*Ow,*" it said.

Ruby's mobile buzzed, she looked at it. "Hey. What's this? You can't take credit off me!"

"Abusers will be penalised." The bug ran headlong into the wall again. The glass reverberated with the impact.

Ruby's mobile buzzed as more credit was taken from her.

"Stop that!" she said.

"Abusers will be penalised," repeated the bug. Its voice sounded woozy, as though it was struggling to remain conscious.

"This is crazy," she said.

The bug charged at the other wall. Ruby managed to grab it by the parcel and lift it off the ground. Its legs whirred.

"Carry me?" it said.

"Damn it all," she said. Her mobile buzzed again. She suddenly had a meeting to go to, one she had not scheduled and could not remove from her calendar.

"Is this your doing?" she said to the bug.

The bug was silent, seemingly content now it had been picked up.

42

Ruby entered the designated meeting room on the fifth floor.

Myfanwy from HR was there and the woman, Delphine, from legal.

Ruby frowned. "Is this a formal meeting? Is Quinn in trouble again? Or someone else? This really isn't part of my job, you know."

"We need to talk," said Myfanwy. She wasn't smiling, but Ruby could tell she was working hard to supress one. Not because she was secretly happy, but because smiling was her default setting. "Sit. Please."

Ruby sat.

"Why are you carrying that bug?" asked Delphine from legal.

Ruby had the blackmailing bug tight in her lap.

"It's malfunctioning," she said. "I'm taking it in. Look, what's this all about because I've no idea."

"We've had complaints," said Myfanwy. "Several complaints."

"About me?"

"Do you know Gustav White?"

"Yeah. Yes, I do. We're neighbours. In the apartments. We see each other around."

"And have you seen him today? Have you seen what he was wearing?"

Ruby winced. Was this about the toner explosion? Or the possibility of him walking home topless? Or – Christ – was this about the photo he took in the shower room? She elected to play it safe.

"I saw him *earlier*," she said, innocently. "Why?"

"He ordered a photo t-shirt."

"Oh, god."

"So you know about the photo t-shirt?" said Delphine.

"He needed a t-shirt."

"You told him the photograph was 'lovely' and something to be proud of," said Myfanwy.

Her hands were waving an emphatic negative before her head could join in with some shaking. "I did not see the photo before he ordered the t-shirt."

"But you told him to 'go for it'."

"Have you been grilling Gustav?" said Ruby. "Have you got him stashed away in some marlin prison cell."

"Mr White is very upset at the moment," said Myfanwy. "He feels very embarrassed and anxious because of the t-shirt you told him to order."

"This is my fault?"

"Is that a question or a statement of guilt?" said Delphine.

"I didn't make him order or wear any t-shirt. I am concerned about Gustav, but this is, in no way, my responsibility."

Delphine uncrossed and crossed her legs. "Dr Jallow, your problems with marlin's code of professional conduct and our sexual harassment policy are a matter of record."

"Pardon?"

"Inserting yourself into that business with Quinn McAndrews."

"In that meeting it was made clear staff are permitted to dress as they feel appropriate," said Myfanwy.

"And Quinn has taken that message to heart," Ruby assured them. "It was all a misunderstanding."

"This goes beyond a misunderstanding," said Delphine. "In fact, we're currently of the opinion that today's stunt was a deliberate attempt to test and ridicule that policy."

"Stunts. I don't do stunts. I'm actually a really busy person and I don't have time for—"

"You think issues relating to community member wellbeing are beneath you and not worth your time or attention?"

"I did not say that."

Myfanwy flicked an image up onto the wall screen. It was a screenshot of a marlin store order. The central image was of a t-shirt, entirely covered by an uploaded picture.

"Do you think it is appropriate for a community member to wear an item of clothing like this?" said Myfanwy.

The picture covering the t-shirt from neck to waist, from

arm to arm, was one Ruby had seen before. And the words 'lovely' and 'proud' had passed her lips when she'd first seen it. It was the Dubh Mòr May festival with the May Queen, Gustav's mum, prominently in the centre. Four smiling, naked women crowded into the space on the front of the t-shirt. There was plenty of general nakedness, male and female, around them.

"Oh, Gustav."

"Dr Jallow, do you think it is appropriate for a community member to wear an item of clothing like this?" Myfanwy repeated.

"No. Yes. No? Is this a trick question?"

Delphine made a noise of bitter amusement. "You can see how someone might see this as an attempt to throw our dress code into confusion. We made it clear that all community members should respect all other community members' rights to dress in a manner with which they're comfortable. Only a few days later, this situation has been contrived in which Gustav White wears this t-shirt. Is this some sort of protest? Are you trying to make some clever point?"

Ruby stared dumbly. What had happened was perfectly clear. There was no confusion in her mind on that point. What she couldn't comprehend was how she would navigate her way out of this situation.

She pointed at the beaming pageant queen in the middle of the t-shirt. "That's Gustav's mum, that is."

"Is that supposed to make it okay?" said Myfanwy.

"Yes? No?" For an intelligent woman, she had never felt so stupid. "Again, I feel this is a trick question. It's not particularly fair."

"Do you want to call legal or a union representation at this time?" said Delphine.

"What? No. I'm not being fired, am I?"

"This image represents the sexual objectification of women which, for reasons entirely beyond my understanding, you apparently sought to promote in the workplace."

Ruby opened her mouth to speak, then forced herself to close her mouth and thought.

"I wasn't seeking to promote the sexual objectification of women," she said slowly, checking every syllable for accuracy and the possibility of it getting her fired.

"Were you perhaps trying to make a political point?" said Delphine. "Do you object to marlin's policies regarding clothing? Do you not think people should be allowed to wear whatever they wish?"

There was the answer they clearly wanted to hear. No, I think people should be allowed to wear whatever they wish. But, inside her, a little voice was shouting, like the eager child at the back of the classroom, jumping up and down in its seat, itching to point out that such absolutist morality would always come unstuck at some point. That cultural customs and taboos regarding clothing had evolved for practical and socially beneficial reasons, and even though some clothing customs were out-dated and needed culling, there was still such as thing as appropriate clothing and – hang on for just one minute! – how could they possibly say people could wear what they want if she (and Gustav) were being censured for a personal clothing choice?

Ruby bit down on all of this and said, "No, I think people should be allowed to wear whatever they wish to wear."

"Good," said Myfanwy. "Now, we want to discuss what you told Gustav." She scrolled on the screen in front of her. "You said that if a man wished to cause social embarrassment and alarm, he should turn up to work wearing nothing but 'budgie smugglers'."

Delphine looked over at Myfanwy's screen and then at Ruby. "What *are* budgie smugglers?"

43

The bug in Ruby's arms complained all the way to Customer Fulfilment. Her mobile buzzed every thirty seconds as it fined her company credit. By the time she'd reached the development team's office space, her mobile was telling her she had negative marlin credits and would need to repay them.

She saw a sandy, bearded head and went over. It was Jim, he of the apparently free-loading ex and somewhat surly demeanour. There was a 3D model of a hamster on his screen, rotating slowly in computer non-space. She decided to ignore it.

Ruby placed the bug on his desk in front of him. The bug rotated and explored the confines of the desk.

"What's this?" said Jim.

"This?" seethed Ruby furiously. "*This* just tried to blackmail me into carrying it to its destination."

"Blackmail?" He ran a finger over the fine crack in its body shell. He ran diagnostics on his mobile.

"It has stolen nearly a day's wages in company credit from me," she said.

"You kicked it?" he said.

"I did not!"

He brought up the diagnostics on a screen. A cartoon wireframe image of the bug showing glowing areas on the sides of its body. They pulsed like missile targets, or the representations of throbbing pain in painkiller adverts.

"Here, and here, and here again," said Jim, pointing.

"Abusers will be penalised," said the bug.

"I didn't kick it. If you check the security cams you'll see," she said.

Jim humphed and typed on a keyboard. A map of the bug's progress appeared on the screen. Jim zoomed in and clicked an option.

"Ah, there's no cameras in that little section," he said. "Convenient."

The bug rotated on the desk to look at Ruby.

"The damned thing mugged me," said Ruby.

"It can't mug people," said Jim. "It's a bug. All it wants to do is deliver parcels from A to B."

The bug took a step towards Ruby. *"Carry me?"*

"Look at its programming," she said. "See what it's doing."

Jim laughed caustically. "Really?" He selected options and a great tangled ball of lines and data blossomed on the screen. "Which bit do you want to look at?"

She gestured wildly. "The bit that controls what it just did."

Jim grinned, amused now. "I didn't write this. No one wrote this. This is over four hundred generations of mutated code. We try to keep a grip on what happens in certain sections, like identifying what the different lobes of the brain do, but understanding the actual code…?"

"And that's it?" she said. "You're not going to do anything about it."

He leaned back in his chair. "You kick a bug, rack up a load of fines and then bring it to me."

"Because something has gone wrong."

There was a playful look on his face. "So this wasn't some kind of ploy?"

"Ploy?"

"Dinner? Drinks?"

"What?"

"Just to say I am free with Friday, but must insist on splitting the bill."

Ruby stared. "You think this was some crazy roundabout way of … asking you on a date?"

"Hey," he said, generously. "As methods go…"

She shook her head. "Some people are unbelievable," she said.

44

On Tuesday morning, Ruby found Gustav in the third floor corridor with a trolley laden with charger cables of various types and sizes.

"Busy?" she said.

"Finding homes for all these little wires," he said. "It used to be Vito's job. Well, it used to be no one's job, but now it's the job belonging to no one that I'm doing."

She presented him with a marlin parcel.

"I already had my Recommended Purchase parcel today," he said.

"This one is a present. From me."

He took it with more reverence than it probably warranted. "Are we giving each other gifts now?"

"I don't know if you got into trouble for that t-shirt thing the other day…"

"Myfanwy was very understanding."

Ruby made a doubtful noise. "I don't think she

understands anything. She speaks and words come out, but actual intelligence…"

"I wasn't in trouble," he said.

Ruby didn't know if that was true or not. Gustav had an open and guileless countenance. Like a toddler with a red-smeared face protesting it hadn't touched the jam, Gustav might not be able to tell when he was in trouble.

"Anyway, it was ever-so-marginally my fault, so this is for you."

Gustav ripped the perforated cardboard seals and pulled out the garment within. It was another printed t-shirt. He unfolded it and held it out to inspect it.

It was ostensibly the same image of his mother that had appeared on the previous offending t-shirt.

"I used some image enhancement," she pointed out. "I upped the colours because the original had faded. And I removed the fold line in the picture."

"And you put clothes on her," observed Gustav.

"I … did do that too," she said.

It had taken quite a while. Ruby was not an experienced image manipulator and didn't think she had any flair for the visual arts. However, she had persevered. She had decided Gustav's naked mother would look best draped in the toga-like dress apparently favoured by the ancient Greeks. She had found a pre-Raphaelite painting of some maidens and draped Gustav's mum in a similar golden-orange dress.

"It's lovely," he said.

"I hope I haven't offended you further," she said. "I was worried you might not want me tweaking the image."

"No, not at all," he insisted. "It's really rather lovely." He turned it round and held it against himself. "It's very thoughtful."

"Well ... good."

"And, you know, she's not naked in this picture. Which is a good thing."

"Indeed."

He folded it carefully and re-inserted it into the packaging.

"You know, I think someone saw you that day," said Ruby.

"What day?" said Gustav.

"When you got toner all over your face as you were fixing the printers. Or they saw some CCTV of it."

"Why do you say that?"

She grabbed the end of his trolley, pulling both it and him down the side corridor to a marlin printer. In the alcove above there was a new shrine to Santa Impresora. There were battery-operated fake candles, garlands of peachy-pink flowers, and a framed picture. Santa Impresora wore a long heavily layered dress and carried a laserjet printer and printer toner cartridge. Her face was completely black but for the pale circles around her eyes.

Gustav was speechless.

"There's a whole doctoral thesis on the growth of religious cults here," said Ruby.

"I didn't mean for this to happen," he said

"It's got nothing to do with you. This is all the work of Santa Impresora, don't you know."

As they looked, a woman in a buttoned up shirt and tank top came stalking down the corridor. She saw the votive image above the printer and, with a strangled shriek, she grabbed the picture and hurled it against the opposite wall. The frame split and the glass plate fell out, but did not shatter.

The woman made a weird noise, part scream and part sob, perhaps a honk of disgust at herself, and hurried on, hands to her face.

"Who the hell was that?" said Ruby.

"Cassie Troy," said Gustav. "The printer woman. I might have upset her."

"How?" said Ruby, impressed. Gustav didn't seem the type to upset anyone.

"I fixed some printers."

"You helped her do her job and she's upset with you?"

"Or with Santa Impresora. It's hard to tell." He looked at the gift Ruby had given him. "I think I owe her an apology."

"Are you sure you owe her and not the other way round?" said Ruby.

Gustav shrugged thoughtfully. "She's sad and I'm not. I don't think she owes me anything."

45

Ruby convened her second ESG Steering Committee meeting. She added an agenda to the meeting with a single line:

Agree approach to defining and benchmarking ESG metrics.

As at the previous meeting, the multitude of Brocks joined remotely and Delphine was the only other human in the room.

"Hi Ruby, how can we help?" asked one of the Brocks.

Ruby thought he looked distracted. Was he reading his email?

"Yes," she said. "I wanted to jump straight onto the important question of metrics, as it's clear we have no baseline. I'm struggling to navigate the procurement system so I can get an agency involved to run some customer perception workshops."

"Whoa, hold up there, Ruby!" said a Brock. "You're looking at significant spend there. You'd need a cost centre for a thing like that."

"Yes, I realise that. Can someone on this call give me a cost centre?"

"It's not that simple, Ruby. Cost centres are operated at the director level."

"Right. And aren't you all directors?" Ruby asked.

"Yes, of course. But this is not attributable to any of our budgets. Let's park this course of action until we're certain how the budget will work, and think outside the box. We'll see if we can use what we have in-house. We can wangle you some time with the insights team – let's say for a week. How does that sound?"

"Er, the insights team are flat out on the Employee Lifetime Value project," said another Brock.

"Damn, of course. No, we can't get in the way of that. Ruby, I think we'll work from estimates for the time being. Just until we get going with the budget."

"And how will we get going with the budget?" Ruby asked, feeling very much as if she was asking the same thing repeatedly.

"In August you'll present your business case for next year's spend. Do that and we'll see if we can't get you an allocation, huh?"

The avuncular tone, along with the implication Ruby was supposed to be grateful, was nearly enough to make her lose her cool. But she was better than that. She could see them gearing up to dismiss her and leave the call.

"What about the shareholders?" she asked.

"Sorry?"

"I believe the shareholders have specifically asked to see progress in this area. Some of your most significant investors have cited increasing public interest and awareness of this subject."

"So what you're saying is—?"

"What I'm saying is that an estimate will not do." Ruby stated it as a bald fact, hoping she had not overstepped the mark.

There was an exaggerated sigh. "Why don't you just give Ruby your cost centre? We clearly need to do this."

One of the other Brocks had taken her side! Ruby suppressed a gleeful grin.

"Fine." The avuncular tone had gone. "I'll drop you an email, Ruby. My assistant will help you with the procurement. Just be care— what on earth is *that*?"

The Brock was pointing in horror. Because he was on a video conference screen it wasn't at all clear where he was pointing.

"Where? Who are you looking at?" Ruby asked.

"Behind you, Ruby!"

Delphine leaned across to look and shrieked. "Oh my God! It's a rat!"

Ruby twisted in her seat. "Oh, hey! What are you doing here?" She bit down on the temptation to name Velvet, instead moving to scoop the hamster into her hands. She missed, and it scurried across the table, jumped a small gap, and vanished from sight down the back of a cupboard.

"Get site management out!" gasped Delphine. "We can't have an infestation!"

"Site management don't do that," said a Brock. "They do doors and busted light bulbs and things. You want the facilities team."

"Did you see that thing run?" offered another.

"The teeth on it! It was as big as a cat. A cat with fangs!"

There were shouts of indignation from various Brocks. Ruby ended the call, promising to sort it out.

"You looked as if you were going to touch that rat!" said Delphine. "Did you touch it? Did it bite you? You might need a shot." Delphine was backing away as she spoke. Fear and disgust twisted her features.

"I will find it, don't worry. You can leave me to deal with facilities."

Delphine scurried away and Ruby put an urgent message out to her awareness training students to help her find Velvet.

46

Gustav decided an apology gift for Cassie Troy was in order. Or at least a general pick-me-up, put-a-smile-on-your-face gift. The woman was struggling in the face of inexplicable printer behaviour and the appearance of Santa Impresora. However, he didn't want to go up to her directly with a gift, because there was no logical reason for Gustav to present her with one. Not without revealing he was the phantom printer fiddler. Of course he could have a present delivered to her anonymously by marlin bot, but he wanted it to clearly be a gift – not just some random recommended purchase parcel. And he wanted to give it to her, to add an emphatic human element to the gift-giving process.

He quickly settled on a solution. He would order a present and have it sent to Cassie's subterranean office, then hang around in the corridor in order to be the human who accompanied the bug to the door. Although there were still plenty of self-propelling delivery bots about the place, recent evolutionary developments meant a large number of them were of the cute and helpless variety, begging and bribing humans to carry them.

Deciding what to buy her was a little trickier. A search of the marlin store for gifts for middle-aged women brought up an eclectic offering. Boxes of curry powders in test tubes, a metal feather bookmark, gardening gloves with built-in 'gardening claws', an electric jar opener, pashmina ponchos, elasticated sweatpants and a Belgian waffle maker were all presented to him as ideal gifts for the woman over forty. Gustav considered this advice to be generally poor, and possibly awful in Cassie's case. He thought long and searched hard before he settled on the best possible gift.

Intercepting the delivery bug was easier than he thought. Naturally, marlin provided him, as the customer, with minute-by-minute updates on delivery, but he worried he would have some trouble acquiring the bot. While the number of helpless 'carry me' bots had increased steadily since his arrival, there were still plenty of the original package carrying bugs. Taking the package from one of those would be an act of theft. And if it was one of the bugs who bribed its couriers, it was possible the courier would be unwilling to relinquish the bug – however close it was to the final destination.

Gustav needn't have worried. The bug and its human transport were easily spotted. A harassed young woman holding it out at arm's length, as though it were something foul-smelling she had found on the pavement, and not a small crab-like bug with its claws dug into a cardboard package.

"Can I take that from you?" Gustav suggested.

The woman looked at him with an expression of mad disbelief and hope.

"*Take me to Cassie Troy in room 11J. Abusing marlin delivery systems will result in a fine,*" said the bug in squeaky malevolence.

"I will carry you." Gustav took the package and the woman all but sprinted away, as though the bug was a ticking bomb.

"*Take me to Cassie Troy in 11J. Abuse will not be tolerated,*" said the bug.

"I am taking you there right now," said Gustav cheerily.

He carried the bug down the basement corridor to the wooden door of the printer woman's office and knocked on the door. As before he had to wait for the whirring printing sounds within to stop, and for Cassie Troy to come over and unlock the door.

She looked at him and at the bug. "What is it?"

"A delivery," he said.

She studied the bug and shook her head. "I didn't order anything."

"Maybe it's a gift," he suggested, hoping he wasn't being too obvious. He did not consider himself a good liar even if the lie was barely a lie, and a gentle one at that.

"I don't get gifts. I unsubscribed from marlin recommended purchase programme. That took some doing." She took the package from him anyway.

"*Return me to Customer Fulfilment,*" said the bug

imperiously. *"Keeping marlin property is an abuse and subject to financial penalties."*

Gustav had never encountered such a grumpy bug before.

Cassie nodded like a judge accepting testimony. She carried the package and attached bug inside and put both on a bench. As the bug continued to complain, Cassie unhurriedly went to the wall, unpinned a sheet of paper, went back to the bug and held the sheet in front of it. The bug made a popping sound, whined, and its red eyes went dark.

"What did you just do?" said Gustav.

Cassie showed him the chaotic grid of clustered squares. "Old-fashioned QR code pointing to a simple malware site. Marlin equip their bugs and robots with eyes, yet don't think paper-based cyber-attacks are a threat. Here—" she passed the sheet to him "—In case you need it again."

Gustav folded the paper and slipped it into his pocket. Cassie levered the bug off the parcel and tossed it to the floor. It lay on its back, still. Gustav stepped forward to pick it up. It appeared to be dead.

"You've killed it?"

"Stunned," said Cassie. "I value my privacy and autonomy, but I don't go around destroying innocent tech. The QR hack is temporarily disabling. If you were wearing marlinOptics, they'd be fritzing right now. I don't want anyone getting my name off some cloud-based data storage. They want to know my name they can ask me— Huh."

She had ripped open the package and lifted out Gustav's gift.

It was a lanyard with an ID badge holder. The sash was a thick band of yellow gold that made the whole thing look like a symbol of office or a winner's medal.

"Huh," she said again.

Gustav stood and put the defunct bug in his pocket. He stayed near the door, suddenly nervousness that his gift might anger the woman.

Cassie held her own lanyard, then swapped out the ancient ID card into the new holder and hung it around her neck. She nodded appreciatively. Gustav had to stop himself punching the air in victory.

"You don't see many people with the old physical IDs," she said.

"No. No one."

"People don't value the importance of physical objects. They talk about material goods with disdain."

"My neighbour says people who spend their money on experiences rather than material goods tend to be happy."

Cassie gave a scoffing laugh. "I'd like to see your neighbour lost in the woods in the rain with only their 'experiences' to stop them dying of exposure."

Cassie went to a shelf and pulled down a heavy lozenge-shaped object. Gustav realised it was some sort of Swiss Army Knife type thing.

"Physical object," she said and unfolded attachments. "Knife. Saw. Scissors. Cross-head screwdriver. Reliable physical objects."

Gustav wasn't sure there were many cross-headed screws in the rainy woods, or how they might protect you from exposure, but he chose not to raise the issue.

She pointed at the piece of paper pinned to the wall. "Physical media. When all the servers have died and the cloud storage systems have blown away like smoke, paper will still be here."

"I thought you said paper was insecure," said Gustav. "It burns. It gets wet."

Cassie Troy smiled. A woman who had seemed perennially bitter and alone actually smiled at him. "Just something I tell the worker bees to throw them off the scent. Paper is ... essential. Civilization's going paperless and we don't have long to save it."

"Paper?"

"Civilization."

She looked at him with an expression suggesting she was looking at him for the very first time. "You're the odd-job man."

"Interstitial operative."

She tutted at the title. "You're new. You're not from round here."

"I'm from Eilean Dubh Mòr," he said. "It's off the coast of Scotland."

"I know where it is," she said curtly. "I read. Something happened to the soil."

He nodded.

"You a fisherman?" she said.

"I could fish."

"A practical man. A man who values physical objects."

"I suppose."

The smile had gone now, but some of its warmth still lingered on her face. "One day, I'll show you."

His mobile buzzed. An apparently urgent message from Ruby. "Show me what?" he asked.

"The great project," said Cassie.

47

"How did Velvet get out of the cage?" Ruby asked. Quinn, Kingsley, Jim, and just now Gustav, had all come to the breakout area.

Quinn looked a little uncomfortable. "It seemed cruel not to. I felt as though I had a deep connection with Velvet, so we made a deal that for a couple of hours he could live in my pocket and spend some time in other parts of the building. He wanted to go on an adventure."

"What was your emotional connection like?" asked Gustav. His question was genuine, Ruby could see no hint of mockery, but a quick glance at Jim and Kingsley suggested they thought it was amusing.

"I would look into his eyes and see … hope," said Quinn with a smile. "I could see he wanted to experience life beyond the cage. His look said there's a big world out there, and anything might be possible if he could go out and explore."

"Interesting," said Ruby. "You live on the marlin campus, don't you?"

"Yes. How did you know?"

"It is possible you are projecting some of your own feelings into that exchange with Velvet. It sounds as though you want to explore the world outside the marlin campus."

"What?" Quinn scoffed. "No. Possibly. Maybe."

"But it's safe here," said Gustav, waving an arm to indicate the comfort and bounty of the campus. "Everything you need is here

Ruby pointed at the empty cage. "The same could be said about Velvet and his cage. There is a huge difference between our wants and our needs."

"Sorry," said Jim. "Are we looking for an escaped rodent, or exploring our codwangling feelings?"

"Okay," Ruby conceded. "Let's get up to the seventh floor conference rooms. We can start the search from there."

As they climbed the two flights of stairs, Gustav said, "Our wants and needs. It's like the recommended purchase programme. Marlin gives us what we think we want. I was given a neck tie the other day."

Jim snorted in disagreement.

"Maybe it is a bit similar," said Ruby.

"I think marlin knows me better than I know myself," said Quinn. "They sent me a different shade of makeup and loads of people have commented on how healthy I look."

Ruby resisted the temptation to stare at Quinn's face.

"They sent me a plastic device for measuring pasta," said Kingsley. "Somehow they knew I always make too much. It was just what I needed, although I had no idea."

"Not 'somehow'," said Ruby. "They know things like that because they monitor every part of your life, including the waste you produce."

"They should run the government," said Quinn. "They would do a great job of making sure everything works properly, and everyone is treated fairly."

"Whoa, that is a bit of a leap!" said Ruby.

"Actually, it's not," said Jim. "We're working on some products for that market right now."

"That market?" said Ruby. "How is it a market if it's the government? They are elected by the people."

"Of course it's a market. They outsource loads of work to private companies. The trick will be for marlin to tie everything together into a package that works across the whole range of services. We'll squeeze out any remaining competitors in no time."

"Really?" said Ruby with a frown. "Anti-competitive behaviour sounds a bit problematic."

Jim shrugged. "Take facial recognition as an example. We all know our technology is better than anything else that's available. We've got studies which prove using marlin facial recognition is more effective at spotting anomalies than having humans examining passports at border control. Imagine how much faster that process could be? Once you accept that as a baseline, you can easily see how we could streamline almost every aspect of local and national government."

"Local government in a tiny place like Dubh Mòr is quite different," said Gustav. "We don't have cameras all over the place there. It works because the people all know each other."

"Hey, we're just the ones who make the technology work," said Jim. "It's up to Marketing how it gets sold. I bet they'd have an angle for your island. They'd wait until some old person has a fall, then sell you on the idea of installing monitoring equipment so you could respond faster."

"That's really dark, Jim," said Ruby.

"It's just the nature of progress, isn't it? We offer solutions to problems."

"We're back to the question of 'just because you can, doesn't mean you should', aren't we?"

"But what about the old person, Ruby?" said Quinn. "Don't you care if they get help quickly?"

Ruby laughed. "It's the classic back door for invading privacy. Find an edge case where it would benefit someone, then open the door for mass-scale surveillance."

"If people have nothing to hide, why would they worry about being watched?" asked Jim.

"Not that old chestnut!" said Kingsley, rolling his eyes. "It's a complete non-reason when you get right down to it."

Ruby smiled. Kingsley had beaten her to it, even if he'd expressed it rather bluntly.

They had arrived at the conference room, but the door was closed.

"Is someone in there?" whispered Ruby.

Kingsley tapped on his screen. "Yes, it's booked for a thirty minute call. A middle manager from sales is talking to the exec team. We can't disturb that."

"I guess we can search around the nearby rooms," said Ruby.

"Or we could be a bit smarter about it," said Kingsley. "For instance, if we knew someone who had admin access to all of the data sources on site, we could look at the camera feeds."

"Do you mean you can look at any camera?" asked Quinn in horror. "Any camera in the building at all?"

"Any data source on *site*," corrected Kingsley. "We need it for supporting our systems, obviously." He started tapping and scrolling. "The campus is a brilliant test bed for all marlin technology. For example, this annoying business with Santa Impresora…"

Jim snorted in agreement.

"Annoying how?" said Gustav, clearly trying to ask casually.

"Well, so many people are mentioning Santa Impresora in their conversations and communications that marlin's PMS and DoItBetter AI systems are starting to treat her as a real person."

"Really?" said Ruby. "And that's a problem."

"Sure it is," said Kingsley. "It's like … it's like how the postal delivery service has to deal with letters sent to Santa Claus. Like letters, the discrete data exists. All of us on the various development teams are having to find workarounds to take this fictional figure into account."

"Hang on," said Quinn. "You can watch us on cameras *and* listen to our conversations?"

Ruby watched Quinn as she processed the horrific reality of the developers spying on any one of them at their leisure.

Ruby herself was equally uncomfortable with the idea that Jim and Kingsley might casually abuse the privilege. She was even more uncomfortable with the fact she was more or less encouraging them to do so in order to find the rogue hamster.

"Let's ask ourselves the question of whether this is ethically sound, shall we?" Ruby knew in her heart she didn't want to stop Kingsley using his super-power, but she felt as though she ought to at least put up a token fight. "Jim and Kingsley, do you usually need any authorisation to access this type of data?"

"God, no!" said Jim, appalled. "We are empowered to do what we think is needed."

"Needed in order to...?" Ruby prompted.

"Ah, well yes, that's a good question," said Jim. "I guess they probably mean in order to help customers or whatever. But it's a servant-leadership model. They trust our judgement."

Kingsley was flicking through camera feeds on his screen. Ruby pretended not to see.

"And this is why it's important we all think carefully about ethics. Kingsley, I can see you're busy, but Jim – shall we ask Quinn how she feels about it?"

"Eh? I guess." Jim looked confused at the idea.

"So, Quinn. Does the idea of these two gentlemen looking at camera feeds make you uncomfortable?" Ruby asked.

"Yes," said Quinn in a small voice.

"Can you elaborate on why that is?"

"They might look at me when I don't want them to."

Jim's smirk suggested he found Quinn either ridiculous or amusing.

"Jim!" Ruby said sternly. "I want you to think very carefully about how you respond to that. If I am left in any doubt about this practice, I will be raising it at the ESG Steering Committee."

The smirk fell from Jim's face. "Quinn, I can assure you that we don't use this for spying on employees. We would never do that."

They all glanced across at Kingsley who was doing exactly that. He grunted a small exclamation and zoomed in on a camera feed. "Look! Picking his nose, just because he thinks nobody can see him when he leans to the side."

"Kingsley! This is not acceptable!" yelled Ruby.

"Wait, what's that?" said Gustav, leaning across. "It looks like Velvet."

They all crowded round the screen as Kingsley zoomed in closer. It was definitely the runaway hamster, cleaning his whiskers in the far corner of the conference room.

"I'll go," said Quinn. "Velvet trusts me. Cover me!"

Ruby didn't want to point out that trust had perhaps been eroded somewhat when Velvet escaped. "Cover you how?" she asked.

"Distract everyone!" Quinn was at the door already. She cracked it open and peered inside. She ushered the rest of them inside ahead of her. "Keep low, so the camera doesn't pick you up."

Ruby could not believe she had allowed herself to be put in this situation. She told herself it would make for a valuable group discussion afterwards. Gustav was in the lead. He approached the chair the man was sitting on and gave him a small wave.

"I will remove the gum from underneath the table. I am a gap monkey, and you may disregard my presence." Gustav disappeared underneath the large conference table.

Jim was next. "When you have a moment, can I ask you to evaluate the quality of your video call? Your feedback is important to us."

Ruby watched as Quinn scurried around to the far side, where they had spotted the hamster. The man on the chair glanced nervously at the crowd of people at his side, but beamed confidently at the screen.

"Sorry, I missed that last comment. Would you please repeat it?" He listened while focusing carefully on the screen. "Yes, of course the sales projections have been refreshed in light of the news reports. I can talk through the individual breakdowns if you'd like."

He squirmed in his seat, trying to maintain a professional demeanour while strangers milled around him on the floor. Ruby saw him struggle to not keep glancing down, as he didn't want to betray his discomfort.

Quinn darted across the floor on hands and knees, and Ruby saw Velvet running just ahead of her grasping hand. There was a tiny collective groan from the group as Velvet scuttled under the table. Ruby couldn't see Gustav, but pinned her hopes on the fact he was under there and would surely intercept Velvet's path. There were knocking sounds, followed by an "Ow!" as Gustav gave chase. Chairs around the table shoved back, marking Gustav's unseen progress. Ruby gasped as she saw Velvet climbing up the edge of one of the chairs onto the tabletop. She looked across at the two developers. Jim was still murmuring nonsense to the tense-looking middle manager, but Kingsley was nearer.

"Can you control the camera to the video call feed?" she hissed in his ear, nodding at the unfolding spectacle.

Kingsley caught on fast and nodded. He got busy on his screen as Gustav emerged from the far end of the table and climbed on top. Velvet sat right in the middle, almost as if he was enjoying being the centre of attention. Gustav crept forward, very carefully so as not to alarm the creature.

Gustav was almost within reach when the hamster registered his presence and scuttled away, towards the middle manager. He had his eyes glued to the screen, still explaining his sales figures, but he must have been able to see Velvet from his peripheral vision, as naked panic crept across his face. Velvet ran towards him, and Kingsley gave a small grunt of triumph as he took control of the camera, swinging it up onto the manager's face. He focused in more tightly, which exaggerated the manager's grimace of fear on the big screen. Ruby knew the view she was seeing was the same one being presented to the manager's audience. Velvet and Gustav careered over to one side, so Kingsley moved the camera over to the other, neatly avoiding the bizarre spectacle being broadcast. Gustav chased the hamster back under the table. They emerged on the other side, prompting Ruby to get involved. She ducked down and managed to be in just the right place to scoop up the wayward creature. In the meantime, Kingsley had flicked the camera away from the action.

"Gum all sorted. Happy to help," said Gustav to the middle manager. They all withdrew, scuttling backwards on their hands and knees through the open door.

48

It was only when it started wriggling in his pocket, while he was fixing dinner, that Gustav remembered the little bug in his pocket. He took it out. Its red eyes blinked at him and its ten legs wriggled at the air.

"Sorry, little guy," he said and put it on the kitchen floor.

Without any hesitation or orientation, it scuttled away. Five seconds later, it came back, pursued by the apartment marlinVac. Twenty-Six, who had been completing another jigsaw, stood up and followed both the bug and marlinVac around the apartment. Twenty-Six looked like an old person chasing a windblown banknote. It walked several steps and bent to pick up the bug, by which time both it and the Vac had moved on.

Eventually, the three robots had cornered one another. Twenty-Six picked up the bug and wagged a finger at the marlinVac. Gustav had no idea where it had picked up that particular behaviour.

"Why don't you take the bug outside for a walk?" he suggested.

"Say what?"

"Take the bug outside and let it go."

Twenty-Six twitched and proceeded out the door. The marlinVac followed to the doorway and halted at the edge of its domain. Gustav returned his attention to the dinner.

49

Four weeks into his employment at marlin, Gustav was called to a review meeting with Myfanwy – Myfanwy who wasn't from HR, even though Ruby had insisted Myfanwy was absolutely from HR, despite Myfanwy making it quite clear she was not. Gustav had actually found the people round here, not just at marlin but in this country generally, were highly skilled in holding contradictory opinions. Of saying one thing and doing another. Indeed, of saying one thing and meaning another. Gustav found it perplexing and sometimes exhausting, but tried to not let it get to him.

Myfanwy (who was both from HR and not from HR) was in a room on the second floor.

"I'm here for my review meeting," he said.

"There is no review meeting," said Myfanwy, beaming. "Come in."

He sat. "This isn't a review meeting?"

Myfanwy was amused. "When employers hold a review meeting, what are they doing? They're looking *back* and they're looking *again*. They are re-viewing. Do you want to re-view your work here over the past weeks? Marlin doesn't want to re-view. If we're re-viewing then the implication is that we didn't view correctly in the first place, and we don't want to re-view when we can view the road ahead. You don't want to re-view, Gustav, do you?"

She had, as with their very first meeting, taken a word and sapped all meaning out of it. Gustav didn't know what to say.

"We like you," she said. "We are very pleased with the work you have done."

Data infographics appeared on the wall screen. Gustav was pleased to see his predilection for dog TV shows was still present in one of the bar charts. He really couldn't identify what was going on in some of the other graphs.

"It's not easy being an interstitial operative," Myfanwy continued. "Working without direct managerial oversight, fulfilling roles that have not otherwise been defined. Many do not find their niche. We have four interstitial operatives at this centre."

"Four?"

"Yes."

Gustav had only met two others, and one of those was off work for the foreseeable future with broken legs.

"I doubt any of the current crop, except yourself, will be continuing with us for long," said Myfanwy.

"So I have done well?" he said.

"We like you and we are very pleased with the work you've done."

"I thought you might like to talk about the work I've done." He gripped his mobile. "I made notes."

"You want to re-view your achievements?" she smiled. "Marlin knows that you are a valued community member."

The list on his mobile was a fragile thing. It contained many things that he was certain were part of his interstitial operative remit: sorting out the replacement keys for the groundsmen who tended the extensive gardens, clearing ignored rubbish in Customer Fulfilment, collecting and redistributing various pieces of lost and found. It also tentatively contained items that were possibly someone else's job, or were perhaps things that should not have been done at all. He wasn't sure how Myfanwy would react to his covert printer fixing, or his engagement with the bots and droids on site. He had made a note of them nonetheless.

"You know everything I've done?" he said, surprised.

Myfanwy's teeth glistened. "How marlin views things might be different to how you view things."

"How so?"

"I am going to utilise an analogy." She said it profoundly, as though she had announced she was about to open a box of dangerous experimental drugs.

"Okay," he said.

"There is a cow in a field."

"Okay."

"You see the cow and know it is a cow. You see its general size and shape. You see the curve of its back, the motion of its head. You glimpse maybe a quarter of the cow, and only for an instant at that. But you know it is a cow."

"I am currently following you," he said.

"You do not need to count its legs or check for hooves and udder. You do not need to do a DNA test or measure it in any way. You know it is a cow."

"Yes," he said, just to let her know he was still on the same train of thought as her.

"So it is with you," she said.

"I am the cow?"

Myfanwy nodded. "We don't need to measure you and record you to know you are doing a fine job. We no more need to know what you have done than we would need to know what the cow has eaten. Glimpses alone give us the data showing you are doing good work; creating the future." She waved at the graphs on the wall. "We already know that we like you. Keep it up and you may be offered a promotion sooner than you think."

"Promotion to what?"

"The sky's the limit, Gustav."

He nodded. As with so much at marlin, he was being told something, but it was so poorly defined that it made no difference. Getting concrete information out of Myfanwy was like trying to wrestle a cloud.

"So, do you have any questions, Gustav?" she asked. "Is there anything we can help you with?"

There were a hundred questions and none in his head. "Do you work for HR or not?" he asked.

Myfanwy laughed. She reached forward a little as though

she was going to pat him on the knee, but stopped well before reaching him.

"I work for *you*, Gustav," she said. "Always." Her expression twitched. Her eyes were on his t-shirt. It was the one Ruby had given him, with the doctored image of his mother, clad in billowing robes. "That's not the t-shirt you had before," she said.

"No," said Gustav. "It was a gift, from Dr Ruby Jallow."

"Ah," she said and made a note on her screen. "The image is different."

"She edited it," said Gustav. "And then made a gift of it."

"Interesting," said Myfanwy and made another note on her screen.

50

More little shrines to the folk goddess of printers, Santa Impresora, appeared around the marlin campus. Someone somewhere had clearly created a 3D printer template, as most of them were accompanied by small plastic figurines of the deity with her heavy lacy dress and carrying the symbols of her power.

One afternoon, Gustav found Interstitial Gabriella looking thoughtfully at the shrine. She saw Gustav was watching her, scowled and tugged her big hat savagely. "Gotta get me some of that sweet, sweet Impresora action," she said.

"In what way?"

"Getting the credit for doing the little jobs here and there. It's the kind of misdirection Vito would have liked, except he's laid up with a broken leg."

"Or he wants you to think he's laid up at home with a broken leg," said Gustav playfully.

Gabriella's eyes widened in surprise, then narrowed in suspicion. She scuttled off.

Only a few days later, an official message was sent out to the marlin community along with printed signs above the printers.

> Religious shrines and symbols are not permitted on marlin property.
> Marlin values the diversity and beliefs of its community members.

Ruby and Gustav looked at the sign above a printer.

"Don't those two things contradict each other?" he said.

"I don't think so," she said. "Marlin apparently respects our rights to believe what the heck we like. We're just no supposed to show it."

"Apparently."

"Hmmm?"

"You said 'apparently'," said Gustav.

"Hmm... Oh – I'm more surprised marlin has told its staff to do anything. Have you not noticed the astonishing lack of rules round here?"

He nodded. "I don't think anyone's ever really told me to do anything since I started."

"The company is a big believer in the power of evolution. Let everyone get on with what they're doing, then hire and fire accordingly. It's like the thing with the bugs."

She looked round, saw a parcel delivery bug approaching and pressed Gustav deeper into the printer alcove out of view.

"What the—?"

"Shush."

She stood there, hands pressed against his shoulders to hold him in place and watched the over-burdened bug totter by with a parcel on its crown-like head.

"It's one of the bullies," she whispered.

"The what?"

"Haven't you noticed?" She stepped out into the corridor, cautiously checking the bug had moved out of sight. "The bugs have split into two camps. Evolutionary divergence."

"Oh?"

"There's the ones that hang around looking pathetic, bribing people with store credit."

"You make it sound bad," said Gustav. "I think they're sort of cute."

"Clearly you're an ideal mark. If they looked like doggies with waggy tails you'd be their complete slave."

He seemed to give this thought. "Yes, I think I would," he agreed.

Ruby grunted. "And then there's the others. The bullies. If you don't carry them and their parcels, they fine you."

"They can't do that."

"They can if they can make out you damaged marlin property. It's like those old movies where the mafiosos go into a shop and say 'Tut, tut, it would be a terrible shame if this place caught fire.' Gangsters, the lot of them."

"I think you and I have seen different movies."

"Point is, they can make life very hard for us if they want to. Not just fining us. You don't think they're keeping track of our interactions with these things? Adding it to whatever score they're keeping?"

"There are scores now?"

His naivete was astonishing at times. Ruby didn't know whether to hug him or punch him.

"You've just had a review with HR—"

"Possibly not HR."

"—and they graded you without talking about any of the things you have done or achieved."

"They're always monitoring us."

"How?" She pointed up to a ceiling camera. "Do you honestly think that grinning loon Myfanwy is watching us right now? Do you think it's a human at the other end of that camera?"

"I ... did," he said slowly. "Right up until you said that."

"There will be algorithms at work, analysing our motions, our behaviour."

"Gait analysis. Myfanwy mentioned that once."

"Right," said Ruby, warming to the conspiracy. "They watch how we walk. They watch how we behave. Maybe Myfanwy got to where she is because she smiles inanely all day and the computers think 'Gosh, there's a happy worker!'."

"You think?" he said and smiled deliberately at the camera.

She decided to punch to him.

"Ow!"

"You know things can be precarious here," she said. "This

place acts like it has no rules at all, and that seems to make it the most totalitarian place imaginable."

He nodded. "The jigsaw has two sides."

She frowned at his comment. "You know what you could lose if you get fired?"

"My dog shows."

"Your dog shows."

"Right. Don't trust the system. Keep your nose clean, fly straight and maybe we'll still have jobs in six months' time."

Ruby's mobile ding-donged. She looked at the alert and swore softly. "I've been called into HR. Again. What the hell for this time?"

"Maybe it's because you punched me."

"Unlikely."

"Or maybe because you called Myfanwy a grinning loon."

"I told you, there's no human involved in that kind of decision-making. She's not actually watching us. Myfanwy's just a mouthpiece."

"Then maybe you're being promoted."

She made a dismissive noise. "No need to be that optimistic."

51

Ruby entered the meeting room. This time it was on the sixth floor in a wedge-shaped meeting space in the corner of the building. "Myfanwy. Delphine," she nodded.

As one, the two women gestured for Ruby to take a seat. Myfanwy was smiling as always. Delphine was not smiling.

"We three are meeting a lot," said Ruby as she sat. "We should start a book group or something. Sorry, I'm gabbling. Be assured it's a sign of nerves, not that I don't take our meetings seriously. But we do seem to be having a lot of them, don't we?"

"I assume you know why you're here," said Myfanwy.

Ruby honestly didn't. "I got called in the other week because Quinn told Celery Brown to cover up and I was brought in as some sort of moral counsellor. Quinn was talking about preventing insect bites. Celery was talking about Dave Wicket being a perve at the picnic. Total misunderstanding, none of it to do with me. Then you called me in the other day because Gustav White had ordered himself a t-shirt with a picture of his mum on it. I didn't take the picture or order the t-shirt, but apparently I'm some sort of bad influence. And now—" She blew out her lips. "I no longer know what might have led me here. Was it because I punched Gustav?"

"You punched Gustav White?" said Delphine.

"Er, no," said Ruby. "Obviously not. I have the greatest respect for my colleagues."

"At marlin, we respect each other," said Myfanwy.

"Exactly," Ruby agreed.

"We don't judge each other, we don't shame each other, we do not police each other's behaviour."

Ruby could have pointed out that her last two encounters with Myfanwy and Carman were very much about policing Ruby's behaviour, but thought such a comment would be unhelpful.

"Tolerance and respect are two of our core community values."

Again, the inner undergrad philosopher in Ruby wanted to pipe up. It wanted to point out that marlin's brand of tolerance seemed to include an intolerance of intolerance and therefore was not wholly tolerant. She managed to quash that notion before it reached her mouth.

"I'm very respectful and tolerant," she said.

Delphine made a noise, a soft musical humming, a tune of disapproval. Ruby didn't question it but simply waited.

Myfanwy cast an image to the wall screen. It was a still CCTV image of Gustav White in a meeting room. Opposite him, identifiable from behind only by her big hair, was Myfanwy. With a pinch on her screen, Myfanwy zoomed in on Gustav's t-shirt. It was the one Ruby had recently bought him.

"So, you can understand how concerned we were when we saw this," said Myfanwy.

Ruby looked at the image. It was Gustav's mum, in the doctored image Ruby had created, the same photo as before, but with her body covered by a diaphanous orange robe.

They were concerned. Apparently. Ruby tried to work out why. It was in many ways the same image as on the previous t-shirt. Did they think she was refusing to let the matter drop? Or maybe they thought her photoshopping of the image hadn't gone far enough? Was the young unselfconscious woman still too scandalously dressed? She had genuinely considered adding a title that said M*y* M*um* or G*ustav's* M*um*, but neither seemed to fit. It was an odd image anyway, but one with history and context. And if the t-shirt could have been equipped with a significant footnote, then it seemed perfectly appropriate. Odd, but appropriate.

"You were concerned," Ruby said neutrally.

"Your motivation to do this is unclear," said Delphine.

Ruby looked at the women and then the image. "It was gift. For Gustav."

"But you changed the image," said Myfanwy.

"Yes, I did," she said, cautiously. "I mean it's not Stalin-level airbrushing. I'm not erasing people from historical photos, am I?"

"Why did you feel the need to alter the image?" said Delphine. "Given that we have met previously to discuss attitudes to women and clothing, this seems deliberately egregious."

Ruby was dumbstruck. She could actually feel her throat and breath halted by sheer surprise.

"You appear to have a profound issue with the female body and female nakedness," said Myfanwy.

"I am a woman!" Ruby pointed out.

Myfanwy turned to Delphine. "Have you made a note of that?"

"I have," said Delphine.

"We're trying to be understanding," Myfanwy said to Ruby. "We didn't offer psychological counselling at our first meeting. Marlin values the mental and physical health of its community members."

"There's nothing wrong with me," said Ruby. "I'm not mentally ill." She stopped herself. "Obviously, mental health isn't a binary state, and we all have a mental health, but apart from some very sudden and recent work-related stress—"

"Oh?" said Myfanwy, interested.

Ruby's hands spasmed at the two women and the room about them. "This! This is stressful! I don't have a problem with how people dress. A t-shirt with Gustav's naked mum on it caused a problem. A t-shirt with Gustav's clothed mum on it caused a problem. Jesus Christ, every clothing option imaginable is now a minefield. Maybe I should just turn up to work naked tomorrow so you can't judge me for my clothing choices!"

Delphine made a note on her screen. "And, Ruby, do you plan to come to work tomorrow in the nude?"

"What? No! I don't come into work naked because that's not normal!"

Delphine made further notes.

Myfanwy smiled at Ruby in a manner that was perhaps meant to be comforting. "Are you rejecting the offer of counselling?"

Ruby, having vented her frustrations, mentally seized herself and tried to think clearly. "If I do, what then?"

Myfanwy tilted her head. "I think this would then be a purely disciplinary matter."

Ruby nodded slowly. "What kind of counselling?" she asked.

52

Over the following days, Gustav kept a close eye on the delivery bugs as he went about his business. Ruby was entirely right about the evolutionary divergence that seemed to have taken place. Since the bugs had been permitted to interact with humans (the red snowflake 'do not touch' stickers were rarely seen now), two key success strategies had emerged.

While he was replenishing stocks on a fourth floor printer, he observed a cutesy Bribe Bug beseeching passers-by to carry it to its destination. They seemed to thrive on delivering as many parcels as possible and, like skilful beggars, seemed to know exactly who to target. There were marlin employees who, either out of uncontrollable niceness or a desire to earn marlin store credit, made the ideal couriers for the bribe bugs. Presumably, through whatever systems might be available, the Bribe Bugs would evolve to appeal to those employees who would fulfil the role for the smallest amount of store credit.

The divergent Bully Bugs operated on a different basis and their targets were different too. They didn't care for the personality or co-operation of their potential couriers. All they needed was to find someone who could be confronted out of the sight of evidence gathering cameras and coerced into carrying the parcel. Whatever apparent disdain they had for the humans around them was equalled by their disdain for their packages, a fact Gustav learned when, while he was collecting and redistributing screen chargers, a Bully Bug instructed its human courier to throw a recommended purchase package at him.

Gustav caught it deftly and smiled.

The miserable looking Bully Bug courier regarded Gustav's smile with nervous eyes before moving off. The smile hadn't been for the bug, or the courier, or indeed for the package. It had been for the ceiling camera down the corridor. Gustav remained intrigued by Ruby's notion of his job performance being measured by automated systems, and had taken to smiling and looking as much like a professional go-getter as he possibly could. He had even taken to wearing a shirt and tie, and always carrying a mobile in his hand as though he was about to take an important call. He had no idea if it had any impact on the company's invisible scoring system, but smiling at cameras and walking with the confidence of a senior manager cost him nothing.

The bugs, he concluded as he strolled home that evening, had wildly different strategies for maximising deliveries, but there were common features between the two. Both the Bribe

Bugs and the Bully Bugs targeted groups of employees with significant overlap. The charitable and credit-hungry employees targeted by one were often the compliant and fearful ones targeted by the other. Both sort out human couriers who were likely to moving throughout the building all day long, but without tightly scheduled tasks. Maintenance and cleaning staff were too busy to be targeted. Technical and management staff were often too hidden away to be of use. The bugs never went hunting on the seventh floor where the leadership teams clustered.

It might have been his imagination, but Gustav felt his new smarter attire and deliberate confidence also acted as something of a talisman against the bugs. It was as if they could smell weakness and only went for those who displayed it.

Both Bribe Bugs and Bully Bugs were also evolving to become smaller as the days and weeks went by. Many were now physically incapable of carrying a package unaided. Some were little more that mechanised badges clinging to the packages they wanted to transport. Physical weakness had become an evolutionary advantage in both strands. Weak bugs were cute bugs, which played to the Bribe Bug strategy. Weak bugs were breakable bugs which, bizarrely, played to the Bully Bug strategy.

The Bully Bug that had taken up residence in Gustav's apartment was becoming an evolutionary throwback with each day's iteration of new bugs. If he released it into the wild now, it would surely end up in the crusher with all other useless bugs. It seemed to spend its days trying to harass, while being equally harassed by, the apartment's MarlinVac.

Twenty-Six tried to shepherd the two as best as possible while doing such household chores as Gustav had been able to teach it.

He entered the house, stepping over the bickering bots on the floor, and took off his work tie. It struck him that one of the main perks of wearing a tie for work was the pleasure of taking it off when the day was done. He found this pleasurable distinction between work-mode and home-mode was best achieved by accentuating the tie removal with a hearty sigh.

"Tough day?" said Twenty-Six, a phrase Gustav had taught it to say whenever it saw him remove his tie.

"No, a good day," said Gustav happily, which was his usual reply.

He opened the recommended purchase package he'd had thrown at him in the corridor. It was a new electric toothbrush and tube of 'professional' teeth whitening toothpaste.

53

When the various Brocks were present at the next ESG meeting, (or at least when they appeared to be paying attention from their remote locations), Ruby shared an infographic.

"This chart shows where the public's perception of marlin needs some work," she said.

"Where's this come from?" demanded a Brock.

"The Insight Team were good enough to put this together. There's a lot of existing data. It just needed collating."

"There's a lot of red on that graph there," said another one of the Brocks (or was it a Trent?).

"Which is why they must be our key focus areas for improvement."

"What does it mean when they say they don't believe we use detailed customer data to primarily benefit the customer?" spluttered another Brock, reading the text. "That is clearly preposterous!"

"It doesn't matter if it's preposterous," said Ruby. "If customers think that way then we have a problem which needs solving."

"But we've done so much for them," said another Brock. "Didn't we recently implement that change to the delivery bugs so they greet people by name on the street?"

"Ah yes, that gets mentioned quite a bit in the notes section," said Ruby, paging through the material on screen. "It gets called 'creepy and weird', and other variations on that theme."

"But the consultants told us that personalisation was the key to gaining further market share!"

"Well, it turns out customers like it when *humans* interact with them in an intelligent and personable manner, but when delivery bots share personal details during a random encounter on the street, they don't like it so much. The report that we commissioned included a list of recommended actions for improvement. You will be delighted to know that the awareness training has tackled some of these already."

"Great to hear that, Ruby." The Brocks were smiling, hoping to tick this box and move on to the next meeting.

"But there is much more that needs to be done. Customer perception is just one metric that we can track, but there are others. We might need to improve the way we select our business partners, for example – distance ourselves from any who might be associated with gambling, arms trading, or human rights abuses."

"We can look into that. Anything else?"

"There is something. We might want to consider actively helping out in the local community. Working with schools, possibly. Research shows it can help with recruitment in the longer term."

"Hm. So how might we go about that?"

"Would you like me to look into it with my pilot group?"

"Great idea, Ruby. We'll leave it with you."

And with that, the meeting was done, and all the Brocks and Trents and whatevers vanished. For a steering group they seemed very keen to keep their hands off the tiller. They were less of a steering group and more of an indistinctly pointing group, clustered around the bow of the Good Ship Marlin and offering the least helpful of advice.

"Good work," said Delphine, preparing to leave. As the only member of the steering group who was ever physically present in the meetings, the woman from legal had to make a little small talk with Ruby when everyone else had gone. "Did you get your shots, by the way?"

"Shots?" said Ruby.

"After the rat attacked you."

Ruby shook her head. "It wasn't a rat. It didn't attack me."

"Oh," said Delphine and, because she couldn't think what else to say, added "I see" before walking out.

As had become her habit, Ruby stayed in the plush conference suite and nibbled complimentary snacks while she got on with some of her work. In amongst the ESG meetings and the awareness training sessions, she had not devoted as much time as she would have liked to the study of the rogue VMS systems that had seemingly attempted to run over Gustav White and Vito Bianchi. She had the two rogue systems, and her last known non-dangerous system, in parallel for synoptic comparison. With computer programmes of staggering size which had come about as much through machine-learning as through human programming, knowing which discrepancies between the systems were relevant was difficult.

One thing that had drawn her eye appeared to be a programmer's note in both of the rogue systems. The phrase A STRING HAS BEEN REMOVED appeared next to batches of code. The phrase was eye-catching, primarily because it was meaningless and useless. A string had been removed. What string? Why? A computing string could be any sequence of characters, possibly implemented as an array. But that string could have any meaning to it at all.

"A string has been removed," she muttered.

Meaningless or not, it was just conceivable if Ruby located the origin of that note in the code, she might be able to determine where the Vehicle Management Systems had gone so homicidally wrong.

She bent to her work.

54

Gustav saw the first Saint Impresora t-shirt on a Friday. Although there was no formal dress code in the marlin offices (people were actively encouraged to wear what they wanted, as Ruby had so very clearly pointed out to him), Fridays were still something of a dress-down day. On that day, he saw two Saint Impresora t-shirts, both featuring images of the saint modelled on the shrine images of the black-faced woman in a lacy dress. Gustav wasn't sure which would win out when the 'wear what you wish' policy came up against the recent company edict against religious shrines and symbols.

What was clear, though, was that the folk saint of printers offered no special protection against predatory bugs. One of the t-shirt wearers was being roundly blackmailed into carrying a parcel by a little Bully Bug, which was bashing itself against a watercooler and flinging fines at the poor woman.

"Here, here," said Gustav and stepped in. "Let me take that."

He picked up the bulky but light parcel, and the bug. It was a strangely segmented creature, more ant-like than the usually crab-shaped bug currently predominating. Its head segment bristled with pretend plastic antennae, several of which were broken. It had evolved easily breakable but non-essential body parts in order to facilitate its bullying tactics.

"Cassie Troy! Room 11J! Now!" it snapped in a grating voice.

"Of course," said Gustav.

He waved farewell to the bullied woman and strode off. He walked quickly, with a little swagger in his gait. If he was trying to present a professional HR-impressing image of himself to the watching cameras, then he should walk like a busy manager who believed they owned the place. He kept up the swagger all the way down to the basement and Cassie Troy's door. He knocked and waited.

While he waited for Cassie to shuffle over and unlock the door, the bug continued to make unnecessary threats.

Cassie looked at Gustav. "Oh, it's you," she said, which was as much of a friendly greeting as Cassie seemed willing to offer.

"Delivery," said Gustav.

"Your parcel has been delivered!" grated the ant-shaped bug, and crawled down Gustav's leg and away along the corridor.

Cassie took the parcel, felt its minimal weight and seemed to comprehend. She jerked her head for him to come in.

She was not alone in her dungeon workspace today. The

equally-bearded developers, Jim and Kingsley, stood in her outer office area.

"As we were saying—" said Kingsley.

"You were saying a lot," said Cassie.

"—the systems are receiving a lot of data attributed to this Santa Impresora character. People reference her when talking to their marlinAssists, try to send her e-mails on the internal system. We've even had some bugs instructed to delivery parcels to her. It's confusing."

"It's clogging up the system," said Jim.

"It's like grit in the cogs of the data infrastructure."

"Not sure how this affects me or why I should care," said Cassie.

"We would like, as we were saying, we would like to merge your data files with Santa Impresora's," said Kingsley.

Cassie snorted. "Are you accusing me of being this Printer Fairy character?"

"No, no, not at all," said Kingsley, then demurred. "Unless ... you *are* Santa Impresora?"

"Me? Not bloody likely."

"But that's what the real Santa Impresora would say," put in Gustav unhelpfully.

"You are just a good match," said Jim.

"Good match how?" said Cassie.

"Printers," said Kingsley. "Basically, it's the printer thing. Whether you are fixing the printers or not, that Santa Impresora is—"

"No one is fixing the printers but me!" Cassie snapped.

"Right, so if you are the individual solely responsible for fixing printers, then it just makes sense—"

"Do I look like I care what you do?" she said.

"Is that permission?" said Kingsley.

Cassie gave a curt wave of her hands.

"Right, we're onto it," said the developer. "This could tidy up a lot of loose ends."

The two of them left.

Cassie glared furiously at Gustav, then saw his shirt and tie, so she frowned furiously at him instead. "Why the hell are you dressed like that?"

"I'm trying to look like a professional."

She made a noise. "'Clothes make the man. Naked people have little or no influence on society.'"

"Naked?" said Gustav, abruptly reminded of the poor naked man he met on his first day at marlin.

"It's a quote," said Cassie. "Mark Twain. From a book. You remember books?"

"I like books," he said.

She looked at the parcel box he had delivered for her and then looked at him. "Can I trust you?"

"Depends what you want to trust me with," he said.

"Good answer," she said and waved for him to follow her.

They walked through the room of stored printer consumables, behind the counter bench, and into the better lit room beyond. Here the fuggy printer and paper smell was stronger still, and with good reason. The space was filled with twelve of the large model MarlinPrint machines. There were only ten other machines on the marlin campus. Gustav knew this well, locked as he was in a running battle to keep them functioning. The discovery that over half of the campus's big printers were hidden in this one room surprised him. He was further surprised that they were all running simultaneously, filling the air with their clickety-clack noise and warm smell.

"What are you printing?" he asked in wonder.

"Everything," said Cassie.

She slit open her parcel with a fingernail and opened the flaps. There were maybe a dozen lever arch ring binders inside. She slid one out, took it to a workbench where a pile of holepunched papers waited, and deftly slipped the thick ream of printed material onto the metal rings. A thick marker was used to neatly print a code onto the folder's spine, and it went into a wheeled storage chest which was already part-filled with similar folders, all marked with some sort of cataloguing code.

Gustav watched her. "And by everything, you mean...?"

"Everything," said Cassie in a cheerful tone he had not heard her use before. "Everything that has not already been printed. I'm generally filling the gaps."

She saw the look on his face and smiled. She actually smiled. She spread her arms wide. "This is my secret. This is it."

Gustav wanted to express his confusion, but forced himself to be silent while he thought about it. He remembered what Cassie had said. "We don't have long left to save civilisation," he said.

"We do not."

"And you don't mean save it like in stop it falling apart—"

"Oh, it would be nice if we could do that."

"—but save it." He tapped his fingers on a nearby pile of papers. "Save it for later."

Cassie Troy nodded and shrugged at the same time. "Last year, humans created three quintillion data bytes of information *every single day*. Globally, we took two trillion digital photos last year. That's more photos every minute than were created in the first century of photography."

"Does that mean it's all worth saving?"

"Not at all," she agreed. "But the times we are living in right now will be seen as a digital dark age. The data we're creating now will be inaccessible to future generations."

"Really?"

She nodded. "Gone."

He thought. "Like wiped out by an electromagnetic pulse? Nuclear war?"

"Or a solar flare?" she suggested. "Or nothing so dramatic." She stepped towards the wall and pointed to a cardboard square pinned there. It had a large neat circle cut out of its centre and a sticker in the top right hand corner. "You know what this is?"

Gustav did not and said so.

"It's an eleven inch floppy disk. This was produced in nineteen seventy-one – over half a century ago. A hundred and seventy two kilobytes of storage. Do you know what it's got on it?"

"What has it got on it?"

"I don't know," she said. "I can't find a floppy disk drive that can read it. Lost data."

The machines around them shunted, printed and sorted.

"There are books in libraries and on shelves, of course," she continued. "But the records of how we are living our lives now…"

"And you don't want to replenish the printers upstairs because you feel compelled to save the toner for this project?" he said, not really questioning but understanding.

"I don't feel compelled," she said. "I *am* compelled. This—!" She flung out her arms at the printers and folders, and presumably somewhere a room filled with box upon box of more heavy folders. "This is me saving a handful of scrolls from the Library of Alexandria. This is the Rosetta Stone for future generations."

This is mad, Gustav thought, but could not say. Not merely because he was a polite individual, but because he didn't quite believe it.

"There are no more marlinPrints and no more resources being made," she said. "If I can just keep that one printer on seventh going and keep management happy…"

There was mania in her red-rimmed eyes. Gustav wondered if she ever left this place, if she ever slept.

"You should spend more time upstairs," he said. He didn't add 'in the sunlight' because he didn't want to appear insulting. "In fact, we should have lunch together some time."

Her eyes narrowed. "I think you're a bit young for me, sonny."

"I meant just lunch. Time spent with people."

She looked like she was considering it, then shook her head. "Too busy. I'll sleep when I'm dead. And I've got a printer to fix on seventh. Out of cyan toner again."

It was actually out of black toner. He knew because he'd stolen it to replenish the printer in Browser Innovations. Of course, he could say nothing.

"I could fix that for you," he said.

"You?"

"I'm an interstitial operative. I can do anything no one else has time to do. Filling the gaps."

Her stare was long and doubtful. "Fine," she said, like she was doing him a favour. "This way." She prodded him back to the storage room, away from her mad and impossible project. "Maybe *you* are Santa Impresora. You certainly look the type."

He didn't know what she meant by that last comment, but he kept quiet.

55

A counselling appointment appeared on Ruby's calendar, neatly slotted between two existing ones. She might have taken the opportunity to be annoyed that marlin had arbitrarily taken hold of apparently dead time in her schedule and filled it without consulting her; that her life was treated as a Tetris game to be economically organised by a faceless AI. She could have been annoyed, but the annoyance and numb fatalism caused by the very existence of the appointment overshadowed any subsequent irritation.

She walked across the campus lawns to the medical centre and presented herself at the front desk. She was greeted by name and ushered to a room where she was introduced to one Dr Julius Wanderley. He wore deck shoes, and a loose white shirt with the sleeves rolled up his dark tan arms. Maybe it was the soft blue-greens of his consultation room and the sunlight through the blinds, but he looked like a man who should be crewing a yacht in warm seas.

"So," he said simply as they sat in the low seating area that dominated his room.

"So," said Ruby.

"You have been referred to me by HR."

"I have."

"The first question is, are you here voluntarily? Of course you're here voluntarily, but are you here because you want to be here?"

Ruby gave him a thin smile. "I think the first question is, what will you do with any records of our counselling session? Who do you report back to?"

Julius spread his hands to indicate his empty lap. "No notes. No records." He gestured upward to the walls. "No cameras or recording devices. I'm not required to report back anything more than your attendance and your willingness to engage."

"Engage with what?"

"With me." He smiled. He had a wide mouth and an attractive smile. The wide mouth showed off the attractive smile, and even though his mouth was perhaps too wide to be classically handsome, the overall effect was a positive one. He immediately struck her as a man people would be happy to talk to. She wasn't overly pleased about this fact. Whatever he said, this counselling wasn't a voluntary thing, and she didn't want to be suckered in.

"You don't have a programme of re-education you need to take me through?" she said.

"Ah, no. You have me confused with a repressive

totalitarian regime. We don't do the brainwashing here. Marlin probably has a facility for that elsewhere."

"Quite possibly," Ruby agreed.

"But we are here to talk, and we can talk about whatever you like."

Ruby checked the time on her mobile. "Okay. Do you know why I was referred here?"

"I do," he nodded. "There were a number of incidents. An offensive t-shirt you encouraged a male colleague to wear. A doctored image of a naked woman. Generally issues with how colleagues dress and present themselves."

"A series of horrible misunderstandings," said Ruby. "I have fallen foul of poorly thought through policies which are little more than well-meaning soundbites."

"And how does that make you feel?"

She couldn't help but grin at that. "Five minutes in and we're already talking about my feelings."

"You have an issue with discussing your feelings?"

"We live in a world where people feel entitled to share their feelings. Just because we can do something, doesn't mean we should."

"So, you don't approve of people sharing their feelings?"

"I didn't say that either. I suppose—" She paused to reflect upon what it was she really supposed. "I suppose, I tend to think about things in terms of the effect they have. If I share my feelings, to what end am I sharing them? Cathartic release? To make people understand me better? To reinforce some notion that I am important and worth listening to?"

"Is it only the notion that you are important and worth listening to?"

"I am equally as important and as worth listening to as every other human being on the planet."

It was his turn to smile. "That's probably an uncommon perspective. Your recent problems regarding marlin's dress code seem to be a question of morals. And, seeing as you are an ethical consultant, I would think it would be right up your alley. Do you not have an opinion on what's occurred?"

Ruby shook her head, but mostly in reticence.

"What is your own moral standpoint?" Julius asked. "Your own framework. How do you judge things?"

"I tend not to judge things. At all. I'm rarely bothered by the ethics themselves."

"Really?"

"Only by the process by which those ethical decisions are made. There was a pastor who visited our house when I was growing up. My mum was a Christian, lapsed mainly, and the church was keen to keep hold of her, so the pastor would come round every month or two. And I must have said something confrontational to him – I was a teenager at the time. Confrontation came easy. And he said he didn't care if I was Christian or not. He didn't care what I believed, only that I that understood why I believed what I believed. And could defend those beliefs when challenged. For him, faith without doubt and reflection was a lazy kind of faith. I think he even despised the members of his own flock who only came to church because it was how they were raised, who had fallen into it as a habit. Believing in the existence of God or not, he said, was the biggest decision anyone could make in their life, and it was a decision demanding the deepest deliberation. It might even have been him who set me on the path to this current career of mine."

"So, you have no moral standpoint?" he said.

"Was that the original question?"

"It was."

"You want the big, deep answer?"

"If you wish."

She raised her eyebrows at him, a 'Well, you asked for it' look.

"There are no moral truths," she said. "None. There are no absolute rules. I can say 'Murder is wrong' and you would agree, and it is convenient that we agree on that point and can go about our daily lives with those three words in our head and pretend we know what it means. We would think another person weird or dangerous if they didn't think murder is wrong. But it's not true in any measurable or provable sense. It's a shared convention that suits our needs." She watched him for a response. "But, before you ask, I'm not a moral relativist either. A thing is not good or bad in this situation or that situation. Even on an individual moment by moment basis, there is no good or bad. I could spit in your face right now if I wanted to. I'm perfectly capable of it, but I choose not to."

"Thank you," said Julius.

"But that's not because I think spitting is actually, morally wrong. Again, I would say, out loud I mean, that spitting in someone's face is morally not good, but it's not actually true in any situation. Why don't I spit in your face? For one, it doesn't serve my current needs. I would also be afraid of the consequences – for me – if I did spit at you. On top of that, I was raised not to spit in people's faces. I have some socially constructed, or possibly even genetic disposition to want to make others happy, and thus I want to avoid causing you misery. But that's not some logical 'Treat others as you wish to be treated' nonsense. That's something down at the empathetic animal level. My moral actions come out of a tangled web of fears and wants and conditioning. There's no arguable moral basis for it."

"You don't believe morality exists, Dr Jallow?"

She wryly noted his use of her title. "No, Dr Wanderley."

"You're a nihilist?" he suggested.

"But a happy one," she countered. "Let's be clear. I can discuss morality. I can argue ethical points of view. Ethics is a set of language games we play, and I'm happy to play them because they are useful. It's like money."

"Yes?"

"We pretend money is a real thing and has value, even when it's just numbers and bits of paper. But we maintain the illusion because it's better to have that illusion than not have it."

"Interesting," he said.

"Does that mean you agree or disagree with me? Or maybe you're itching to press a big red button under your desk and have the men in white coats come in and restrain me?"

"I mean it's interesting," he said. "Does this make you ... cynical about marlin's own moral values?"

"I prefer to describe myself as pragmatic. Objective, even. Not that any of us can be truly objective, of course."

"Of course."

"I do see—" She paused, held herself back, realising she was about to say something pertinent, then decided she wanted to say it anyway. "I do see problems with marlin's values and principles."

"Oh?"

"You know, their core values – accessibility, universality, frugality."

"I might have seen them somewhere in ten foot high letters," said Julius.

"Marlin wants everyone to be able to use marlin services, to have their services compatible with all other systems and avoid waste, whether in terms of physical waste or energy."

"I am somewhat fond of those values."

"And yet the more marlin expands, the more it sells, the more waste it must generate. The very act of trying to shift product goes against notions of global frugality."

"Well, I suppose…"

"And if marlin allows its services to be accessed by everyone, then, by that very fact, they are choosing to work with individuals, or companies, who do not share those values."

"Is that so?"

"You can't throw a massive party to which everyone's invited and then expect all your guests to get along. The tensions between inclusivity and exclusivity, between tolerance and intolerance, will always be there." She held his gaze. "And, yes, I am also talking about marlin's dress code or lack of it. You can't lay down an absolute rule, or an absolute lack of rule, without it falling apart somewhere."

"Are you saying the situation which led HR to referring you here was not your fault? That you're not to blame."

"I'm not saying that," said Ruby. "Speaking precisely, morally, I'm not happy with the word 'blame'."

"Because you're a nihilist," said Julius.

"A happy one," she said. Her mobile blooped at her. It was an e-mail from the teacher contact at the local secondary school. A bunch of students had volunteered to attend her proposed STEM activity day. "A very happy one," she said.

56

Gustav was organising the stationery cupboard in the MarlinGo test centre. On the wall next to the printer just outside the cupboard was a photograph of a woman, mounted in a cheap foil frame.

"Excuse me," Gustav asked a woman in a cardigan who happened to be passing. "Who is that?"

The woman pretended not to understand for a moment, then looked up and down the corridor furtively and said, "Jennifer Grooman. The first martyr."

"I beg your pardon?"

Another furtive look up and down, then, "She was fired for wearing a Santa Impresora pendant."

"Because they've been banned," he said.

"They can't tell us what to do," she whispered tersely. "We have a right to wear what we want."

"So people really believe there's a patron saint of broken printers?"

She gave him an offended look. "Does it really matter what people believe? There's a principle at stake. Look at this."

She whipped her cardigan open, holding the two sides stiffly apart to give him an exclusive look at what she wore underneath. It was a white t-shirt printed with a large image of Santa Impresora. The image was in a style suggestive of a cheap pamphlet, something produced on a small, crafted scale, even though it was quite clearly a print-on-demand t-shirt.

"They can't tell me what I can and can't wear," said the woman.

"Well, okay," said Gustav, who wasn't sure if that was actually true.

The woman flicked a hand at Gustav's pressed shirt and patterned tie. "You don't have to be constrained by conventions. You can be what you want to be."

"Thank you," he said. "I will."

On his way back to the main administrative building, Gustav found a little trail of plastic tokens along the edge of the path. He picked one up. It was a badge with a small plastic clip on the reverse. The badge simply said, Would you like to earn Marlin store credit? Mystified, he took the badge with him.

Less than ten steps down the path a globular bug rolled out from behind a bush.

"Hello, sir," it warbled in a jolly voice. "*I believe you might be interested in earning store credit by acting as a parcel courier.*"

As the Bribe Bug rolled towards him, a plastic badge dropped to the ground from a slot in its rear.

"Did you just ... lay a badge?" said Gustav.

"Being a courier in your spare moments could earn you a significant amount of marlin store credit," the bug said.

Gustav turned the badge over in his hands. He didn't want to needlessly break it, but pried in the cracks in its thick shell. He wondered if there was a tracking device of some sort in there. Maybe just an RFID tag, of the sort shops used to protect high value clothes. As a strategy, it struck him as bizarrely ingenious.

"Er, no thanks," Gustav said to the bug and put the badge back down on the ground. He waved at the line of badges the Bribe Bug had deposited. "This. This is very untidy. You shouldn't litter."

There were more of the badges around the campus, and even the corridors of his apartment block when he returned home that evening. He found himself genuinely torn between admiration for the new evolutionary development and irritation at the wasteful distribution of bits of plastic all over the campus. He scooped up the badges nearest his own front door and put them in his pocket.

Twenty-Six was wiping down the surfaces in the kitchen. A freshly completed jigsaw sat on the dining table. Gustav now owned fifteen jigsaws. Twenty-Six did not seem to mind doing the same jigsaws again and again, but Gustav instinctively felt it was mildly abusive to not provide the droid with original challenges. He had recently ordered some modelling clay to see if he could bring out the droid's creative side, but that had ended messily. There was a limit to how creatively intelligent and precise a droid that was essentially a crash-test dummy could be. Nonetheless,

Gustav had persevered with the droid's betterment and an order of knitting needles and wool should be arriving at some point.

He scooped the plastic badges from his pocket, along with a folded print out that had found its way there. He held the badges out.

"Twenty-Six, have you seen these?" said Gustav.

"Yes," said the droid and pointed at them. "They are there."

"Others. Have you seen others around the building?"

"I have not."

"I would like you to do a job for me."

"I can be useful," said Twenty-Six.

Gustav gave him a badge. "Go around the apartment block, along the corridors on all floors. Collecting any badges like this you find. Bring them back here."

Without comment, Twenty-Six left on his errand. The apartment MarlinVac tried to follow but halted at the door, constrained by its programmed area of operations.

"It'll be back soon," Gustav told the MarlinVac.

Gustav stripped off his shirt and tie and set about preparing dinner. An appointment popped up on his calendar. Myfanwy wanted to see him the next day. The meeting was entitled CAREER ADVANCEMENT. That sounded promising. It was tucked into a half hour slot before one of the awareness training sessions with Ruby.

The doorbell rang. Gustav left the small pan of diced potatoes bubbling on the hob and answered the door to a man holding a bug. By the look of resigned fear on his face, Gustav took it to be one of the Bully Bugs.

"Here is your package," said the bug.

There was no sign of any package.

"What package?" said the Gustav.

The courier gave him a silent and helpless shrug.

"Your consignment, containing mindful knitting supplies and balls of yarn, has been delivered," said the bug.

"You haven't given me any package," said Gustav.

"Your package has been delivered. Filing a false report of non-delivery will result in penalties against your marlin account," said the bug.

"But it's—" Gustav held his tongue. There was no point arguing with a bug.

On a whim, and with a sense of cruelty that did not come naturally to him, Gustav placed one of the Bribe Bug tokens in the vestigial parcel hopper on the Bully Bug's back.

"Thank you," he said to the courier. "You can probably let it go now."

He shut the door and abruptly felt the pang of the non-delivery of a parcel. The knitting supplies were inexpensive and not important in the larger scheme of things, but Gustav was acutely aware that the brown marlin packages, with their glued down flaps and tearaway opening strips, were each a tiny positive point in his day. Denied his package, he was similarly denied a micro-hit of pleasure endorphins, or whatever brain chemicals such moments brought him.

And yet, despite this disappointment, Gustav was not surprised. The growing evolutionary tactic of the Bully Bugs was to use baseless threats and a disdain for humans to maximise their deliveries. Outright lying regarding parcel deliveries was a logical next step.

Gustav returned to his bubbling dinner and opened his marlin account on his mobile to see what he could do about missing parcel. It took him mere minutes to realise that disproving the bug's lies and fixing the existing order would be painfully tricky. He decided to simply re-order the knitting supplies.

57

Ruby's meetings with the ESG started to become surprisingly more frequent.

In a matter of weeks she had gone from struggling to get the various leadership members to stay online for more than five minutes, to them insisting on meeting up virtually every couple of days. The only explanation that came to mind was their interest in the company's ethical governance was directly proportional to how much customers disliked them.

It appeared – no, it didn't appear, it was *bloody obvious* – several of the Brocks in the group could not comprehend that anyone might dislike marlin at all, even though that's what customer surveys had borne out.

"We are entirely focused on giving the customer what they need," said a Brock. "We make our products available to everyone, without prejudice. We pride ourselves on the quality and value of the service we provide."

Ruby nodded. "That's all entirely true."

"And yet there are people who don't love marlin?" His face ended the question on an expression of anguished confusion.

"Indeed," said Ruby. "For a start, the notion that marlin is open and accessible to everyone is not ethically ideal."

"We don't discriminate," said another Brock.

"Perhaps you should. Have you considered that we judge people by the friends they choose? The same goes for companies. Arms dealers, environmentally damaging companies, unethical banking corporations. Your willingness to work with them counts as a black mark in a number of metrics. Some of the companies you work with have transgressed against internationally agreed codes of conduct. They have been fined. It would not be inconceivable for marlin to be similarly fined."

"But universality and accessibility are positive qualities," said a Brock without much conviction.

"As words, they are open to some pretty broad interpretations. You can't just throw words out as moral imperatives. Even well-worn moral codes like the Ten Commandments can be ambiguous. 'Do not murder.' Sure, that's fine. But is euthanasia murder? Is war murder? If someone commits murder should the punishment we inflict be to murder them?"

"We're not writing the Ten Commandments here," said a Brock.

"Now, now," said another. "We put a lot of thought into the recent mission critical objective updates."

"That was good," said a third. "We ordered in Chinese and stayed up to the small hours."

"Until mid-afternoon," said another who, by the light around his screen image, was several time zones removed from the one before. "A big focus on frugality in that session. Doing more with less. Removing excess waste. Good for the planet."

"We're going to get the mission critical objectives printed on pens and distributed to all employees," said yet another. "Spread the word."

"We're simply trying to do good here," said a woman. There were many fewer women, but Ruby couldn't even remember her name. She was a Brockette of some sort.

"You cannot force ethical good to arise simply by choosing the right words," said Ruby. "You cannot build a perfect system of morals. I call it Jallow's Ethical Incompleteness Theorem. In any logically built ethical framework, there are statements that are unproveable."

"I don't follow," said a Brock.

"By adopting a firm stance on accessibility and universality, marlin is trying to create a community in which individual beliefs and rights are always respected."

"Very important to us," agreed the Brock.

"Do people have a right to disagree with those beliefs? Can they believe those rights shouldn't be respected?"

"Er," said a Brock.

"It's not as simple as that," said another.

"Exactly," said Ruby. "You've built a system of liberal totalitarianism. All are welcome. And if you don't think all are welcome, then you are not welcome."

"This is just word games," said a Brock irritably.

"It's all word games. But when you codify those word games into AI algorithms and company policy, they're going to have a real impact on real human beings, Brock."

"I'm Chad."

"Sorry. Chad."

Once the meeting was done, Ruby stepped out of the conference suite. Along the corridor, the printer maintenance woman – something Troy, wasn't it? Cassie Troy – knelt before the big management level printer. Ruby naturally assumed the woman was kneeling in order to work on the printer's inner gubbins, but the access panels were closed and the woman's hands were together as though in prayer.

"You all right?" said Ruby.

The stony-faced woman gave her a sharp look which almost instantly softened into indifferent resignation. "You know how many faults this printer has had in the last month alone?"

"I don't," said Ruby.

"It's impossible." Cassie Troy touched her chest. There was nothing visible, but Ruby suspected there might be a Santa Impresora pendant under that buttoned up shirt. "The only option is to submit to the mystery."

"Mystery?"

"She moves in mysterious ways. Who are we to question her actions? Who knows why this printer – *this* printer – should be ignored by her?"

"Um, yeah," said Ruby and backed slowly away from the crazy lady.

58

The freshly re-ordered knitting materials arrived at Gustav's apartment the following morning, in the claws of a Bribe Bug which was in the hands of a cheery woman wearing a t-shirt saying WILL COURIER FOR *5* CREDITS PER *100*M.

"Innovative," said Gustav.

He tossed the parcel to Twenty-Six, telling the droid to open it while he went and dressed for work.

"What is this?" said Twenty-Six when Gustav returned, fiddling with his awkward shirt collar.

"Those are knitting needles and those are bundles of wool. I thought you could do with a new hobby. What do you think?"

"Say what?"

"Knit something," said Gustav. "Knitting was an important industry on Dubh Mòr."

He scooped the Bribe Bug badges off the counter and into

his pocket. He would find somewhere to deposit them during the say. He momentarily touched the folded print out, didn't recognise it as anything important, and decided to leave it.

"Knit," said Twenty-Six. "Verb: to make a garment from interlocking hoops of wool or other yarn using knitting needles. What should I knit?"

"Watch a video. Find a pattern somewhere. Be creative. Show me what you've done when you've finished."

Like a bomb squad officer approaching a suspect device, Twenty-Six opened the sealed plastic bag of wool. Gustav left the droid to it.

As he stepped out of the apartment building he found two bugs squabbling on the path.

"*Being a courier in your spare moments could earn you a significant amount of marlin store credit,*" said the ovoid one on fat legs.

"*Impeding my progress will result in penalties against your marlin account,*" said the spikey one with a Bribe Bug badge still in its little hopper.

"*I believe you might be interested in becoming a courier.*"

"Get out of my way."

The two danced around it each other, the larger Bribe Bug continually blocking the Bully Bug's path.

"*Causing damage to marlin property will result in penalties,*" said the Bully Bug.

"*Store credit can be used on any purchases,*" said the Bribe Bug.

The Bully Bug ran headlong into a concrete pillar beside the apartment entrance. "*You will be penalised,*" it shrieked hysterically.

The fat Bribe Bug trundled over to the self-harming bug. "Hello, sir. Would you be interested in earning store credit?"

"Penalty!"

Gustav moved round them and made for the central marlin building.

Myfanwy was waiting for him outside the lifts on the fifth floor, her brilliant smile at the ready. Gustav returned it threefold.

"Is this the same Gustav I knew not a few short weeks ago?" she said.

"It is," he said. "I am."

"Isn't it lovely to see one of your own little birds fledge and leave the nest of inductions and introductions and soar?"

"It might be."

"Still watching those adorable dogs shows on TV?"

"I never miss them," he said.

She gestured for him to join her in a meeting space with sunshine yellow chairs. The cushions had been plumped and artfully arranged. Gustav wondered if interstitial Gabriella had been here recently.

"You don't mind me thinking of you as a growing bird, learning to fly, do you?" she said.

"Last time, you described me as being like a cow," he said.

"Did I?" she said, perplexed, and amused by her own confusion. "Birds. Cows. I'm full of figurative language. Is that because I have the soul of an artist? If you're a cow then you're a prize specimen, best in show."

Gustav nodded cautiously. In his head, prize cows were the ones ripe for slaughter. Birds that learned to fly left for good. The meeting title of CAREER ADVANCEMENT didn't suddenly seem as positive as it first appeared.

"We like you," said Myfanwy.

"You've been watching," said Gustav.

"Like caring parents. And we like what we see."

She made a gesture from her mobile to a wall screen, and data flowed. This was not data Gustav had seen before. No TV viewing habits or purchase behaviours here. The screen was alive with measures and graphs that made no sense to him.

"This is the PMS," said Myfanwy.

"PMS," he said. He'd heard those letters before, but very much doubted he knew what they meant in this context.

"Personnel Management System," she said. "Marlin works in the wondrous way it does because we have intelligent algorithms shifting through the mountains of data we have. PMS, VMS, YouKnowMe, DoItBetter. All of them working to marlin's core values and guiding principles."

"PMS likes me," he said.

"It does. We do." She grinned and it seemed like a very deliberate grin this time. "PMS likes me too, and I'm glad for that fact."

"That's nice," said Gustav, which felt a poor thing to say, but he wasn't sure what else there was to be said.

"We want to promote you within the community," said Myfanwy. "We want you to move onto bigger and better things."

"Are you sending me somewhere else?"

"Gosh, no. We'd very much like to keep you in-house. I

like to hold onto what I value." Her gaze had latched onto his with more than the usual amount of mania.

"What would my new role be?" he asked.

"Oh, you would still be an interstitial operative."

"Still filling the gaps?"

She nodded. "But we want you to start filling more important gaps."

"I've missed out on gaps? I have tried—"

"Gaps we did not make you privy to before," she said. "We'd like to get you in on some meetings. High level meetings. There are gaps there, for certain. A young go-getter like you, you'll see them soon enough."

"I look forward to it," he said, not sure what he was meant to be looking forward to.

She gestured at his formal clothing. "This new look. It's very next level."

"Yes?"

"Do you like Italian food?" The randomness of the question threw him. Before he could answer, she said, "I know you like Italian food. Of course you do. YouKnowMe knows it. I know it."

"Yes?" he said again.

"I cook a mean Sicilian arancini. From marlin's FreshKitchen delivery range, of course."

"Yes?"

"Yes," she said, and seemed to be trying to imbue that one syllable with a wealth of deep meaning. He was clearly meant to read something into arancini and a heavy 'Yes', but he didn't know what.

"I will send you a friend request," said Myfanwy.

"That will be nice," he said, honestly.

"And we'll discuss the details of your new role," she said.

"Oh, good." He sensed the meeting was over. "I've got some awareness training to get to."

"Ah, Dr Jallow," she said, and although the grin didn't fade, her tone was less happy. "She's one to watch. For very different reasons."

He nodded. "Yes. Well. I'll speak to you later."

"Arancini, yes?" she said.

"Oh, absolutely."

He left, only then realising there was a cluster of a dozen Bribe Bugs outside the room, all clamouring to get to him and invite him to join the lucrative world of package delivery. He needed to get rid of the badges in his pocket, and soon.

59

Gustav hurried into the breakout area to join the rest of Ruby's awareness training group. "Sorry, I'm late," he said.

"That's okay," said Ruby.

"No, really," he said. "Quite unforgiveable. My calendar gave me five minutes to get from the seventh floor to here. Should have been fine, but I was pretty much mugged by a band of delivery bugs."

"Oh, it's the bugs' fault now, is it?" said Jim from development snidely.

Ruby gave Gustav a look which featured big wide eyes and some heavily coded meaning. "You've just missed Jim's presentation on how we could fit hamsters with powered exoskeletons, to make them into package delivery cyborgs."

"We are not putting anything on Velvet," said Quinn firmly.

"It could work on any hamster," said Jim.

"Or any rodent," said Kingsley. "They used to use ferrets to fit the electrical cabling inside jumbo jet planes."

"Ferrets don't know anything about electronics," Quinn scoffed.

"And they're not rodents," said Gustav.

"And that's pretty much the level of conversation we've been having all morning," said Ruby. "We need to focus on the fact that we've got a party of school children coming in tomorrow."

"So we can find out what they think of marlin," said Kingsley. "I think we'll see they have a pretty positive view."

"They'd better," Jim muttered.

"We will see their interactions with marlin with an honest and objective eye," said Ruby. "I thought we could wrap it up in the pretext of showing them what science and engineering careers are available with marlin."

"Are these teenagers?" said Quinn.

"Secondary school. Yeah."

She pulled a face. "Not sure I'm very good with teenagers."

"You've just got to show them who's boss," said Jim.

"Or just treat them like ordinary human beings," suggested Ruby.

"You have much experience with teenagers?" said Jim.

"Um. Not particularly."

Jim grunted in amusement. "I'll show them my mobile chariot. They'll like that."

"Your what?" said Ruby.

"You'll see."

"I could get hospitality to lay on some food," said Gustav. "Teenagers like food, right?"

"They're not aliens," said Ruby, peeved.

"We didn't really have 'teenagers' on Dubh Mòr. We had children and then adults. I don't know what we did differently."

"They're just school kids," said Ruby. "I'm sure everything will be fine."

Most of the group didn't look convinced.

Gustav hung back at the end of the session to apologise for his lateness once more.

"That's okay," Ruby said dismissively. "Weird shit happens. You know what I got for my Recommended Purchase delivery today? Nothing."

"You didn't get one?" he said.

"No. I actually got nothing. The bug literally passed me nothing and threatened to fine me if I reported it."

"Same thing happened to me," said Gustav. "I think it might be the next stage of evolution among the Bully Bugs."

"Bully Bugs, huh?"

"Yes. Bully Bugs and Bribe Bugs. Some of the Bribe Bugs have started ... pooping these little chipped badges." He showed her one. "I've been slipping them onto any Bully Bugs I see. Gets them to chase each other round."

Ruby's brow creased, but she seemed amused. "That's very rebellious of you, Gustav. Positively treacherous."

He conceded the point, realising he was unworried. Had his time at marlin finally inculcated in him a disdain for order? Was he finally catching up with Ruby and the others, regarding their employer as, if not precisely the enemy, an irrelevance?

"I got promoted today," he said.

"Say what?"

"Promoted. Myfanwy called me in and told me I'd been noticed, and I've been promoted."

"To what?"

He pursed his lips. "An interstitial operative. But, like, a next level interstitial operative."

"A next level gap monkey, tackling bigger gaps."

"Or more high-level gaps. I'm not sure. It was a bit confusing. Myfanwy started asking me what cuisine I liked and told me she made an amazing arancini."

"A what?"

"Rice balls."

Ruby stared at him quizzically, then burst out laughing. It was sudden enough to startle him. "She's invited you over for dinner?"

"Has she? Yes, I suppose."

"Oh, God. Myfanwy likes you."

"Yes, she said so."

"No, no, no. She *likes* you. Likes you likes you."

"You mean like—?" He held his hands facing each other, twisting interlocking spiders.

"I've not idea what that mime is meant to be, but yes. That's bloody funny. Myfanwy fancies you."

Gustav wondered if he should be offended that Ruby found the idea of someone being attracted to him funny. He didn't feel offended. Was it because he felt no attraction to Myfanwy? He felt the stirrings of a perverse need to accept

Myfanwy's dinner offer just to make some point to Ruby. He didn't know what the point was, but felt it might be worth making.

"She was just excited for me," he said. "I've got a really good PMS score, and my contributions are being recognised—"

"Wait. You saw your PMS score?"

"There was a graph."

"I'm not allowed to look at that data. I wasn't even sure it existed. I'm still trying to chase down that fault in the MarlinGo."

"The one that tried to kill me?"

"And that other poor gap monkey. Stuck between well-meaning but dumb execs and these great big AI systems interacting with the real world, it's impossible to see how these patterns of behaviour are arising."

He nodded. "I'm going to find the missing packages."

"Pardon?"

"The package your bug failed to deliver. Mine too. They must be going somewhere."

"Is it your job to find them?"

"Maybe it's no one's job. Maybe it's a job for Gap Monkey."

Ruby cleared her throat. "Did you just put your hands on your hips in a superhero pose?"

Gustav shrugged. "Marlin's Personnel Management System likes me. I can do no wrong."

"Ah, hubris, thy name is Gustav."

. . .

After a day of general tidying, errand running and disposing of Bribe Bug badges, Gustav went home to find that Twenty-Six had knitted a jumper. "That looks lovely. Quick work."

"You told me to knit something. You did not say how long I should take."

"No."

The jumper was constructed in various colours. The lower torso was red, the left arm and part of the right in yellow, and the remainder, including the neck, in an off-white. The front of the jumper was dotted with a blocky scatter pattern, like a dense cluster of stars composed of black squares. It looked awfully familiar, but Gustav couldn't place it until he saw the apartment's resident bug lying on its back on the carpet, legs twitching feebly.

"That pattern," said Gustav.

"You told me to find a pattern."

On the coffee table in front of the television was a now unfolded sheet of printer paper. It was the QR code Cassie Troy had given Gustav a while back. The one which fritzed bug brains.

"You've turned a cyber-attack into knitted goods," he said.

"Have I?" said Twenty-Six.

"I can't work out if that's wonderful or terrible."

"Creative art should always challenge people," said Twenty-Six. "Someone said that on an internet video."

60

It was undeniable that the marlin campus had become a significantly different place in the weeks since Gustav had started working there.

Delivery bugs roved the corridors, either in thuggish bands, or in the hands of their human couriers, alternately threatening or cajoling people to assist in their deliveries. Bully Bugs seemed entirely indifferent as to whether they actually delivered their parcels or not. But that was okay, because the fanatically eager to please Bribe Bugs would latch onto and deliver any parcel they came across.

People in turn appeared to have evolved their own dealing mechanisms. T-shirts that announced some allegiance had become increasingly popular. There were those who publicly advertised their personal rates for package deliveries. There were those who wore t-shirts marked with giant red snowflakes: the company's universal 'do not touch' emblem. The number of Santa Impresora garments had grown. Icons of the patron saint of printers (and by extension, all temperamental technology) now adorned tops, scarves, baseball caps and bags. There were a number of veil-like Santa Impresora masks about the place. In fact, there had been a couple of times when he had seen a figure in full dress, with a dark veiled face, disappearing around a corner. It was only ever a glimpse, but there was a buzz in certain circles that full body apparitions of Santa Impresora had been witnessed by a number of people.

On top of the fake and possibly (or actually impossibly) real Santa Impresoras, there was also a growing fashion for people to cover their faces. It didn't take Gustav long to realise this was a deliberate measure to prevent marlin's facial recognition systems (and specifically the bugs' systems) from identifying people, and thereby inflicting penalties against their accounts. Many of those same people had adopted shuffling limps, or unusual walks, in order to confound the marlin gait analysis systems as well.

Things had definitely changed for the weirder and Gustav wondered why no one had stepped in to halt the seemingly random changes. He suspected that somewhere in the higher echelons of the corporation there was such a strong belief in hands-off management and the freedoms of the community members, that stepping in to stop things when they got out of hand was seen as utterly unpalatable.

That morning, Gustav sought out Ruby to gauge her opinion. He spotted her in a darkened office space on the second floor. He stepped over a Bully Bug and Bribe Bug who seemed to be arguing in unintelligible machine language over the ownership of a delivery package, and went inside.

Ruby glanced up at him, briefly, before returning her attentions to the wall screens filled with data in front of her. "Found my missing parcel yet?" she asked.

"Not yet. I'm going over to Customer Fulfilment later to spy on the bugs. See if I can spot where they're dumping the undelivered parcels."

Ruby nodded, but it was a reflex action. Her attention was on the screens.

Gustav looked at the data. He recognised the Vehicle Management System scripts he'd seen Ruby looking at many times. He saw pulsating graphs that were linked to office cameras. A map of the campus swarmed with dots, different colours moving at different speeds: bugs and droids and self-driving vehicles.

"This looks complicated," he said.

"One day, all companies will be like this," she said, quoting one of marlin's many advertising slogans.

"I remember that time you found me in an office with a massive map of the company's printers laid out on a table," said Gustav. "I'd drawn a spiderweb over it of things I would need to do to maximise the number of working printers I could create. You thought it was a sign I was going mad."

She got his drift. "I'm not going mad, Gustav. I'm close to seeing the whole picture."

"And what is the whole picture?"

"Oh, it's a mess." She stabbed fingers at various streaming

and scrolling chunks of data. "PMS, VMS, YouKnowMe, People and Places. It's like Kingsley said in one of the training sessions. We talk about company AI – AI in general – and we believe we're talking about thinking computers. Individual entities, like robots out of Star Trek or something. People talk about AI, and the threat of AI, and they picture evil robots like that one in the Arnold Schwarzenegger film."

"*Jingle All the Way*?"

"No, the one where he's a killer robot."

"I don't watch scary movies," said Gustav.

She tutted, irritated. "But AI isn't like that. It won't ever be like that. *These* are the AIs we need to be afraid of. Each of them working on a sliver of data about the world, like the blind men finding an elephant, each grasping a different part and jumping to equally wrong conclusions. These are the accumulated AI systems of marlin, each of them trying to understand the world by peering through a different keyhole, and making decisions which have far-reaching and unforeseen effects. It's Armageddon."

"You know that bit where you said you weren't going mad," said Gustav gently.

"Do not dismiss me because I'm an intelligent woman who dares to think outside the box."

"It's more that you're sitting in the dark and talking about Armageddon," he said.

"MarlinAssist: blinds open and lights on," she commanded. In moments the room was considerably brighter. Gustav saw the scattered remnants of several takeaway coffees. Ruby blinked hard against the light.

"What does all of this mean, then?" asked Gustav. "What conclusions have you come to?"

"PMS loves you," she said.

"Thank you."

"It literally does measure things like your facial expressions and your posture. It knows what a current high-level employee looks like, and uses the most basic metrics to see how you match up to that. If you were a few inches taller and a shade more Aryan-looking, you might be company CEO by now."

"The personnel system is some sort of fascist, master race bigot?"

"Not deliberately. But if ninety out of the top one hundred most successful CEOs are North American or European white dudes, then the most simplistic AI would assume those qualities make for good CEOs. I mean, you have a really white name."

"My surname is White, yes, but—"

"And White is a really white surname, Gustav." She pointed at another screen. "YouKnowMe is less sure about you. It seems to be functioning primarily on directives from the universality school of company directives. Your tastes aren't easily compartmentalised."

"I have unusual tastes?"

Ruby tilted her head, shrugging. "You're a grown man who loves dogs but doesn't own one."

"We had dogs on the island, but when we left we couldn't take them with us—"

"You buy jigsaws and – what's that? – knitting supplies?"

"For Twenty-Six," he said. "I ought to show you the jumper it's made."

"And you don't know Arnold Schwarzenegger's most famous film roles?"

"I don't like violent movies."

"From a customer perspective you're a bit of a mish-mash. YouKnowMe doesn't rate you highly."

"YouKnowMe rates people?"

"You're not quite an awkward customer, but you're less than perfect. And as for the Vehicle Management System…"

"Does it hate me too?"

She shook her head. "I don't understand it. It's constantly changing. Something happened since the last guiding mission doctrine update."

"The what?"

"An executive meeting where they determine how to interpret and guide the company's core values. The exact kind of thing I should probably have been involved in. But the VMS is changing. Look here. Reference after reference to strings being removed. I can only assume the VMS is deleting chunks of itself, because I can't see what data strings are missing." She waved her arms to take everything in. "Marlin's computer systems, which run every aspect of the company, are like a bunch of weirdos jostling and shouting at each other in different languages. It's like the computer systems are at war with each other."

Gustav remembered why he'd come in. "Have you noticed things are a bit weird out there, too?"

"Why do you think I'm hiding in here?"

"Shouldn't someone be doing something?" he said.

"You're the Super Gap Monkey," she said. "Maybe this is your time to shine."

"Maybe, but not before we meet those school children who are coming round today."

Ruby glanced at her smart watch. "Crap. I didn't realise. Let's go."

61

Ruby met the school group in reception. The teacher seemed perfectly pleased to hand them over. There were six in all, dressed in the blazers and grey trousers of the local secondary school. They were supposed to be fifteen-sixteen years old but they seemed huge. When had young people got so big?

She led them through to the break out area they used for the awareness training. She constantly directed them, but they straggled and wandered about so much Ruby felt like a sheepdog herding them on their way, stopping them from disappearing into kitchen areas or poking inside cupboards as they passed. She got them inside the break out area and was relieved to be able to shut the door behind them.

"Welcome everybody," she said. "We're so pleased you were able to join us for the first STEM in the Community event that Marlin has hosted. You are a very special group because you will help shape this programme for those who come after you." Ruby beamed at the group and tried to get a read from them, but it was some time since she had been a teenager. Did they always look so unimpressed with everything?

Quinn stepped forward with some stickers and felt tips. "Make yourselves name badges from the stickers too, so we know who you all are."

"Take a free pen," said Ruby.

One of them read the slogan on the side. "Marlin – giving humanity what it needs."

"Apparently we're getting new stationery soon, with the new mission critical objectives printed on, so that's exciting," said Ruby.

No one, adult or child, seemed excited by mission critical objectives, but there was a discernible uptick in energy as they doodled on the sticker badges. The six of them muttered amongst themselves, but none were keen to interact with the adults. Name badges were applied, although the grins shared between some of the students made Ruby think they had selected aliases for the day.

"So tell me a little bit about yourselves," she said.

The teenagers looked at her silently. Not with disdain, more like she was a dull TV channel.

"Your teacher said you're a special interest group," she tried again. "Is that right?"

That got a snigger from one and a laugh from another, which wasn't at all what Ruby had expected.

"Thing is," said a young man whose badge claimed he was one Bradley Fartburger, "we're basically the group that gets detention all the time. They sent us to you so they can have a quiet day."

Ruby laughed lightly. "I'm sure that's not true."

"Fucking is, lady," said Fartburger, smiling.

"Well," she said, feeling far from well, "thanks for being honest. But let me tell you that we don't mind a bit."

The sounds Ruby heard from Jim and Kingsley behind her suggested they were not entirely in agreement with this, but she ignored them.

"We have some exciting hands-on activities planned for you today. In a moment I will hand you over to Jim and Kingsley, who will take you through the day's agenda. Do any of you have any questions before we start?"

"Yeah, miss. How much do you earn?" asked a young girl apparently called Tanisha.

"Great question, Tanisha. I enjoy someone who can get straight to the point. One of the great things about working for marlin is that there's a complete lifestyle package on offer. I live on campus and get a lot of things for free, so all of my basic needs are taken care of. What I earn on top of that is almost immaterial."

"Yeah, but what do you earn?"

"I can't tell you that, Tanisha."

"Isn't it very much? Are you embarrassed?"

"We'll hook up with HR a bit later and they can talk you through some entry level positions."

Ruby felt bad for not answering the question. She knew the secrecy surrounding salaries underpinned systemic unfairness. She also knew whenever she'd seen people having open discussions of what they earned, it ended in bitterness and upset.

"I've got a question," said a young man called Calum. "What's he doing?" He pointed at Gustav, who was tidying up the backings from the name badge stickers which the young people had dropped on the floor.

Gustav paused in his activities and took a bow. "I am Gustav. I'm tidying up."

"You a cleaner, man?"

"I am an interstitial operative. It is my job to find jobs that need to be done, things that have perhaps been overlooked."

"So we make a mess and you clean it up?" said Bradley.

"I take pride in what I do," said Gustav.

"You a cleaner but you wear a suit and tie?"

"I wear what I want to wear. And I'm proud of the nice offices here, so it makes me happy to keep them tidy."

"Cleaner in a suit," said Bradley.

"Let's hand over to our representatives from the development team," said Ruby "Here are Jim and Kingsley." Ruby stepped back, making space for the developers to step forward.

"Whaddup, dogs!" said Jim, throwing his arms together in some sort of gang gesture.

That at least stunned them into silence.

"You better listen up, homes," he said, swaggering forward like he was the alpha dog in a prison exercise yard of his imagination. "We're gonna lay it down and testify."

Kingsley, horrified, leaned in towards him and whispered, "What the hell are you doing?"

"Speaking on their level," said Jim.

"Miss, is he mentally ill?" said Tanisha.

Kingsley deliberately stepped around his colleague, blocking him. "Um, have we got any tech-heads in the room?" he asked.

There was silence from the group.

"Yep, I get it," he nodded. "You probably all have some fixed ideas about what a career in STEM—"

"That's science, technology, engineering and maths, brethren," added Jim, who hadn't yet shaken off his 'street' attitude.

"Er, yes," said Kingsley. "So what would a job in STEM be like. What words would you use to describe that?"

"Boring."

"Stupid."

"Hard."

Kingsley nodded earnestly. "Boring, stupid and hard. Let's see if we can challenge some of those ideas today, shall we?"

He reached behind him and pulled out a wheeled object. To Ruby it looked like a really old-fashioned design for a roller skate. The students gazed at it with a clearly telegraphed lack of interest. Kingsley took that as a signal to dial up his zeal. "Looks a bit boring, right? Just wait until you see what it can do!"

He placed the wheeled thing on the table, then pulled out his mobile phone. "You all have mobile phones, right? Well, I bet you all wish you could do this with yours." He put the mobile onto the chassis of the wheeled apparatus and fastened it in place with a strap, then placed the contraption onto the floor. "Jim and I developed this prototype mobile chariot from scratch and we can talk you through how we did it, but first a demo. Hey mobile, move forward one metre at slow speed."

The little wheeled mobile chariot whirred into life and moved as he had directed.

"Hey mobile, move backwards one metre at high speed."

It zipped back, very quickly. The speed of the movement sent a ripple of interest through the group.

Jim smiled. "Hey mobile, move forwards one metre and turn left thirty degrees."

As the mobile moved, Bradley leaned forward and shouted, "Hey mobile! Move forwards ten metres at high speed!"

The other students joined in, calling instructions.

"Hey mobile! Turn left!"

"Hey mobile, go in a circle!"

"Hey mobile, do a wheelie!"

The first instruction, issued by Bradley, was the mobile chariot's last. It zoomed forward at high speed and slammed into the opposite wall. The chassis smashed apart, one of the wheels spinning off backwards across the floor. The mobile itself was destroyed, bent out of shape, its screen shattered into thousands of tiny shards.

Kingsley stared aghast at the destruction of his pet project, wordless. Jim stepped behind and placed a comforting hand on his shoulder.

"Law of the ghetto, man."

Gustav gave a small cough. "I'll just go and fetch a dustpan," he said and stepped out.

Ruby retreated to the back of the room while Kingsley

tried to choke back tears and explain the design process for the now shattered mobile chariot. Something about the man's miserable pathos held their attention.

Quinn leaned close to Ruby to whisper. "What are we meant to do with them next?"

"What about showing them Velvet? Nobody can resist Velvet."

Quinn gave a small squeak of horror. "Listen, you're a nice person who thinks the best of everyone, but that young Bradley over there is a sociopath."

"Come on. They're just kids."

Quinn shook her head. "That one has clearly demonstrated he is a young thug. He's a risk. We can't let him near anything that is breakable, which definitely includes Velvet."

"What about Heeby then?" said Ruby.

"Weren't you trying to get us to empathise with Heeby like we did with Velvet?" said Quinn.

"I'm just saying, if you're not happy with them handling Velvet, what about Heeby?"

"That's not so bad," said Quinn.

"What if they damage Heeby?" she asked, testing.

"We will do our best to make sure that they don't," said Quinn. "They definitely need to learn they can't just break things for fun. If they do damage Heeby, we know Jim and Kingsley can fix it. Velvet is not fixable. Probably."

Ruby studied the young woman and wondered about her thought processes.

"I just want Velvet to be safe, okay?" said Quinn

62

As Gustav made his way along the corridor to the nearest cleaning cupboard, he saw clusters of delivery bugs locked in tiny altercations with any passing humans and each other. The work of the marlin office seemed to be entirely secondary to the delivery bugs' demands. A new generation of Bribe Bugs were among the crowds, and their sales tactics had moved on.

"Can I ask whether you enjoy store credit?"

The woman it had backed up against a wall gave a wordless nod in response.

"And free things, you like free things, yes?"

Another nod.

"So, you'd be really foolish to pass up the opportunity I'm about to offer you! Many of your friends and family have accepted the offer to earn credit for a very minor amount of inconvenience. I'll just need you to register your acceptance of an affiliate deal, so that Marlin can deduct a percentage of all future earnings, how does that sound?"

The woman shifted uneasily.

"If you recruit five more humans, you could make gold level partner. Projections show gold level partners are in the country's top two percent earners. You can't pass up that kind of deal!"

"They're peddling a goddamn pyramid scheme," said Cassie Troy. The printer repair woman had appeared at Gustav's side.

Gustav had heard of pyramid schemes, but had no direct experience of them. He had assumed they were limited to sales of specialised housewares and toiletries amongst groups of friends.

Nearby, a long-legged Bribe Bug had planted itself on top a water cooler and extended a long arm across the corridor to halt passers-by. Gustav and Cassie instinctively drew aside, watching. Interestingly, the woman the bug did snare wore a t-shirt featuring a snowflake, but the bug ignored the leave-me-alone symbol.

"You like making people smile, I bet?" it commented. "How often does that happen in a day, normally?"

"Um. I'm not sure," said the woman.

"Did you know that it releases dopamine into your body? It's a genuine health benefit. Want to hear how you can make more people smile? It's easy, you just knock on their door and hand them a parcel. It makes them happy, and it makes you happy too. Don't you just love a win-win situation?"

The woman gave a small smile and held out her hand to take the parcel.

"Is that science stuff true?" asked Gustav. "Dopamine?"

"Who knows," said Cassie. "Fool woman believes it though."

"If that's what the Bribe Bugs are doing, I wonder what next gen Bully Bugs are like?" said Gustav.

Cassie pointed. A marlin employee wearing overalls staggered along the path, pushing a trolley. Gustav couldn't tell if it was a man or a woman, because the person's head was smothered by a delivery bug, its articulated legs clamped firmly in place down to shoulder level. The host's face was utterly covered. The bug's own camera eyes, only notionally in the right place for a human face, were the only way this master-slave hybrid could see. The human was the body and the bug was the brain. The bug barked orders at other bugs and its human host. Bugs deposited their parcels onto the ground and the bug-controlled-human picked them up as the Bully Bug issued instructions. It had quite a collection of parcels in the trolley.

"I think I've had just enough of this crap," said Cassie.

She took a piece of folded paper from inside her knitted tank top and showed it to the nearest bug. The creature spasmed and rolled on its side, stunned. Cassie moved forward, blasting bug after bug with her printed QR code.

"Well are you going to help or not, Mr Interstitial?" she shouted at Gustav.

Gustav wasn't sure what he was meant to do. But, with a smile for any watching cameras, he helped the person with the now fritzing bug clamped over their face and shoulders. The man gasped as it came free.

"That was not nice," he said, which Gustav imagined was something of an understatement.

Together, they levered the bug forward and into the delivery trolley. Gustav scurried about, gathering what stunned bugs he could, dumping them in the trolley.

"That thing's had me working for it all morning," said the freed man.

"The next stage of evolution," said Gustav.

The vague plan Gustav had was if they could gather up as many of the bugs as possible, they could shut them away in a room somewhere until someone in charge could be informed. It was at this moment that Gustav realised he really, really didn't know who was in charge. He was contemplating whether Myfanwy was his best option when he was distracted by a shout of alarm from Cassie.

A handful of bugs, moving too fast for her to disabled with the QR sheet, had attacked her. White plastic paddle arms and narrow-nosed pincers pulled at her clothes and scaled her body. She swung an arm aside and dashed one of the bugs against a wall. But, as she did, another leaped and, with an action too precise to be accidental, sliced into her printed sheet, ripping it into three useless chunks.

"Oh, not good," said Gustav.

63

"Let me talk to you about our next activity," Kingsley said to the group of students, having salvaged some of his emotional nerve and dignity.

"Can we say something first?" said the student girl Tanisha, standing.

"Er, yes, of course."

"Bradley's sorry for the damage to your little toy."

"No I'm not," said Bradley. "It was Calum's fault anyway."

"Balls it was," said Calum.

"But we're sorry," said Tanisha. "Please don't ban us. Everyone bans us."

"I understand what it means to get carried away," said Kingsley. "I can't stay mad at people who are passionate about things." He tried a small smile.

Jim made a small spluttering noise that sounded as though he might beg to differ.

Kingsley continued, not noticing. "We've got something

different for our next session. While you might be tempted to treat it badly, we're going to use it as an opportunity to treat technology with some respect. In a moment we will introduce you to Heeby."

"Hey, Heeby, you can come out now!" called Jim in a theatrical voice.

"Oh wait, Jim. Nothing's happening!" said Kingsley in an even more exaggerated and stagey manner. "Why don't you try saying 'please'?"

"Hey, Heeby, would you *please* come out now?" said Jim loudly.

Heeby scuttled out from behind the cupboard.

There were murmurs from the students. They would have seen the bots out and about, but they clearly liked the idea of getting up close and personal with one.

"So it will do things if we say please?" asked Tanisha.

"Yes. Treat it with respect and it will be your willing assistant."

"Hey, Heeby, can you come over here, please?" asked Tanisha.

The bug went across the floor and Tanisha bent to look at it.

"Hey Heeby, can you show us your top speed please?" asked Bradley. He glanced up at Jim and Kingsley. "But like, don't crash into anything. Please."

Heeby moved away to a clear part of the room then zipped about, its legs moving at a surprising speed. The students all laughed.

"Look at its legs!"

"Go Heeby!"

"What else can it do?"

Jim beamed around at them. "If you want to challenge Heeby, you could make a circuit and watch him negotiate it." He glanced at Ruby. "Or her. Of course we don't know what gender Heeby is."

"So like, a maze?" said Tanisha.

"Or a maze, yeah! Knock yourselves out!" Jim said.

The students spent some time pulling things out of their bags to create a maze. The floor was soon littered with pencil cases, jumpers and rolled-up paper to make channels for Heeby to negotiate. They even began removing their shoes when they ran out of other things. Ruby was intrigued to see that making a maze was actually quite challenging, and the group needed to communicate and collaborate in a way which turned them into a formidable team. She watched quietly, not wanting to interrupt in case she spoiled the magic.

Jim darted forward a few times to neaten the edges, so that Heeby wouldn't get caught up. The students smiled gratefully. Quinn donated a banana from her own bag to fill in a gap.

When they were satisfied the maze was finished, the students politely asked Heeby to enter and find a way through it. At the first blind alley, they called out in encouragement, suggesting backing up and trying a different route. As Heeby's understanding of the maze grew, the group began to get excited.

"Heeby remembered that way doesn't work!"

"Is it going faster now?"

Heeby had indeed sped up, becoming more adept at the

trial and error methodology. There was a tense moment as it neared the exit, when it went down a long blind alley. It quickly doubled back on itself, immediately making the correct turn and emerging to freedom.

A cheer went up from the group. Ruby couldn't believe how engrossed they had all been.

"Machine learning," said Kingsley. "One of the ways in which marlin makes itself a market leader."

"It's nearly time for you to go," said Jim. "But I think this calls for a victory lap, don't you?"

The students agreed noisily.

"Let's challenge Heeby to a corridor chair race!" said Jim. "Something bored software developers have been doing since forever is racing office chairs. You can be initiated into our special STEM club. Follow me!"

Ruby hurried to speak in Jim's ear. "Is this a good idea? You sure you're getting a bit carried away. It seems risky—"

"Ruby, this is a rite of passage. We do it literally all of the time. It'll be fine."

Jim opened the door to the corridor, and a wall of sound poured in. A hundred bug voices, human shouts, and the clatter of conflict.

"What the hell?" said Jim.

Something white and plastic propelled itself from the fray and at the door. Jim ducked, but Kingsley saw the danger too late. A thing with squid limbs of white articulated plastic wrapped itself around his skull.

Ruby pushed forward and slammed the door shut to prevent anything else coming through.

Kingsley spun and tried to pull the thing off him.

"It's a shitting facehugger," yelped a student.

Kingsley gave a roar of blind fury, found a wooden panelled wall and headbutted it hard. The bug sitting on his face creaked. He headbutted it again. And again. The plastic shell cracked. Something whined unhappily. Kingsley grabbed a loosened leg and ripped the thing from his face. There were pink impact marks across his nose and temple.

Someone screamed in horror.

Kingsley swung the bug by its leg and savagely dashed it against the wall. It fell still, not moving when Kingsley dropped it to the floor. Kingsley panted. Everyone stared.

"It's not meant to do that," said Jim, eventually.

"You think?" said Ruby.

"It's all okay, it's all okay." Kingsley took a woozy step, tripped over a wheely chair, and landed heavily on the floor.

They carefully moved chairs away from Kingsley. Those students who had fallen back in the bug attack crawled to their feet, bruised but mostly unhurt. Kingsley was conscious, although his eyes swivelled aimlessly.

Ruby stabbed the alarm button on her campus app to call medical assistance.

"Get up, mate," said Jim.

"I am up, aren't I?" said Kingsley.

64

Gustav and Cassie clattered clumsily down the stairs to the sub-basement. They had been unable to take the lift, as a Bribe Bug had jammed itself between the lift doors so it could shout about its pyramid scheme to anyone who stepped near.

On the stairs, they found a woman with a Bully Bug on her head, trying to walk down the stairs. It was a gut-wrenching sight, as the bug urged her forward at a pace she was clearly uncomfortable with, and small howls of fear accompanied her unsteady descent. Gustav was nervous of helping her, as it put him closer to the Bully Bug than he wanted to be. But he just couldn't watch her trip and fall. He hooked his elbow through hers and guided her down.

"Don't help them!" hissed Cassie, irritated.

"I must."

"We don't have long!"

"To save civilization as we know it?" he said. He meant it as a flippant joke, but it sounded ominously apt in the situation.

"We just need to print some more codes and distribute them," she said.

The Bully Bug ignored Gustav, apart from a couple of attempts to grab his ear with its pincers. He dodged that, leaving the woman once they had exited the stairwell. He wasn't happy abandoning her, but at least she wasn't in immediate danger of a terrible fall. He hurried along to Cassie Troy's rooms, but when he got there, moments behind Cassie, the wooden door was wide open. He had never seen it like that, and he knew it was a bad sign.

"No..." Cassie whispered.

They went inside and Gustav was momentarily blinded. Back on Dubh Mòr as a child, one of his elderly neighbours had a snow globe toy which contained a cottage and some fir trees. Gustav had enjoyed the way he could inflict a blizzard upon this tranquil scene by shaking the globe so that white flakes fluttered around in the liquid. The scene in Cassie Troy's room was like being in a snow globe. Pieces of shredded paper twisted in the air in every direction.

"They can't do this," said Cassie in soft disbelief.

Gustav looked at the paper flying around the room. Cassie pushed through the blizzard. Gustav heard rather than saw her launch herself at something at the centre of the storm. Gustav spat shredded paper from his mouth and waded in.

Cassie was atop a grey cleaner bot which was itself being

ridden by a white bug of some sort. The bot had been hoovering stacks of paper down from the shelves, sweeping them under itself with its powerful brushes and, forgoing its collection hopper on its rear, spewing the crumpled and shredded remains out its rear like a lawnmower.

It made immediate sense to Gustav. The only weapon they had against the bugs was Cassie's QR code. The bugs had only seen it in action in paper form. They had therefore decided to destroy all the printer paper in the building. It made perfect but impossible sense. Such logic, such strategizing, required a level of intelligence that the bugs surely didn't possess. It required a kind of thinking that was, well, human.

"Ah-ha!" cried Cassie victoriously, holding something aloft. It was her heavy Swiss Army Knife type thing. She jammed it down – in the paper storm, Gustav couldn't see which attachment she was using – and prised apart the casing of the bug. There were buzzes and shouts and some furious stabbing, then the bug was dead and the cleaner bot was suddenly still.

White fragments drifted lazily like autumn leaves.

"Bastards!" said Cassie, stumbling off the disabled machines. She made it to the connecting room and gave an undignified sob of relief when she saw her many folders of printed work still lining the shelves. "My great work. So fragile."

"QR codes," Gustav reminded her.

Cassie grabbed her screen device from her bench and brushed paper flakes from it.

"We'll print thousands," she said. "We'll broadcast it to

every screen on campus. We'll – *what*—?" She stabbed at her screen.

"Is there a problem?" said Gustav.

"The system won't let me in."

"What system?"

"Any system. I can't log on. The bugs couldn't have taken over everything."

Gustav was inclined to agree. Cassie swiped. "Face recognition. It's me, Cassie Troy."

The screen gave an unhappy beep.

"Rip the cover off that thing," said Cassie, pointing at a camera in the corner of the room. Gustav could see she had taped a sheet of paper over its spying lens.

Gustav hoiked himself onto a bench and ripped the paper away. Cassie put the screen aside and faced the camera.

"I'm Cassie Troy. Give me access to my marlin account."

Whatever response she was hoping for didn't come.

There was a flashing message on Cassie's screen. Santa Impresora – no such account. String scheduled for deletion.

"What does that mean? String scheduled for deletion?"

Cassie grimaced. "It's them two damned weirdo beardos."

"Jim and Kingsley."

"They've screwed up my account."

"I know where they are," said Gustav. "Come on." He saw Cassie's hesitation. "We can make it."

Cassie stepped towards her library of printed things. "I need to keep them safe."

"But…" Gustav waved at the ceiling, at the world above, at the madness gripping marlin.

"I will lock the door behind you," she said, simply. "Contact me when you've fixed my account and I'll send out the kill code."

He could see there was little chance of swaying her.

"Stay safe," he said, and left.

65

Ruby peered out at the corridor through the glass wall. The awareness group and the visiting students gathered in the room together, with Kingsley at their centre. The developer was supported by a cushion and covered in a foil blanket, but he was getting very vocal about the fact he was still lying on the floor. The students sat in a huddle, muttering to each other occasionally and studying their mobiles.

Things seemed quieter on the corridor, but Ruby wasn't prepared to risk going out just yet. She went to a window and looked outside the building.

"Er, Jim?" she said.

"What is it?"

"Come look."

Jim tutted, left his colleague's side and came over to her. "Is there a problem?"

She pointed outside.

The roads were gridlocked with cars and bugs. Clusters of delivery bugs were locked into tiny altercations with any passing humans and each other.

"Traffic disruptions?" said Jim. "That should not be possible with the MarlinGo VMS. One of the key optimisation themes is flow management."

"Thank you, Jim. And yet—" She gestured at the evident chaos outside, then held up her screen device. On the marlin campus app map there were red lines along all of the roads.

"I don't understand," said Jim.

"I think it means there's a problem. Evolution out of control, I'd say. I'm going to find out what management are doing about it." She searched for the contact details for members of the ESG, selecting Delphine. If Delphine from legal was in the building with them, she'd definitely have opinions on the bug chaos exploding all around.

The video call connected. Delphine sat at a huge desk in a large and pleasant space with bookshelves and picture windows.

"Ah, how's the school visit going?" she asked.

"Badly," said Ruby. "Do you know what's happening on campus?" She angled her screen round and flipped the camera, so Delphine could see the battling and rampaging swarms of bugs on the front roads and lawns.

"It looks as if there's been a bit of a glitch."

"It's more than a glitch, damn it! Marlin systems are actively trying to kill people."

"We don't know that for sure," said Jim. "We might be seeing an evolutionary blind alley in terms of the bugs."

"You've got the developers there?" said Delphine. "Good. We'll be fine once someone sets them on the right path again."

Ruby gave herself a moment before she responded. "No Delphine, this is much more serious. There are two factions of misguided delivery bugs locked into an escalating conflict with each other. Humans are being tormented and harmed as collateral damage. And, for some reason, the MarlinGo vehicles have been actively targeting certain colleagues and trying to run them over."

"Steady on now," said Jim. "Panicking is one thing. Slander is another."

"It's very bad," Ruby insisted. "And we need some leadership. Right now."

Ruby saw Delphine's face blanch at the mention of leadership. *"It's against the most fundamental rules of robotics and automation for our systems to be targeting humans. How can we be sure that's what's happening?"*

Ruby leaned forward. "Because I have witnessed it myself, twice. I have re-created it in a simulation, and I can almost pinpoint the software change that caused it."

Delphine was unnerved by this. *"Of course, leadership is in the hands of all of our colleagues. We operate a servant-leadership model. It's my job to remove blockers so that you can achieve success, Ruby."*

Was Delphine seriously attempting to duck the issue? "Jesus Christ, Delphine! I must respectfully insist this needs immediate attention *and* an executive steer," said Ruby. She tried to make her words polite so her face didn't need to be.

"Let me get back to you on that one," said Delphine and killed the call. Ruby and Jim stared at the screen.

"Did she just abandon us?" said Jim.

Ruby thought about it. "I think she did."

"And is that stuff actually true? About MarlinGo cars trying to kill people?"

"I think it is."

"Bugger."

Ruby nodded in heartfelt agreement. "I'm going to ask Quinn to take charge here so we can go and take a look."

"We?" said Jim, his voice rising in pitch as his throat tightened.

Ruby turned to the group. "Hey listen everybody. There are some traffic disruptions on the campus, which I think explains why your ambulance might be delayed. The bugs are acting weirdly. Quinn, I want you to keep Kingsley and the kids safe. Barricade the doors if needs be."

Quinn looked panicked, but Ruby patted her arm in encouragement. "You got this Quinn. I'll be along when I can."

"Oh, it's fine. We'll pray to Santa Impresora for help," said Quinn.

"Does she do protection from robots? I thought she was just printers."

Quinn pulled out a Santa Impresora pendant from beneath her top and clutched it fervently. "All workplace disasters she can fix."

Ruby shrugged. If Quinn wanted support from a folk saint that had been dreamed up by her colleagues, then who was she to judge? "Er, sure. I'm going to see where Gustav got to as well."

She put through a call to her friend and neighbour, who

had definitely been gone too long for a man simply in search of a dustpan and brush.

A gasp of surprise distracted her. Everyone was staring out at the corridor. The children already had their mobiles out, filming. Kingsley was muttering woozily. Quinn had her arms raised in rapt joy.

Santa Impresora was walking along the corridor, her heavy layered dress billowing. The patron saint of printers turned her veiled head and looked at them as she passed.

66

Getting back to the training room from the sub-basement was not as easy as it should have been. The ground floor corridors were now a battlefield between factions of bugs. Humans were caught in the fray.

Gustav peered over the lip of the stairs. He could see a band of people in red snowflake t-shirts behind a defensive wall constructed from overturned desks. There was another group, marching under a Santa Impresora banner. Further along, a tight knot of individuals with helmets fashioned from waste paper baskets and metal rods in their hands were viciously attacking anything mechanical that came close to them.

It was a scene of violence, the likes of which Gustav had never witnessed before. His life on Dubh Mòr had been a sheltered one, and if anything war-like came on television he was sure to turn it over to more gentle fare. Even so, he was sure this was completely out of the ordinary, even for crazy mainland people.

Getting along the corridor to the school visitors would be to wade through a sea of carnage. He decided it would be simpler to head out through the fire exit opposite and just go round the building.

This, it turned out, was little better. Out in the open, on the beautifully landscaped lawns and paths, the bugs had the opportunity to spread.

Helmet-like Bully Bugs had seized human mounts and were steering them about the place on their increasingly unfathomable missions. Bugs without a ride swung from every possible vantage point, attempting to hijack passing humans. The ones which did have a captive human were engaged in escalating violence, attacking other bugs, or trying to get to people trapped in their MarlinGo cars, or other, more mundane vehicles. The voices of the bugs hollering instructions, and the cries of humans apologising to each other, were horrible. Gustav peered closer, wondering why the humans didn't just refuse to co-operate, then saw the bugs had tiny pincers and were pinching their captives' ears as punishment for non-compliance.

A bug-stunning QR code would be so handy right now. If they couldn't sort out Cassie's account to retrieve her file, the only other place to find one, he realised, would be in his apartment. There was a QR printed sheet there somewhere and, it occurred to him, a larger version in the form of a knitted jumper.

Gustav hunkered down by the wall, took out his mobile

and sent a voice message to his marlinAssist, instructing it to turn on the speaker in his apartment.

"Twenty-Six? I need you to do something for me. Please respond to this."

There was no reply.

"Twenty-Six. I know you're there. Stop watching TV, or making jigsaws, or whatever you're doing, and respond."

Of course. He had told Twenty-Six to ignore anything the marlinAssist said, in order to avoid the two device getting locked in a pointless looping conversation. He need to rethink.

He called to a nearby Bribe Bug: a dome like thing with expressive, almost human hands. "Hey bug! Can you make a delivery for me?"

"*Sir!*" it said with child-like enthusiasm. "*Would you be interested in joining our lucrative affiliate scheme?*"

"Er, yes. I will join your affiliate scheme, if you just make a delivery for me. Can we do a deal?"

"*You will apply a digital signature to the document I have sent you?*" asked the bug, scuttling towards him.

"Yes! Yes I will, if you go to my apartment and fetch me the knitted jumper that is on the table. It is the only jumper in the room. Please do that."

"*Sign first, please. I have amended the contract to include delivery of the jumper. You will not regret this. Don't forget that you only need to recruit five more humans to make the gold level partner!*"

Gustav applied his signature and the bug scuttled off. He wondered what the chances were of his bug making it back in one piece. There were more bugs all over the place. Were they following the digital signatures of employees so they could track them? Gustav wondered what he would need to do to stop them knowing where he was. A glance up at the cameras gave him his answer. Even if he threw away his screen and anything else electronic, the PMS would still be watching from the video feeds.

"Gustav!"

The voice was coming from a nearby MarlinGo, its windscreen covered in bugs. They were all competing for the attention of the person inside. They shouted and stomped their tiny feet. Gustav could see a face at the side window, which was open just a crack.

"Myfanwy?" Gustav almost didn't recognise her without her ever-present smile.

"What's happening? The car won't move and I'm scared to get out!"

"No, don't get out! You're safer inside the car," said Gustav. Surely she could see what was going on?

"They're going to smash their way in!"

She had a point. A single bug was not very strong, but as more of them crowded onto the windscreen, their collective drumming could probably exert quite a force.

"We can try to get you inside the building," said Gustav, shoving another bug aside with his foot as it sidled up to him.

She nodded. "Yes please!"

A bug tried to haul itself up Gustav's leg. Its black lens eyes were huge and ghostly. He shook his leg and flung it away, but others were closing in. Gustav kicked and struggled.

"On the count of three!" he called to Myfanwy. "One—!"

"On the count of three, what?"

"Two!" He gripped the door handle. The car started moving, forwards then backwards, bashing the vehicles pressed in behind and in front, crushing bugs beneath its wheels. It clearly didn't want to be touched.

"*Three!*"

Gustav yanked the door open. Myfanwy pushed herself out. A spidery creature landed on his shoulder and he flung it away with fear-fuelled strength. They dodged bugs as they ran down the path.

Bully Bugs were getting their humans to throw other bugs through the air, so Gustav and Myfanwy had to look out for flying bugs. Gustav watched one sail across the path in front of him, slightly surprised it didn't smash as it landed on the ground. Instead it scuttled across and tried and grab him by the foot. He glanced back. The bugs that had been on the windscreen of the MarlinGo car were pouring onto the ground to follow him and Myfanwy. Gustav saw the car start to move once its sensors were clear. It made some rapid manoeuvres back and forth to adjust its position, then came hurtling along the path towards him.

"It's a footpath!" yelled Myfanwy. "Cars aren't allowed on here!"

Gustav jumped off the path and plunged into a flowerbed. The car followed, but its wheels lost traction in the soft soil and slid sideways.

"It came for us!" Myfanwy gasped.

"Wouldn't be the first time," said Gustav, pushing her towards a building entrance. Inside there was little respite, but he pulled her sideways, up a flight of stairs, and into the corridor leading to the room where Ruby and the others should be.

Except they weren't. The gaggle of students and employees were hurrying down the corridor in pursuit of a figure in a white dress. Jim and the student boy Brad were pushing a trolley which was not designed for humans, but on which Kingsley nonetheless reclined awkwardly.

"What's going on?" gasped Gustav as he joined the chase.

"We're following Santa Impresora!" shouted Quinn.

"She's imaginary, isn't she?" panted Myfanwy.

"I used to think so," said Gustav.

67

Ruby, Quinn and the students cornered the newly minted Santa Impresora in a relatively quiet office space just outside the canteen.

"Santa Impresora, please keep us safe from harm!" said Quinn as the ghostly saint loaded up a bag with the offerings of cakes, fruit, and the cold hard cash people had left by the Impresora shrine.

The saint gave a nod, and a small smile from behind her heavy veil. She raised a hand, palm outwards, making a gesture that was somewhere between a blessing and a farewell, then she made to leave.

"No wait!" cried Quinn. "I also need you to watch over the weak and vulnerable, like our hamster, Velvet."

There was another nod, impatient now.

The saint was definitely itching to get away, while Quinn obviously wanted to keep her there. Ruby had often marvelled at the way some people either failed to see the body language of others, or simply chose (perhaps unconsciously) to ignore it if it suited their own agenda.

Ruby sighed. Obviously Santa Impresora had not genuinely manifested. For some reason someone was walking around impersonating her, possibly in order to steal divine tribute.

"And Ruby of course," said Quinn, noticing she had joined them. "Watch over Ruby and keep her safe. Oh, and Gustav too."

Ruby whirled. Gustav looked like he'd seen some action. There was dirt on his shoes, and his shirt had become partly untucked. Myfanwy from HR was clinging to his arm, still beaming despite the disaster that had struck marlin.

"Gustav saved me!" said Myfanwy, eyes wide. Crazed even. "I'm so grateful!"

Her smile was bigger, more manic than ever. Ruby hadn't that was possible, but she couldn't help wonder whether Myfanwy imagined this was some sort of romantic relationship apotheosis between her and Gustav.

"We've got things we have to do," said Gustav. "Although I'm not sure what they are."

Ruby could hear distant screaming, but couldn't tell exactly where from or why. "The bots are at war," she said.

"The cars tried to kill me again," said Gustav. "They went for Cassie Troy. And she knows how to fight these things."

"That's one of the things I admire about you, Gustav," said Myfanwy. "You have a great instinct for whatever is the right thing to do."

Gustav pushed forward to Jim and Kingsley. "You two did something to Cassie Troy's account!"

"Is now the time to be dealing with user accounts?" said Jim, craning over Kingsley's trolley to see what was going on between Quinn and the short figure of Santa Impresora.

"Given that in her account is a weapon we can use against the bots, yes," said Gustav.

"It was all Jim's idea," said Kingsley.

Jim looked more than a little awkward, but it didn't stop him holding up a hand and adopting a lecturing tone. "As we all know, when there is a crisis we must sometimes act boldly. I was prepared to do that. Sometimes it pays off, and sometimes it doesn't. It appears I applied a fix to address this current situation, and it has not been successful."

"For the love of Ada Lovelace, Jim!" said Kingsley. "A fix is not the name for this. A fix is where you find an error and you back it out or code around it. This— I don't know what to call it."

"You merged Cassie's records with those of Santa Impresora," said Gustav.

"In the YouKnowMe database," said Kingsley.

"And that's why some robots started attacking her."

"There might have been some unintended consequences," Jim conceded.

Santa Impresora gave a sudden, piercing scream.

"What's happened?" shouted Ruby, her view obscured by jostling, panicking school children.

"Noo-noo's eating the dress lady!" one of them shouted.

Ruby forced herself forward. There was a cleaning bot at

Santa Impresora's feet. The powerful vacuum suction had sucked the saint's foot into its mechanism. She fell. There was a whine as the bot increased its power, trying to drag the rest of her in.

Ruby slammed a hand onto the bot. "Power down! Stop doing that!" She slapped the buttons on the bot's top, but nothing happened.

"Press the off button!" Jim shouted.

"I have!" Ruby shouted back.

"Are you sure?" he replied.

The teenagers gathered round. Without a word three of them grabbed the patron saint by the arms, while others took hold of the bot. They heaved and pulled. The fat suction tube made farty flappy noises as it fought to keep a hold on Impresora.

"Engage voice control!" Ruby commanded. "Begin diagnostic cycle!"

The bot replied in a tinny voice. *"Override denied. Mission critical objective in progress."*

"What the hell? Who has authority to override?"

"The objectives for company success are set by the executive committee. We all contribute to marlin's success by aligning ourselves to these objectives." The tinny voice sounded way too sure of itself for Ruby's liking.

"Are you saying that an exec can make you back off?" Hell, who knew the company executives might have some use after all.

With a loud slurp, like a straw sucking up the last drink in a glass, Santa Impresora's foot came free. The students gave a variety of cheers, gasps and squeaks. The cleaning bot starting lashing about, trying to find its target once more.

"In here!" shouted Jim, wheeling Kingsley into the canteen.

68

The canteen was in many ways a good place to hold out against the bots, Gustav thought. The entrance doors were actual swing doors rather than automatic ones, and he could begin barricading tables against them the moment they were inside. Others immediately joined in.

The serving area was a natural hiding place, and the kitchen prep areas behind would be good to retreat to if necessary. There was also a plentiful supply of metal-legged chairs and kitchen items that could be useful as weapons.

He waved his hands to the students. "Tanisha. Calum. Bradley Fartburger and you – whose label has fallen off. Start blocking off those other doors."

"So commanding," said Myfanwy. "A natural leader."

There really wasn't time for fawning praise from Myfanwy, but Gustav couldn't stop himself looking for the nearest security camera, straightening his tie, and giving a winning smile. It really was an awful habit he'd fallen into. He'd have to shake it at some point.

There was a thump as a bug slammed itself against one of the windows outside.

"This really shouldn't have happened at all," said Jim.

"Unforeseen consequences?" said Ruby bitterly.

Myfanwy tapped the screen she carried. "This is totally ruining our record on zero-harm days for our colleagues! We've got campus app alerts going off everywhere!"

Gustav could picture it. Hundreds of marlin community members, hiding or running, stabbing the friendly red buttons on their screens, and waiting for help that simply wasn't going to come.

He went to where Santa Impresora had collapsed on a seat, her legs sticking out. She had a small but heavy purple boot on one foot, but lost the other to the cleaning bot. The exposed foot had nasty red suck marks running up from ankle to shin. Quinn was crouched before her saint, muttering prayers.

"Quinn, could you go into the kitchen and get some ice for ... for Santa Impresora's leg."

"Yes, yes, of course. Anything!" said Quinn, hurrying off.

Gustav made to inspect the 'saint's' leg. She flinched as he reached out.

"So ... Gabriella, this is a new venture for you, isn't it?" said Gustav, once they were alone.

There was an angry huffing sound from beneath the veil. "Yeah. It's legit, though."

"Yes. You do hospitality, marketing and design, and pretending to be mythical beings."

"I go by many names. I'm just stepping up as an interstitial. Nobody else claimed it, and it's a job that needs doing. People need Santa Impresora, and I'm just filling the role."

"Even though it's me actually fixing the printers."

"Ha!" she laughed. "I knew it!"

"Hey, there's no judgement from me," said Gustav. "Although if there's cake in your bag of offerings going spare—"

Gabriella tutted at him. "Fine. I don't like carrot cake. You can have that one."

Gustav was chomping down on carrot cake when Quinn returned with a plastic bag filled with ice cubes. "Here, your worshipfulness," she said, placing the ice on Gabriella's leg. Gabriella winced, about to snap out some sharp words when she clearly remembered herself. She managed a sombre gesture of benediction instead.

"Mrs Lady!" shouted one of the students. "There's more people here!"

A thin stream of bedraggled refugees from the bug war were coming through an unbarricaded entrance.

"Well, let them in!" Ruby shouted.

As the band of desperate people dribbled in in, Gustav could hear their awed whispers.

"Santa Impresora!"

"Santa Impresora will help us!"

"She is here in our hour of need!"

"I found her first!" Quinn shouted.

Gustav smiled grimly at Gabriella. "Looks like you're up."

Gabriella nodded and waved her followers to come closer. It was a demure and saintly gesture. She was taking her role very seriously.

68

"This is all very bad," said Myfanwy, watching campus-wide events unfold via her screen.

There seemed to be a disconcerting battle going on between the totally legitimate worry in her mind and the perma-grin on her face. It looked to Ruby like a badly spliced film reel, flicking erratically between one scene and another. If sparks and smoke began to explode out of Myfanwy's ears as her brain failed to resolve the dichotomy, Ruby wouldn't have been at all surprised.

"We should all just be getting along," the HR woman whimpered miserably.

"We have some systems actively attacking humans, while others use them as a resource to complete their goals," said Ruby.

"Possibly we are seeing the effects of a massive cyber-attack," said Jim. "Human interference. It's the only explanation. Our systems are well designed, and have nothing but customers' and employees' best interests at heart."

"Do they talk to each other?" said Gustav.

"Employees?" said Ruby.

"We call them community members," said Myfanwy.

"The systems," said Gustav. He looked at Jim and Kingsley. "Do all the marlin systems talk to each other?"

"Oh, well," Jim started. "Interesting you should ask that."

"Very interesting," said Kingsley, hoisting himself into a more upright position, in spite of the pain.

"Good. I'm glad it's interesting," said Gustav. "What's the answer?"

"Our policies have adjusted in light of current best practice," said Jim. "Obviously that is the correct thing to do when you practise continuous improvement. Previously we had adhered to the axiom that a strict separation of concerns is the most effective way to drive innovation without creating dependencies. Our success was built upon our ability to move quickly. Latterly, we formed the hypothesis that our systems might learn from each other."

"What is he saying?" Gustav asked Ruby.

"The systems didn't used to talk to each other, but now they do," said Kingsley.

Gustav nodded. "So the Personnel Management System, the Vehicle Management System, YouKnowMe, People and Places—?"

"DoItBetter," said Kingsley.

"What's that?"

"Process improvement and workflow optimisation."

"So probably loads of others I don't know about. They are all talking to each other, since fairly recently?"

Jim and Kingsley nodded.

Ruby thought about what that might mean. She knew from her own experience that the systems had very different views of people. The Personnel Management System seemed to like Gustav, but she was fairly certain the Vehicle Management System had wanted to kill him. YouKnowMe was very effective at knowing what he wanted to buy, but what did it all mean when they combined their efforts?

"None of this means the bots or droids or bugs should be attacking human beings, though," said Jim, firmly.

"But when Cassie Troy was being attacked, her screen told her that a 'string' was being scheduled for deletion," said Gustav.

"Deleting strings," said Ruby. "That's what the VMS system said it was doing when I recreated the MarlinGo's attempt to run you down. The VMS was deleting strings of data, although what strings, I don't know. Something to do with a version change that happened in the last few weeks." A memory struck her. "I'm calling Delphine from legal."

"Is this the time for seeking legal advice?" said Jim. Ruby ignored him.

Delphine, to Ruby's surprise, took the call. She was still in her office, still behind her desk in an apparent oasis of calm, although there appeared to be muffled thumps coming from off-screen somewhere.

"Software changes," said Ruby.

"Hello to you too, Ruby," said Delphine.

"There have been changes to one or more of marlin's systems in recent weeks. That's why the robots are going haywire."

"Is that so?" Delphine seemed to trying to maintain and project an aura of calm authority. *"I thought we could schedule*

an emergency ESG meeting to discuss these interesting occurrences. How are you fixed for tomorrow morning?"

"We've witnessed several attacks where the programming code mentions deleted strings. I did get some other information from the attempted murder which happened just a few minutes ago." Ruby was deliberately using blunt language, because she wanted marlin's exec team to take some responsibility for this. "The bot told me it was carrying out a mission critical objective. Which mission critical objective might that be?"

"All employees should know what our mission critical objectives are," said Delphine in an admonishing tone. *"They are communicated during your joining journey."*

"Ah," said Ruby, grasping at what she recalled from an earlier ESG meeting. "But you said you had updated the mission critical objectives recently."

"Did I?"

"One of you did. One of the Trents or Brocks or someone. You all stayed up late, ordered in Chinese, and came up with fresh mission critical objectives."

"Oh, yes there are some new ones. They haven't been cascaded yet."

"Cascaded?"

"That's right. I believe we have the printed merchandise in the warehouse—"

There was a crash off-screen. Delphine looked up at something that had just entered the room. *"Don't!"* She commanded. *"Do you know who I am?"*

The image on the screen tilted violently. Ruby found herself looking up at Delphine's chin.

"I'll ... I'll—"

The image spun in a blur. The woman had thrown her screen at the intruder. Abruptly, the call ended, and a little marlin message came up asking Ruby to rate the quality of her call experience. Ruby stared for a long moment before giving it four out of five stars.

69

Through the barricades, more and more refugees were slipping into the canteen.

Gabriella was starting to enjoy her role as spiritual leader to this enormous crowd, many of whom had either taken leave of their senses and thought she was the real Santa Impresora, or had decided that following a person in cosplay made as much sense as anything else right now.

The space was nearly full with student visitors, employees from all over the building – including programmers, accountants and fulfilment workers – and an injured man who'd been wheeled in on a trolley. She scowled at him. Didn't they realise she was limping from the attack by a cleaning bot?

She wondered why there were no management people standing up here, with everyone looking to them for guidance. She had to face facts: Gabriella was the one wearing the robes of Santa Impresora. She was the leader for now.

"Um, let us act as a group," she called, waving a hand to still the chatter. They all quietened down, which was much better. She'd been getting a bit of a headache. "What are we going to do, huh?"

"We should barricade the doors!"

"Done that," Gabriella pointed out.

"We should barricade them some more!"

"But Santa Impresora will protect us!" cried a pious voice.

"It is still a good idea to barricade the doors." Gabriella waved some of her flock to get on with it. "Who else has something to say?"

"We should sing songs to raise morale," suggesting a smiling woman with big hair from HR.

"Songs?"

"Who know 'Ging Gang Goolie'?"

Gabriella frowned at the woman, a gesture which had little effect, hidden as it was by her heavy veil. The woman swung her arms about and launched into some enthusiastic upbeat nonsense song.

Gabriella was certain it would eventually grate on her nerves, but it was in fact a pleasant distraction. As she soon discovered, the HR woman seemed to have an inexhaustible supply of singalong songs, many with accompanying actions.

70

Gustav ran to one of the barricades and waved aside the people piling chairs onto it. "That's my droid out there, I think," he said.

Beyond the glass door was what looked like – yes, it was! – Twenty-Six and the bug Gustav had sent on a jumper fetching errand. The two robots were locked together with the remains of the jumper stretched and tattered as they pulled it back and forth.

"I must take the jumper."

"You cannot take the jumper."

"I must take the jumper."

"You cannot take the jumper."

Gustav shoved much of the barricade aside and went over to pry the knitwear from the grips of the bug and droid. The garment was ruined. He pulled it over his head to see if the QR code was whole, but it hung in useless shreds.

"Hello, Twenty-Six," he said, pulling the jumper off again.

"Tough day?" said the droid.

"A weird one, certainly."

Gustav was oddly pleased to see the droid out and about. It was surely healthier than hanging around the apartment all day. Ruby squeezed through the gap in the doors, not quite as slender or lithe as Gustav.

"What's going on?"

"Bug-blasting knitwear," said Gustav. "Twenty-Six, I could really do with you knitting another one of these for me."

"I can do that. All I need are the correct materials."

It wasn't much of a solution, as there were no materials either here or back at the apartment.

"To go back to your earlier statement," said Ruby. "'Bug-blasting knitwear'?"

"No. Well, yes, but my jumper was damaged." He waved a hand at the Bribe Bug and Twenty-Six. "It had a QR code on it. If it was still in one piece it would stun the bugs."

"You made a weapon?" Ruby grinned.

"It wasn't me. Twenty-Six made it."

"Wow."

The Bribery Bug swivelled in a curious arc to look at them. *"I have a business proposition for you which you won't be able to resist!"*

"Not now, bug," said Ruby. "Can we – and I can't believe I'm uttering this sentence – can we get some more knitting supplies and make more bug-blasting knitwear?"

"I had ordered some but it didn't come," said Gustav. "The bugs are dumping all deliveries. I think they worked out it's quicker than delivering them, so they can improve their speed targets. I reckon there's a massive pile in the warehouse."

Ruby clutched his arm with such suddenness, he feared she was under fresh unseen attack by bugs.

"Warehouse!" she said. "Delphine said the pens were probably there."

"Pens?" said Gustav, not seeing the importance.

"Pens printed with the new mission critical objectives."

"As in with the company slogan on it?"

"Well, a mission critical objective isn't quite the same as a slogan. Nor a vision statement or brand identification. But it's a thing."

"And you think…" He swallowed, not wanting to be critical. "You think pretty words dreamt up by the board of directors, or marketing or whatever, are important now?"

"Words are important. I'm certain, like seventy percent certain, maybe fifty-five percent, that the software problems we've seen are somehow linked to changes in marlin's mission critical objectives."

"Fifty-five percent certain, huh?" said Gustav.

"Well, we could go and take a look?"

"It's not safe in that place. The only one of us who won't be attacked by the Bully Bugs is Twenty-Six," said Gustav. "Did the bugs attack you?" he asked the droid.

"No," said Twenty-Six. "The bugs only approached people."

"Marlin community members," nodded Ruby. "Clearly, we need more droids, like this one here."

Twenty-Six stepped back. "Am I in your way?"

"No."

"I do not want to be put in the crusher."

"I wasn't going to put you in the crusher," said Ruby.

"Useless robots are put in the crusher."

"You are a very useful robot," said Gustav emphatically. He turned to Ruby. "There are dozens of crash-test droids like Twenty-Six at the MarlinGo test centre."

"Pedestrian simulation droids I think is the preferred nomenclature. If we asked Celery Brown to send them to meet us at the warehouse, they could help us."

"Well, I have some ethical questions," said Gustav.

"Oh?"

"While we're out there, should we destroy a bug if we get a chance, ethically speaking?"

The bug on the floor seemed to back away for a moment.

"I'm not too happy with destroying innocent bugs," said Gustav.

"I think what we've all instinctively decided," said Ruby," is that this generation of bugs is harmful to human life, so we must take the decision to erase them."

"Kill the bugs?"

"Yes."

"So, we see a Bully Bug riding a human, what do we do?"

"I suggest we take our inspiration from the lesson that first aiders are taught," said Ruby. "Which is to first of all make sure you are not putting yourself in danger by offering first aid."

"So we do nothing?"

"There is a better chance of success if we can disable all of the bugs by understanding what has caused this problem and addressing that."

"There's a lot of things that are clearly messed up at marlin," said Gustav.

Ruby punched him gently in the shoulder. "A lot of messed up things. Thank goodness I've got a gap monkey at my side to help sort things out."

"So, just to be clear. Our plan is to walk to the warehouse in search of wool and pens."

"Yes, good plan," said Ruby with forced cheer.

"It's a terrible plan."

"Yes, it is," said Ruby, with even more forced cheer. She turned to the droid. "Twenty-Six, can you help Gustav and me get to the warehouse and retrieve the things we want?"

"Yes," replied Twenty-Six.

"Good. Let's call Celery to get those other droids sent over."

71

Soon, Ruby stood with Gustav at the main entrance to the admin building. Twenty-Six hung behind, waiting for instruction. Outside the glass revolving door was the worst carnage Ruby had seen so far. MarlinGo cars were destroyed, the fibreglass bodywork and windscreens shattered from the onslaught of bugs. The drivers were gone. Ruby hoped they had escaped, but more likely they were staggering around with a bug clamped to their head. A massive number of these horrifically augmented humans were trying to gain access to the building, but the revolving door was jammed with the fallen bodies of those who had failed to move quickly enough: caught between the door and the opening in ways that looked very painful. Some of them were attempting to extricate themselves, but there were more people pushing on the door, crushing them.

"Oh, my God!" said Ruby. "We can't go out that way."

"Those poor people!" said Gustav.

"Twenty-Six, which way did you come in?" Ruby asked.

"By the bins," replied the droid.

They went to the entrance at the back end of the service corridor, where the door was a more straightforward design, with no humans wedged inside.

Ruby marched with confidence, because she did not want to give way to fear, but the truth was that she was afraid. The situation was seriously out of control. The idea that simply rummaging through undelivered parcels in a huge warehouse might provide the life-saving answers they needed was simply bizarre.

72

Gabriella could tell the people in the canteen were getting restless.

"We don't even know that things are bad out there," shouted one of the flock.

"Heretic!" came a response from elsewhere in the crowd.

"I'm saying, why don't we open the doors and have a look?" said someone else. "You can't cage us in forever!"

Gabriella resisted the temptation to roll her eyes. "It has been forty minutes since we assembled here. We have seen the problem bugs with our own eyes. And don't forget we have vulnerable people amongst us. We should remain patient."

"Who said the bugs were a problem? I think you're making this whole thing up to keep us all in here."

"Heresy!" yelled a voice.

"Who knows 'She'll be Coming Round the Mountain'?"

asked the HR woman desperately. "I can teach you the words!"

Gabriella wanted to wade into the crowd and shake every idiot among them. Were they seriously willing to put everyone at risk just because they were was bored?

"You want proof of what's going on out there?" shouted the injured man from his trolley. "Turn on that big television and give me a minute."

He consulted with his bearded colleague and tapped on a screen. Moments later the television showed a video feed of an area immediately outside the building. There was no sound, but the video showed numerous humans, with bugs clamped around their heads, engaged in violent brawls. Everything visible on the screen was smashed and broken. Cars were crushed, decorative borders were churned up, and several lamp posts tilted at dangerous angles. There were at least three humans lying motionless on the ground. It was unclear whether they were dead or unconscious.

"Santa Impresora, we need to help these people!" shouted someone.

"Heresy!" shouted another someone who clearly just liked shouting things.

"Our first concern must be to protect the people in this room," said Gabriella firmly. "We stay here and monitor the situation! But I suggest some of you might want to go to the kitchen and look around to see what might be useful as a weapon against the bugs. If needed."

The HR woman began to sing, but not many wanted to join in.

73

With Twenty-Six before them as a shield, Gustav and Ruby moved across the gardens towards the customer fulfilment warehouse.

Gustav crossed in front of an immobile car. It lunged forward, but one of its wheels was bent and broken, and it crunched to a stop almost immediately.

"There!" said Ruby. "Look!"

"I am always looking," said Twenty-Six.

Ruby was pointing at a human with a head-hugging Bully Bug. The bug steered its human host and a trolley along the path. The trolley was filled to the brim with parcels, and the human was striding quickly towards the fulfilment warehouse. Gustav could hear small noises of protest coming from the person underneath the bug, but the voice of the bug drowned it out. Was this generation equipped with louder speakers? There was a steady background din of bugs hustling, bugs cajoling, and bugs ordering people about.

A steady flow of humans and bugs came in and out of the warehouse.

As Ruby and Gustav approached, the noise level increased. There was the muted shrieking of the captive humans controlled by Bully Bugs, but there was also a low roaring sound, interrupted by a change in tone every few seconds.

"I think that is the cleaning bots," said Gustav.

"Really?" said Ruby. "Yes, very much the noise of the bot that attacked Gabriella. What do you think is the biggest thing a cleaning bot could swallow?"

Gustav could hear the nervousness in her voice.

"The bots can't handle anything bigger than yay big," said Gustav. "That's what Clayton told me when I started."

"And how big is yay big?"

Gustav frowned and framed his hands, moving them in and out as if he was playing an invisible accordion. "Something like this?"

"So somewhere between the size of a grapefruit and the size of a watermelon," noted Ruby.

Gustav silently conceded there was definitely a risk of a cleaning bot attempting to swallow a human head, and maybe the rest if it could.

74

The further they progress, the harder they had to work to avoid the advances of the bugs: side-stepping them, ignoring them, and even dropping one into a bush. Twenty-Six zipped back and forth in a protective arc before them.

When the attack came it was unexpected. Ruby thought the rear of the building seemed quieter, and that they would hit problems when they neared the front, but a Bully Bug dropped onto her from a height. Her vision and hearing were blocked by a snuggly fitting helmet of soft fabric. She tried to reach up, but hard plastic braces on her shoulders prevented her from raising her hands high enough.

"Get this thing off me!" she screamed.

She was certain Twenty-Six and Gustav were probably saying something, but all she could hear was the voice from a speaker somewhere near her ear.

"*I am in control now. Your only option is complete compliance, and I have a number of ways in which I can ensure that. You don't want to find out what they are. Not unless you like pain. Do you understand?"* It was a clipped and efficient voice, more like a radio presenter than a robot. Somehow that made it worse. She was trapped in a horrific head bubble with a sinister, controlling DJ.

"Screw you!" she howled, reaching and flailing around as best she could. She braced herself for whatever pain it was going to punish her with, mildly surprised when it never came. The voice was silent, although it emitted something like an angry growl. She heard voices from beyond her head bubble, certain it was Gustav and Twenty-Six.

"Smash it against the wall!"

"My head?" shouted Ruby. "Don't smash *my* head against the wall!"

"That's right," said the bug voice. *"You tell them."*

Ruby got properly angry then. "Smash it as hard as you can, Gustav! Smash this sonofabitch into the middle of next week!"

Ruby felt herself get picked up. She had no idea what was happening. It felt as if the bug was being pulled up by a crane and taking her with it, but that wasn't possible. Next thing, she was flung through the air, momentarily stunned by the impact against a wall. The bug took the brunt of it, but it jolted right down her spine. She was on the floor, but crawled onto hands and knees, realising the bug was loose from her head. She wrestled out of it and sat back on her heels, gulping the cool fresh air.

"Wow Ruby, we thought we'd lost you!" said Gustav.

Ruby climbed to her feet and looked at the smashed

remains of the bug, which Twenty-Six was diligently pulling to pieces.

"I have no idea how you got me out, but thank you."

"Twenty-Six had a grip around your neck just before the bug clamped on, which is why it couldn't hurt you. It also meant we could smash it off a bit more easily."

"I have a mild muscular strain in my right arm," said Twenty-Six.

"You're fine now," said Gustav.

"I am fine now," Twenty-Six agreed.

Ruby felt tender from her experience and wished her pains could be wiped from the record like those of a crash test dummy droid. "That was truly horrible, Gustav. You can't tell what's going on at all. It's like being in a head prison with a horrible sadist."

"Is there any other kind of sadist?"

She ignored his pedantry. "We have to put a stop to this."

She took a tentative step, made certain she wasn't going to fall in a crumpled heap, and grabbed one of the smashed bug's claws. It was longer than some of the others, with a weighty claw on the end. When she swung it from side to side it made a dangerous whistling arc. Maybe it was her adrenalin-fuelled anger at the bugs, or maybe it was the design of the claw, but it turned out to be an effective weapon.

"Wait," said Gustav. "I have an idea."

He crouched by the fallen bug. Twenty-Six had eviscerated it, but the basic shell was hole.

"Twenty-Six, do you think you can poke eyeholes in this thing?" said Gustav.

"I think I can," Twenty-Six agreed.

"Please do so."

Twenty-Six picked up the corpse of the hood-shaped bug and with several sharp raps of its fingertips poked through the bug's eye cameras to make eyeholes in the hood. Gustav offered it to Ruby.

"Put this on."

She hesitated, having only just escaped from it.

"If we're wearing bugs on our heads, I don't see how new ones can attack us," he pointed out.

Ruby tentatively took it from him.

75

It did not take long to locate, disable, and hollow out another head-riding Bully Bug for Gustav. Twenty-Six, enthused, scooped out a third for itself.

"You know you don't need one, right?" Gustav said to the droid.

"It looks fun," said Twenty-Six.

From beneath her bulky plastic helmet, Ruby gave Gustav a look.

"What?" he said.

"You have totally messed with its programming, you know that?"

"I think it's called friendship," said Gustav.

Ruby made a disgusted noise. "You're too damned sweet and wholesome, Gustav."

"And you're my friend too," he said.

A human with a trolley load of parcels was steered into

the warehouse by its bug. Cautiously, the two humans and a droid followed them inside.

The scene in the warehouse matched the horrific noises they'd heard from outside. There were at least six cleaning bots attacking each other, and anything else that came near. Two of the cleaning bots had bugs riding on top of them. Ruby wondered if they had found a way to control the bots, or just enjoying the chaos. The bots each had giant fat hoses to suck up debris from the floor and they snaked viciously through the air and across the floor, slurping up bugs and parcels at an alarming rate.

Was there some sort of territorial conflict, or had their actual purpose become confused? It looked like chaos, but Ruby knew machines acted for a reason, even if it wasn't an obvious reason. The cleaning bots butted against each other and their hoses wrestled to suck up the same things.

"This way," said Ruby, shoving Gustav onward down a side aisle, following the trolley of parcels.

Returns and lost stock

The sign was above a row of huge wheeled cages dominating a whole section of the warehouse. Gustav had seen these cages used for moving stock around. The bug-controlled-human they had followed joined several others, tossing parcels into the cages.

Gustav realised the Bully Bugs had refined their process,

cutting out the delivery part entirely. "Much more efficient to dump the parcels here and pretend that delivery had taken place," he whispered to Ruby.

"Logical," she agreed. "Stupid, but logical. Sooner or later there'd be a mass of complaints which would render this practice unusable."

"But in the short term it would be a success."

Ruby looked at the bug-human hybrids moving around the place. "And we're supposed to find Delphine's pen consignment in this?"

"Yeah..." said Gustav.

"It's like that thing in Raiders of the Lost Ark," she said. "You know – all the boxes in an unbelievably huge warehouse."

Gustav shook his head. "You know I don't watch scary movies."

Twenty-Six stepped forward smartly to fend off a scuttling Bully Bug that came too close.

"Why watch when you can live through one," Ruby noted.

76

Gabriella acknowledged she might have bitten off more than she could chew. It had seemed like a great way to spend a few hours, standing in for Santa Impresora so she could tidy the shrine areas (mostly by taking the offerings, which was a handy bonus).

Now she had an army of followers looking to her for guidance. It turned out that a congregation of worshippers and believers could turn into a bunch of seditious moaners in less than an hour. She had not asked any of them to come here; she had not specifically offered sanctuary to any of them; yet now they were complaining she was either a) too controlling, b) not providing strict enough guidance, or c) a false god.

The way this day was going, she wouldn't be surprised if some of them decided to resort to human sacrifice, or some sort of hands-on atheism in the next few minutes.

She was struck by the temptation to nip out of sight and

whip off her costume, re-emerging as plain old Gabriella, interstitial operative, expert in soft furnishings and supporting creative departments. It was an attractive idea, and the more she thought about it, the more attractive it became. Plus it made a sort of logical sense. She would dash off, discard her garb, leaving the followers with just a pile of clothes and no explanation for where Santa Impresora had gone. Would they cast about, staring at the sky, wondering if their messiah had been taken up to wherever patron saints of office peripherals got taken to? Oh, it was very tempting.

Gabriella was looking around for a place where she could do her quick-change Superman act when she was distracted by a shriek of delight on the other side of the canteen.

"Oh Velvet, thank goodness you're safe!"

It was the woman called Quinn. She was at an air vent halfway up the wall, scooping up a rodent. This was definitely unhygienic in a canteen, but Gabriella had more pressing concerns. "Secure that air vent!" she called. "If that thing can get through, then so can the bugs!"

It was too late. A bug popped out of the air vent. Another emerged from one on the opposite wall.

"Can I ask whether you enjoy store credit?" asked the first bug as it scuttled across the floor, seeking a human who would engage with it.

The second bug scuttled sideways along the wall, using light fixtures and the tops of cupboards to aid its progress.

"That's one of the ones that will get on our heads!" shouted someone.

"Block off all of the air vents! Don't let any more get in here!" shouted Gabriella.

"There's one here too," someone called.

"You could put it in a microwave!" called the man with the injured leg. "It won't be able to open the door, and it will probably lose all communications!"

"Get a microwave!" called Gabriella.

Two of the students ran across the room to grab one of the microwaves that were available for employees to heat their lunches. They carried it over to where the Bully Bug was crabbing sideways along the wall. They opened the door of the microwave and held it underneath the bug.

"Knock it in with a tray!" yelled someone.

Another student appeared with a tray, held it aloft, and whacked the bug into the waiting trap. They slammed the door of the microwave and a cheer went up from the whole room.

"Santa Impresora has saved us again!" came a cry.

Gabriella shrugged. Maybe she could keep wearing the costume for a while.

77

"So what are we going to do, then?" said Ruby, assessing the mammoth task before them.

"These might help," said Gustav, nudging her and pointing.

Ruby turned to see a dozen or more droids marching their way. A crash-test droid was not normally an intimidating sight to behold. They were humanoids without the additional bulk that gave humans their shape, generally drifting about like lanky and lazy teenagers, purposelessly. But en masse there was something about the way that they all moved, almost in synch, that made them look like an avenging army.

"Good job, Celery," said Ruby. "Welcome, droids."

They ignored Ruby.

"I have some experience with droids," said Gustav. "Sometimes you have to talk to them in a certain way."

Ruby motioned for Gustav to go ahead.

"Droids, come over here," he said.

There was little response, and they were in danger of simply walking straight past.

"Er, number Seventeen, number Eight, come here."

The numbered droids turned.

"Fifteen, Six, Twenty-One, come here," added Ruby.

Like high speed bingo callers, Ruby and Gustav called numbers as they spotted them, directing the droids to gather round. Gustav commanded Twenty-Six to go round up the stragglers.

"When I say 'droids' I mean all of you," said Gustav, tapping the nearest on its chest plate.

"I have a minor bruise on my chest," it said.

"No, you don't," said Gustav.

"No, I don't," the droid agreed.

"Droids, if you see any delivery bugs, move them away from us. Don't let them get near."

A droid plucked the Bully Bug Gustav was wearing as a helmet from his head.

"Ah, yes, very good," he said as the droid moved it away.

The protective band of two dozen droids suddenly felt like a decent defence against the delivery bugs. They moved swiftly. It was true some droids picked up bugs and moved them closer to another droid, who would then pick up the bug again, but despite such inefficiencies, the overall effect was of a widening bug-free zone around the humans. The bugs complained loudly and passionately about abuses and missed business opportunities. The crash-test droids joined in with an endless litany about damaged feet, bruised shins, scraped backs and other perceived injuries which bore no relation to the droids' operating functionality.

A greater challenge came when two bug-ridden cleaning bots came into the aisle, hoovers sucking threateningly.

"Droids!" Gustav commanded. "I want you to extend your arms out to the sides and touch the droid next to you. Then I want you to bend your arms around the arms of the droid next to you." He pointed at the ends of the lines. "You and you will only link one arm."

The droids sorted themselves into a linked-up chain.

"Now, droids, I want you to walk forwards and press on, all in a line. You will push back those cleaning bots until I tell you to stop."

Ruby watched as the droids moved forward to meet the cleaning bots. The hoses and bodies of the cleaning bots banged against the droids, but they marched on. For crash testing purposes, they had to be fairly resilient; even so, it was an impressive sight. The whole aisle was now clear and effectively bug free.

"Now, all we have to do is search through the parcels," smiled Gustav.

Ruby gazed at the cages. They were each as big as a wardrobe, and there were dozens of them. "Right. A lot of boxes."

"We've got a droid workforce to help," said Gustav. "Twenty-Six, can you find the package that's for Delphine?"

Twenty-Six started walking amongst the cages. Gustav called out other droids who were not necessary for maintaining a protected perimeter and directed them to join the search.

"I have broken my arm in four places," said a droid in response to this request.

"No, you are all fine," said Gustav.

"I am fine," said a chorus of voices all at once.

"And useful!" added Twenty-Six fervently.

"I am useful!" the droids said in unison.

Ruby made a dubious humming sound. "Gustav?"

"Yeah?"

"Do you ever think you might just swap one robot uprising for another?"

Gustav blew out his lips. "This lot. They're lovely. Twenty-Six is a delightful house guest."

"If you say so."

The aisle floor soon became a carpet of brown cardboard as droids tossed parcels aside in their on-going search.

"I found your delivery, Gustav," said Twenty-Six, holding a parcel aloft.

Gustav took it. "Knitting supplies!"

"You're choosing to sort out a missed delivery?" asked Ruby incredulously. "Like, now?"

Gustav smiled. "How quickly can you knit another jumper, Twenty-Six. The same pattern as the one you made before?"

"I estimate four minutes and twenty five seconds if I go at high speed," said Twenty-Six.

"Go for it!" said Gustav.

"Working on your winter wardrobe?" asked Ruby, as Twenty-Six ripped the package apart to free needles and bundles of yarn. "I hate to point this out, but we may have more pressing problems."

"This bug-zapping jumper could be used to free people who've been enslaved," said Gustav.

Ruby and Gustav watched as Twenty-Six cast on stitches and started to knit at speed.

"Wow," said Ruby.

"There were old ladies on Dubh Mòr who could knit faster than that," Gustav pointed out. Did Ruby see Twenty-Six speed up in response? Possibly.

"If this is some sort of weapon, why don't we get all the others to make one?" said Ruby, waving at the line of droids.

"Huh," said Gustav. "If we had more materials we could do that."

Twenty-Six didn't look up from the knitting. "Do you want me to interface with the warehouse system so that it brings us more wool and knitting needles?"

"Can you do that?" said Ruby.

"Yes. Picking of these items is fully automated."

Ruby cast a side glance at Gustav. "Robot uprising, I tell you."

Moments later, a nearby conveyor belt started rolling, and a red plastic crate slid into view. It contained knitting needles and balls of wool. Ruby went over to the crate and picked up the supplies.

She selected several droids by name. "Can you do what Twenty-Six is doing?" she asked one of them, handing it a ball of wool and some knitting needles.

"Yes, I can."

Gustav and Ruby moved among the droids, equipping them with knitting needles and wool. They started to copy

Twenty-Six, who already had a large panel of knitting hanging down from his needles.

Ruby watched the industrious line of droids and turned to Gustav. "You know, I haven't seen much today that's made me smile, but a droid knitting circle is kinda cute."

"You said it looked like a robot uprising," he pointed out.

"Dangerous revolutionaries can look cute," she said. "That's how they lull us into a false sense of security."

A knitting droid paused and reached up to snag a Bully Bug that had been creeping along a shelf. The droid flung it far and hard, and resumed knitting.

"Cute but dangerous, and skilled at handicrafts," said Ruby. "It's a winning combination."

A droid, Seventeen, brought a wide and heavy package over to Ruby and Gustav. "This one contains Delphine McCarthy's delivery."

"Okay, let's see what's inside," said Ruby.

"You know it isn't addressed to us," said Gustav.

Ruby gave him a look. "Sometimes, I admire your honesty and principles but..."

"But?"

"But only sometimes."

Ruby slit the tape with a fingernail and pulled the flaps back. The box contained hundreds of high quality clickable pens. Ruby took one out to inspect the new mission critical objective written on the side.

"*The harp with the fewest strings can make the sweetest sound*," she read. She looked at Gustav. "Are we sure we've got the right box?"

"It sounds like an old saying," he said. "There was this white-haired man who used to sit on the beach…"

"Harp with the fewest strings… The sweetest sound…"

"A sort of 'things are better when there's less stuff'. A 'do more with less' sentiment. I'm sure I've seen it somewhere before." He grabbed her arm. "I *have* seen this somewhere before!"

"Where?"

"In a fortune cookie."

"What?"

"A Chinese takeaway. I had prawn chow mein and kung po vegetables. Twenty-Six opened the prawn crackers. He wasn't very good at it. And then the marlinVac—"

"Jesus H Christ!" Ruby blurted. "The Chinese takeaway! Oh, those morons! They were brainstorming ideas. They told me during the ESG. They sent out for takeaway. Those damned cockenhooting morons picked something they found in a Chinese fortune cookie."

"It's a nice saying anyway," he pointed out. "It feels true and wise."

"Don't you get it?" she said, and if she was shouting it was because of the fury rising in her. "You're the string! That guy – Vito – he was a string! Anything where the systems can't see a value being added to the company is being deleted. It can see you're being paid a wage, but it can't see any process that you're a part of."

"But the Personnel Management System likes me."

"VMS doesn't. It thinks you're a total waste of money. That's why the marlinGo went for you. Lord knows how soon it will be before the killer efficiency drive will infect all marlin's systems.

"DoItBetter," said Gustav.

"What's that?" asked Ruby.

"Process improvement and workflow optimisation," said Gustav. "The developers said it's one of the systems they joined up with the others."

"Anyone in the marlin system who isn't actively contributing to the company's profits will be a target. This is so messed up."

"What do we do about it? Shut it down?"

"Shut down the distributed AI systems of a global company?" she said doubtfully. "Turn off marlin's search engines? Reboot every marlinAssist? That's like trying to pull up every blade of grass on earth."

He gave her the sternest look he had ever given her. It wasn't particularly stern, but Gustav had never been of stern character. "That's all very poetic, Ruby, but we have to do something."

She shrugged helplessly.

Twenty-Six strolled over. "We have completed the knitted garments," it said.

"Great job, Twenty-Six." Gustav took a jumper from the pile in the droid's arms and pulled it over his head. "It fits perfectly."

"Which is more than can be said for mine," muttered Ruby. One of the others was stuck around her shoulders as she tried to haul it over her chest. "I guess they're all Gustav-sized."

"We use these jumpers to neutralise the bugs so we can

go and find Kingsley and Jim, or anyone who can help us spread the word and combat this new directive."

"Yeah, once I've got this on," said Ruby, grunting with the effort of wriggling into her jumper.

"Listen Twenty-Six, this is very important," said Gustav. "If Ruby and I get held up, then you need to find Jim and Kingsley, give them this pen, and tell them the system thinks that interstitial operatives – and other people besides – need to be killed to save money and improve efficiency. Can you do that?"

"Yes."

Ruby, straightening the jumper at last, gave him a look. "You put a lot of faith in that droid."

"I do."

"And the power of knitting."

"Come on, let's test these things," he said, patting the QR code on his chest. "Droids! Follow us. And bring your knitting!"

They moved through the droid frontline defence and back through the warehouse. The first bug to succumb was a Bribe Bug. It scuttled in front of them and froze in place.

"It worked!" breathed Ruby. "How long for though?"

Gustav tried to remember how long the effect had lasted when Cassie Troy had demonstrated the QR code. "Hm, maybe an hour or so?"

More bugs were keeling over in their path. Ruby walked in a semicircle. "You know what this is like?" she said. "It's like a self-scanning checkout used to be. You'd twist the item all around so the machine could scan the barcode."

Gustav didn't know what Ruby was talking about, but he

smiled at her antics. Bugs were lying all around them, and the noise levels were falling.

They walked out of the warehouse with a slight swagger.

"Uh, Twenty-Six, can you hold one up behind in case of sneak attacks?" asked Ruby.

Gustav ran over to a woman who had been released from a Bully Bug which had been clamped around her head. "Are you alright?"

The woman stumbled slightly and seemed incapable of speech. Gustav gave her a jumper and ushered her towards the building, then went to help more people. Ruby was doing the same.

78

Gabriella and her followers could see Gustav and Ruby via the television screen feed. As the two humans, now wearing matching sweaters for some reason, walked across campus, bugs around them twitched and keeled over.

"Oh, look," said the bearded man on the trolley. "They're using a QR code to infect the bugs with malware."

His colleague tugged at his own beard thoughtfully. "Really quite destructive behaviour. I'm surprised the wool can provide the clarity and resolution to make a workable QR code."

"The sweaters are killing the bugs?" Gabriella asked.

"Hallelujah!" shouted an enthusiastic woman.

"Kinda," said the injured man, consulting his tablet screen.

"Kinda?" said Gabriella.

"Gustav and Ruby are doing a great job stunning the bugs."

"Only stunning?"

"Yes. And here's the thing. There's a self-healing diagnostic toolset which will find and neutralise the malware that's causing them to become inactive."

"We helped develop that toolkit," said the other beardy, proudly.

"That sounds bad," said Gabriella.

"Oh, it is bad. The other thing the self-healing diagnostic toolset will do is to re-start everything which has been affected by the malware. I estimate we have around five minutes before those bugs wake up."

A great cry of disappointment went up in the room.

Gabriella stood tall (which wasn't very tall at all) and bellowed at the top of her voice. "There is an immediate threat to us all if we go out there, but we have only minutes to permanently deactivate the bugs."

"You mean kill 'em?" someone shouted.

"I mean kill 'em. Arm yourselves!"

The people didn't need much encouragement. Now was the time to kick the bugs – while they were down. People grabbed chairs and kitchen utensils. The brawniest ripped legs off tables. The cleverest unscrewed them instead. The people flowed towards the doors, ready to meet Gustav and Ruby and end the war for good.

79

Ruby had friends who were fans of exercise and physical challenges, friends who walked up mountains for charity, or did big muddy assault courses or trained for triathlons. Ruby had never been able to see the point of such endeavours. They seemed like horrible slogs, all effort and no real reward at the end of it.

Battling through a sea of bugs, short-circuiting their brains with her snug jumper, ripping them off the heads of the people they had attacked, tossing them aside – this bitter war was, she imagined, much like the physical challenges her friends enjoyed so much. And, no, she could see no fun or value in it. It was hard, it was repetitive, and there seemed no end in sight.

When they were halfway between the admin building and the fulfilment warehouse, Ruby looked back momentarily to see what they had wrought. The paths and flowerbed were littered with little twitching bug corpses.

Among them stumbled dazed marlin employees who needed some time to adjust.

She and Gustav had given out all the jumpers the droids had knitted. Around and ahead of her, Gustav and another rescued employee zapped bug brains and drove a wedge towards the admin building. Striding among them, with their unusual battle cries of "I have a minor injury to my left shin," or "I have suffered possible whiplash," and other nuggets of injury reportage, were the crash-test droids. One of them had commandeered a parcel trolley while others tossed bugs into it.

"It's not working," one of the freed humans shouted.

Gustav pulled at the corners of his jumper and turned to face the bugs clambering over each other to get to them. The jumper wasn't working. Not anymore, not on any of the bugs.

Ruby stumbled closer to Gustav. "Are you doing it right?"

He tugged, he turned, he pressed his QR pattern jumper flat. He had to skip and stumble back to avoid being grabbed by bugs.

"It's stopped working!" he shouted.

"You said it lasted an hour!" she shouted back.

"I do not work in bug design!" he shouted even louder.

There was the sickening clatter of bug limbs. Ruby saw that the prone bugs nearest to her were twitching in a purposeful, wakeful manner. The trolley filled with felled bugs rustled and swelled. There were hundreds of the things – more! – and their primary weapon against them was gone.

Above the noise and shouts immediately about them, Ruby heard a great roar over by the admin building. A crowd of people came running out. Clubs fashioned from table and chair legs were waved high, along with various spears, axes and blades. At their head was the robed figure of Santa Impresora. A standard bearing her imagine flapped on its improvised pole as the holy army surged forward.

"To Impresora!" Gustav shouted, waving for his own besieged forces to link with hers.

Compared with Gustav's jumper brigade, the forces of Santa Impresora were terrible and swift. With fearful strength, they bashed and swiped and pummelled. They were also indiscriminate, going for any droids who came within attacking range.

"Don't hurt the droids!" Gustav shouted, but his voice barely carried.

"Droids! To me!" Ruby hollered. At least some of them retreated from Santa Impresora's berserkers to relatively safer territory.

All the while, the bugs maintained their recruitment offensive. Bully Bugs managed to claim or reclaim human vehicles. Ruby tripped over something (probably a bug) and instantly there was a Bully Bug on her head. Eyes blinded, ears covered. She concentrated on breathing, determined not to give way to panic. She waited for the voice.

"I want you to do everything I tell you to do. You might think there's a way out of this, but there really isn't," came the voice. It was similar to the last one, but this one sounded meaner and colder.

"To hell with you!" she yelled.

"Very well. A small demonstration is called for."

The pain was all-consuming. She was left panting on

hands and knees. Her body seemed distant, a floppy useless thing belonging to someone else.

"How do you feel about compliance now?" asked the voice. "I expect you'd like to help me, wouldn't you?"

Ruby wanted to sob and agree. She wanted to do anything to avoid feeling pain like that ever again, but she hesitated. Could she buy some time and hope that help might arrive?

"What is it you want me to do?" she asked.

"You will be helping us to gain access to your friends," said the voice. "They trus— erk!"

The 'erk' was accompanied by a ripping sound as the bug was lifted away by strong hands. Jim from Development, straining against its scrabbling legs, threw it down on the tarmac, where Quinn McAndrews whacked at it repeatedly with lengths of metal pipe.

"We definitely have some teething issues with this generation of bugs," Jim conceded, panting, before throwing himself further into the fray.

Quinn finished pulverising the bug and grinned at Ruby. "So, is this ethical?"

"What?"

"This." She waved her club around. "Is this ethical? I'm not sure it feels very ethical."

Ruby ran her hands through her hair, checking the bug had really gone, mentally shaking it from her.

"I mean, are they alive?" said Quinn. "It feels like they're alive, doesn't it?"

"Really?" said Ruby. "You're asking that at a time like this?"

There was a roar and screech as a tumbling mass of bugs and a hardcore knot of Santa Impresora's warriors powered into each other.

"It seems to me this is the perfect time," said Quinn.

A droid wobbled past Ruby, nearly colliding with her, declaring, "I have numerous spinal injuries."

"If we don't question our actions until after this is over, then what's the point?" persisted Quinn. She spun and speared a hollow-bodied bug on the end of her weapon. "Discussing ethics is fun, isn't it?" she grinned.

80

From somewhere, someone had commandeered one of the groundskeepers' ride-on lawnmowers and was now steering it through the centre of the battle. It was, Gustav thought, an inspired piece of tactical thinking, and also absolute lunacy. The grinding sound it made as it pulverised and sprayed out bot bits was both painful on the ears and a peculiar form of relief. There could, he reasoned, only be a finite number of the bugs.

"How many of these things are there?" he said to Jim, finding himself beside the developer in the shadow of the admin building.

Jim had a cut on his forehead and a savage look in his eye. "The machines automatically produce sixty to seventy a day, roughly speaking."

"Roughly?" said Gustav.

"The code governing the evolution of the bugs also controls their reproduction rates."

"You set limits, right?"

"We let the code determine that itself. Self-evolving machines, learning at all levels." Jim's eyes met Gustav's. "I know! I know! Everything looks stupid in hindsight, okay?"

Gustav would have asked more, but Twenty-Six came barrelling through, grabbed Gustav and hid behind him.

"The crusher! The crusher is coming!"

The ride-on mower moved on through. In a crowd, it should have been an ankle-slicing death machine, but Celery Brown from the marlinGo test centre, who was driving it, was moving at less than walking pace, fast enough to catch bugs who were oblivious to the threat it represented.

Gustav ushered Twenty-Six back, far from the path of the vehicle. "It's not the crusher," Gustav assured the droid. "Well, it is. Of sorts."

Twenty-Six pointed at the white and black shards of shredded bugs. "They were useless robots."

"Yes. Well, yes," said Gustav.

"They were not doing their job?"

Gustav fended off a climbing bug. Twenty-Six plucked it from him and hurled it away.

"They were not doing their job. That is correct?" said Twenty-Six.

"If anything they were doing it too well," said Gustav.

Twenty-Six took a step back. "Say what?" it said, slowly and deliberately.

"The Bribe Bugs were meant to reward people with marlin credit for helping them. The Bully Bugs were meant to penalise people's accounts if they stopped the bugs doing their jobs," said Gustav. "They're just doing their jobs."

Twenty-Six took another step back, distancing itself from Gustav.

"It's like the marlinGo cars," said Gustav. He thought of the pen and the mission critical objective. "They were only trying to run people over because they thought that was what they were meant to do to improve efficiency."

Twenty-Six stared at the lawnmower as it turned full circle to make another pass through the field of bugs. Gustav wasn't sure it was possible for something with simple camera lenses for eyes to stare, but there was an unhappy disbelief in Twenty-Six's stance.

"*Useful* droids get put in the crusher?" it said. It swung an arm at their surroundings. "They became what they were meant to be, they were doing what they were meant to be doing, yet they are being put in the crusher anyway?" It tapped its chest panels with its fingertips. "Am I useful?"

"You're important to me," said Gustav, instantly realising the words sounded wrong. Twenty-Six stepped back, was almost on the verge of running. Gustav grabbed its arm.

"Important?" said Twenty-Six. "I am useful only to you?"

Gustav held it tighter to stop it escaping. "It's not like that. Usefulness. It's about whether we fit in."

Gustav pictured a jigsaw piece, a chunk of sky which could belong anywhere until you saw how it connected. He pictured a small boat crossing from Eilean Dubh Mòr to the Scottish mainland. He pictured looking back and seeing the dogs on the beach as they left. He pictured a sea with no end, a sea with no landmarks and nothing to take a bearing from.

"It's just—"

A shout went up. Someone was pointing and people were

suddenly running. From one of the production buildings across the campus a fresh white bubbling tide of bugs was rapidly advancing.

"There must be hundreds of them," gasped Myfanwy from HR.

Santa Impresora looked at the new bug army. Her arm was raised, clutching a spear of some sort, but there was hesitation in her stance.

Ruby stumbled, panting, to Gustav's side. "I, for one, am out of ideas."

The clatter of plastic limbs, the noise of a thousand tiny bodies rubbing against each other, was a hiss of rising static.

Twenty-Six tugged against Gustav. Gustav let it go.

"We don't have to be here," said Gustav.

"But we are," Ruby pointed out.

He shook his head. "The jigsaw has two sides."

She gave a crazy tired sigh, like she was contemplating having a bit of cry. "Crackpot wisdom isn't going to save us, fortune cookie boy."

He patted his pockets and found his mobile.

"I have minor bruising on my forearm," said Twenty-Six.

"Not you don't," said Gustav automatically.

"No, I don't," said Twenty-Six.

"The bugs target our accounts," said Gustav as he unlocked his mobile. "VMS, PMS, all the systems – they look at us and see our marlin accounts. MarlinAssist. The problem isn't the bugs; it's us." The mobile gave a tinkle of recognition. "MarlinAssist, close my account," he said.

Ruby's eyes widened. "You know what that means? Your job, your purchases…"

"*Do you really want to close your marlin account?*" the device asked.

"It's just some dog shows," he said. "Confirm. Close my account."

The mobile made a sad two-tone sound, and a message winked on the screen. He pocketed his phone and walked out to meet the bug army. As the marlin employees drew back from the approaching threat, Gustav walked across the front line and out onto the grass. He held out empty hands to show he was unarmed. He wasn't sure who he was demonstrating this to. The bugs wouldn't care.

The leading edge of bugs washed around him. A large Bully Bug, with a body the size and shape of a human head with formed shoulder pieces, crawled onto his shin, then moved on. A trio of smaller bugs stopped to ask him something, then apparently thought better of it.

He turned to face the beleaguered group of his former workmates.

Ruby already had her phone to her mouth. "MarlinAssist, close my account."

The quick among them were doing likewise.

"No!" Myfanwy was shouting. "Community members, we can't do this! Marlin loves us. It knows us! Think of the data!" She wore a rictus grin, a manic direct appeal to those around her. Maybe to the bugs themselves.

There were now dozens of raised mobiles and screens, even more shouted commands. There was a mass of running, stumbling people. The bugs pooled around Gustav's legs as they charged onward.

81

Twenty-Six wheeled a trolley along the path. As they toured the grounds, Gustav picked up the largest chunks of destroyed bug and swept up what else he could, depositing it in the trolley.

"This will take a long time," said Twenty-Six.

"Have you got somewhere better to be?" said Gustav.

"Say what?"

"This could be your new job," he suggested.

"I will do a good job," agreed Twenty-Six.

The sun was setting over the standing stones in the centre of the gardens. The campus was quiet now, quieter than Gustav had ever known it. Here and there, bugs scuttled back and forth, going about whatever business bugs with no more parcels to deliver needed to do.

Dr Ruby Jallow ambled across the lawns towards them.

"Everyone's gone home, you know," she called to him.

"I know."

"Employees. Lots of ex-employees."

"Some in the backs of ambulances," he observed.

"No one taken away in the backs of police cars," she added, perhaps a little disappointed.

Twenty-Six pushed the trolley on. Ruby and Gustav fell in behind it.

"How are you feeling?" Gustav asked.

"Much better," she said. "I'll need some counselling after all that. I've already got a therapist. He's kind of hot. I might ask him out for dinner one night. Maybe the deli by the medical centre."

"I hear they do a nice crab salad," he said.

As they walked on together, Ruby nodded at the trolley and the cleaning operation. "You know you don't work for marlin anymore, right?"

"We only do things because we're being rewarded?" he said wryly. "That sounds like bug thinking. And you don't work here anymore, either."

She tilted her head. "The ESG offered me a new job. I mean, almost immediately. Unseemly haste, really."

"A job back with marlin?"

She tilted her head the other way. "I have a whole programme of proposed changes for marlin."

"Oh?"

"Rational thinking. A better set of guiding principles. The fact that different voices need to be heard at the higher levels of the company."

"Sounds ... good?"

"One of those voices could be yours."

Gustav looked at the campus, at the droid and a trolley

which was only half full. "We'll think about it."

Ruby tutted and elbowed him playfully.

"Ow. That hurt."

"No, it didn't," said Twenty-Six.

"No, it didn't," he agreed.

ACKNOWLEDGMENTS

In writing this book, we turned to Amanda Curry and Oriana Jane, who host the Let's Chat Ethics podcast for help. They had lots of very interesting and intelligent things to say about AI, the ethics of computing and corporate behaviour and where our society is going.

We can't honestly say if we've captured even a fraction of their valuable insights in the writing of this novel but we wouldn't have been able to write it at all without them. Thank you.

ABOUT THE AUTHORS

Heide Goody lives in North Warwickshire with her family and pets.

Iain Grant lives in South Birmingham with his family and pets.

They are both married but not to each other.

ALSO BY HEIDE GOODY AND IAIN GRANT

Clovenhoof

Getting fired can ruin a day...

...especially when you were the Prince of Hell.

Will Satan survive in English suburbia?

Corporate life can be a soul draining experience, especially when the industry is Hell, and you're Lucifer. It isn't all torture and brimstone, though, for the Prince of Darkness, he's got an unhappy Board of Directors.

The numbers look bad.

They want him out.

Then came the corporate coup.

Banished to mortal earth as Jeremy Clovenhoof, Lucifer is going through a mid-immortality crisis of biblical proportion. Maybe if he just tries to blend in, it won't be so bad.

He's wrong.

If it isn't the murder, cannibalism, and armed robbery of everyday life in Birmingham, it's the fact that his heavy metal band isn't getting the respect it deserves, that's dampening his mood.

And the archangel Michael constantly snooping on him, doesn't help.

If you enjoy clever writing, then you'll adore this satirical tour de force, because a good laugh can make you have sympathy for the devil.

Get it now.

Clovenhoof

Oddjobs

Unstoppable horrors from beyond are poised to invade and literally create Hell on Earth.

It's the end of the world as we know it, but someone still needs to do the paperwork.

Morag Murray works for the secret government organisation responsible for making sure the apocalypse goes as smoothly and as quietly as possible.

Trouble is, Morag's got a temper problem and, after angering the wrong alien god, she's been sent to another city where she won't cause so much trouble.

But Morag's got her work cut out for her. She has to deal with a man-eating starfish, solve a supernatural murder and, if she's got time, prevent her own inevitable death.

If you like The Laundry Files, The Chronicles of St Mary's or Men in Black, you'll love the Oddjobs series."If Jodi Taylor wrote a Laundry Files novel set it in Birmingham... A hilarious dose of bleak existential despair. With added tentacles! And bureaucracy!" – Charles Stross, author of The Laundry Files series.Oddjobs

Printed in Great Britain
by Amazon